PRAISE FOR *CITY OF SPIES*

"Through the eyes of a young girl, *City of Spies* brings to vivid life a crucial episode in the history of the United States and Pakistan, at the moment of the Iran hostage crisis. The tensions and confusions of that time are intensely relevant today. Sorayya Khan's rich and compelling novel is a gem."

—Claire Messud, author of *The Woman Upstairs*

CITY
OF
SPIES

ALSO BY SORAYYA KHAN

Five Queen's Road

Noor

CITY
OF
SPIES

SORAYYA
KHAN

Originally published by Aleph Book Company, New Delhi 2015

Published by Little A, New York
www.apub.com

Amazon, the Amazon logo, and Little A are trademarks of Amazon.com, Inc., or its affiliates.

The text of the Intizar Husain epigraph is from *Basti*, published by New York Review Books © 1979 by Intizar Husain. Translation copyright © 2007 by Frances W. Pritchett

ISBN-13: 9781503941571 (hardcover)
ISBN-10: 1503941574 (hardcover)
ISBN-13: 9781503941588 (paperback)
ISBN-10: 1503941582 (paperback)

Cover design by Faceout Studio

Printed in the United States of America

First edition

For Naeem and our Islamabad,
and our children, Kamal and Shahid

They had left their cities, but they carried their cities with them, as a trust, on their shoulders.

—*Intizar Husain*

AUTHOR'S NOTE

This novel is based on real historical events, but for the purposes of the story, certain details have been altered.

PROLOGUE

My parents tell me that we are defined by the wars we have lived, regardless of whether we can name them. They did not have the luxury of not knowing their wars. My mother's war is the Second World War and, as a result, wherever she goes, she carries with her memories of German soldiers, Allied bombings, and the taste of tulip bulbs. My father's war is the Partition, and despite everything that has gone wrong in Pakistan, his belief in his country remains as steadfast as when he battled the British Empire for it. Currently, we all live the War on Terror, an endless war that will outlive our children. But the war of my story, the war we shared long ago, whether we knew it or not, is the Cold War. And Pakistan, unluckily lodged far from the US and close to the USSR, was but one playground where both superpowers spread mischief.

This is a story of thirty months that some claim changed the world; I know it changed mine. My name is Aliya and the story happened in Islamabad, a city of spies, when the streets of Pakistan's capital were emptier than anyone today can imagine. No one I grew up with believed anything worth mentioning could happen in our quiet town. More than thirty-five years have passed. I travel the world as a journalist, and the names tossed around by children on the yellow school buses of my childhood—Addis Ababa, Laos, Jakarta, Teheran—have become places where I've lived.

The beginning of this story is simple if you have an eye for color, a gift for geography, and a mind for fractions. My father, Javid, is brown and Pakistani; my mother, Irene, is white and Dutch; and my siblings and I are *half-and-halfs*. We lived a quiet life in Europe where my father worked for the United Nations until I was five. Then the 1971 war happened, Bangladesh was born, and the leader of what remained of Pakistan, Zulfikar Ali Bhutto, appointed my father chairman of the country's Water and Power Development Authority (WAPDA).

I imagine it would have been hard for anyone to say no to a prime minister (or president, which Bhutto was still called in those days), but my father had a more complicated explanation for accepting the job. He shared it with us some months later, after he'd shifted us all to the new capital, Islamabad, and we were able to talk to him about the move without weeping. He explained that when your country called on you, it was your duty to run right back to it with arms outstretched and fall on your knees, ready to deliver whatever it needed—water and electricity, for example. My brother, Amir, who at sixteen was much older than me and had left behind a girlfriend in Europe, told him he was crazy and, consequently, went to bed without dinner. My sister, Lehla, older than me by six years, couldn't rise above sarcasm and asked my father if he was joking. I was six then. I hear his words as clearly as if he'd spoken them yesterday, but I don't remember reacting to them. My mother tells me that I was the least unhappy of the three of us, or at least I was wise enough to know I didn't stand a chance competing against my brother or sister when it came to complaining about the move. They were way ahead in the noise department.

In those days, Islamabad was an empty city, and the proof of this was the wide streets and large parks that contained neither cars nor people. But if you'd required a photograph for evidence, you would have hiked to Viewpoint in the Margalla Hills. There, from a flat rock that looked out on the sparse city, Islamabad's two Seventh Avenues resembled airport runways without lights. Each time we hiked the trail during our first summer, I prayed the endless tarmac would reach up and take me away from the "godforsaken" place to which my father had brought us. I'd once overheard my mother use this precise adjective for Islamabad in a late-night argument with my father.

Amir, Lehla, and I were among the few Pakistanis to attend the American School of Islamabad. My father had tried to get us enrolled in Pakistani schools, but when principals learned we didn't speak Urdu, our "mother tongue," we were denied admission. I was glad. We'd gone to American Schools in Europe and, therefore, knew what to expect, but the unfamiliar prospect of going to a Pakistani school as a half-and-half made me nervous. Luckily for us, the government of Pakistan had just permitted the American School to build a large campus forty-five minutes outside the city. In return, the institution was required to admit a handful of Pakistanis on full scholarships because, of course, no Pakistani, except maybe the prime minister, could afford to pay the thousands of dollars of tuition. That's how we ended up in the American School, spending forty-five minutes every morning riding a yellow school bus to the red-brick buildings on the outskirts of Islamabad.

All I've said above is true, but as a rule, truth is as wide and all-encompassing as you let it be, and there is always more of it.

ONE

M y story begins on the heels of July 4, 1977, when I was eleven. Without the events of that early Tuesday morning, I wouldn't have a story to tell—more than that, a prime minister would still be alive, and so, too, would his youngest fan, a little boy I hardly knew. But my summer began as all Islamabad summers once did, with the promise it would never end, and without any of us knowing what was in store.

My mother was in Cairo visiting Amir, who'd convinced my parents that he would die if they didn't allow him to attend Al-Azhar and study Islam. She'd been gone only a week when my father decided we should spend the summer in Lahore with our grandfather. It was already so hot in Islamabad that my rubber sandals left marks on the pavement; Lahore would be worse. Lehla wanted to stay home before she left for college in America, because in Islamabad she would be able to sneak out to see her new boyfriend while our father was away.

But my father resolved that leaving two young girls alone at home all day wasn't a good idea, and try as we might, we weren't able to persuade him otherwise. He had our servant, Sadiq, put matching red suitcases on each of our beds, while he stood there with his hands deep in the pockets of his trousers and calmly pointed out, "Either you girls do it or I will ask Sadiq to do it, and I think you'll want to have a say in what you pack." Sadiq's English was worse than our Urdu, but his eyes grew larger and larger, understanding enough to silently plead with us for the scene to end. It was in moments like this that Sadiq seemed more like us than a grown man with a wife, a baby, a toddler, and a young son. But it was the realization that we would have to stand watch while Sadiq counted our underwear that sent us hurrying to the closet.

My father couldn't accompany us to Lahore because he was a VIP and always had more important things to do in his capacity as chairman of the Water and Power Development Authority. In fact, WAPDA's main office was in Lahore, but my father commuted back and forth almost every day on a forty-five-minute Fokker flight. No one talked about it, but we lived in Islamabad so we wouldn't have to live with my grandfather, who refused to give up his dilapidated house on Queen's Road in Lahore and move in with us.

We were driven to the airport, whisked on a VIP shuttle to the stairs of the aircraft by my father, and deposited on the airplane. Messages were crossed, however, and as a result no one was in Lahore to meet us. Lehla and I took a taxi from the airport to the house, an act for which my grandfather never forgave my father. "You let them take a taxi all by themselves? Throwing your daughters to the dogs?" he fumed a few days later when my father visited, as if he were responsible for our resourcefulness. "God help the water and electricity supply in this country with you in charge!" Lehla and I moved closer to our grandfather to make sense of his hoarse whispers. An operation gone awry had damaged his vocal cords and left him with more of a raspy whisper than a voice.

If she had been there, my mother would have joined my grandfather in his outrage, but she was in Egypt, where, we privately joked,

Amir was learning how to become a better Muslim. A few years earlier, when he first returned to Islamabad for a vacation, my mother, a tall woman, crumpled at the sight of him. His head was shaven, he wore a starched white cap to match his shalwar kameez—the baggy pants and long shirt most Pakistanis wore—and he put his arms around her only when it appeared she might fall. "Mannetje," she murmured, her Dutch endearment for him, although we spoke English. "I hardly recognize you." My sister and I recognized him all right. He may have been bald and fanatical about saying his prayers five times a day, but he was up to his old tricks, stealing a smoke on the upstairs veranda when he thought no one was looking. He'd tried to convince Lehla to join him in Egypt for her university education, but she stood her ground. "What kind of an education are you getting? Smoke carries! You think Daddy doesn't know you smoke?" He giggled, then, with a smile as wide as his face and voice octaves lower than ours. He said, "I've really missed you two," and we believed him, even though he tried to force math on us.

"Why do you like math, anyway? It doesn't even make sense," I said.

"Except for God," he solemnly said, "numbers are everything."

"They aren't cigarettes, though, are they?" I replied and earned a swat on my ear just as Sadiq walked by. His arms were full of our freshly laundered clothes, but he stopped to gently tell my brother to be nicer to me.

We spent the month of June and part of July at Five Queen's Road—a place which, for some reason, we only referred to by its address. We slept on rolled-out mattresses in the living room, where the only air conditioner in the house was installed. The machine was ancient, but in a summer so hot that newspapers were filled with worry that the rain might never come, even barely cool air was welcome.

One morning when my father was visiting, I woke up just when he rose to say his prayers. He had a travel shortwave radio in his hands and was adjusting its antenna. He was not a tall man; in fact, he was two inches shorter than my mother, but when he stood above us as we lay on our rolled-out mattresses, he was a giant. He tried to hop over both Lehla and me in one go, and I was very lucky his foot missed my head.

He suddenly called, "Abaji, Abaji," as if he'd forgotten his father was deaf, and then, remembering, shouted louder and louder as if that would make a difference.

"What *is* it?" Lehla cried, annoyed at being woken up so early.

Knowing I wouldn't be able to sleep again, I wrapped a chaddar over my pajamas and wandered into the next room. "What's wrong?" I asked.

My father handed me the newspaper he was holding and said, "Have you seen this?" fully aware that I couldn't have. Below the large bold print of the heading *Pakistan Times*, the newsprint was missing. "This is censorship."

Lehla groaned from the other room, where she lay with a sheet over her face and complained about early mornings and loud voices.

"There has been a coup," my father said after a moment. "The prime minister is in custody and martial law has been declared."

Martial law sounded like the Marshall Plan I'd learned about in school, but clearly it wasn't the same thing. I studied the formal portrait of a military general splashed across the front page of the *Pakistan Times*. The general's eyes were cast down, as if he were posing reluctantly, like a Pakistani bride. He had a bushy mustache and sleepy eyes and a row of medals pinned across his shoulders.

My grandfather had been at the mosque, and when he returned he took a seat at the head of the dining table.

"Abaji, you have heard?" my father asked. He placed the newspaper near his father's plate. Without glancing at it, my grandfather pushed it away. He fashioned a bite-size packet of halva and poori on his plate and put it in his mouth, his dentures clicking. I wished I could eat my halva as skillfully. Yunis, Sadiq's much older brother and my grand-father's trusted servant, brought him the lukewarm glass of water he consumed at the same time every day. Yunis didn't look anything like his brother, but the most compelling thing about him was that he was Christian, not Muslim like Sadiq. At Yunis's bare feet, and half his size, stood Sadiq's son, Hanif, who spent school holidays with his family at my grandfather's house. All of us watched my grandfather drain his glass of water in one long gulp.

The three radios in the house played different newscasts—the BBC, VOA, and Deutsche Welle, offering the news in British English, American English, and German—with equal solemnity.

"Allah," my grandfather finally said.

"Allah," my father replied, both men invoking God in what was an ironic precursor to the general's plans to introduce Him into every aspect of our lives and the country.

"God save your job," my grandfather said to my father as he put more halva in his mouth. My father had lain down his cutlery in an effort to listen. "Not that you're any good at it."

My father tried to explain to us what had happened. "The army has taken over. The Constitution has been suspended, the national assembly has been dissolved, and the governors and chief ministers have been fired."

"What will there be instead?" I asked.

"Whatever the general wishes," he answered without hesitation.

"What about what I wish? I wish I were in Islamabad," Lehla mut-tered later. "Not only do we have to sleep on the floor and share our beds with ants, now we're stuck in Lahore because of a coup!"

A little while later, the telephone rang, and I beat Lehla to it. My mother had heard the news in Cairo on Amir's shortwave radio, which had been a gift from my father.

"Are you all right?" she asked. "Shall I come home? Is your father there?" In her absence, I'd almost forgotten her Dutch accent that made her *f*s sound like *v*s.

"Mama," I said to my grandfather, almost apologetically, handing the heavy receiver to my father. We all looked at each other while my father encouraged her not to alter her plans and to enjoy the three remaining weeks of her vacation.

My grandfather beckoned us. "Your mother has lived under occupation once," he said and paused. "Your father," he said, as if he belonged more to us than to him, "should not make her do it again."

"Pardon me?" I asked.

"The Germans," he whispered. "Don't you know about her war?"

"Oh, *that*," Lehla said, as if she knew exactly what he was talking about.

We weren't interested in my mother's war or, really, any suggestion that she'd lived a whole life before having us. But my grandfather's reference melted into our experience of that morning, and by the afternoon, Lehla was claiming to have seen tanks and soldiers in the street. My grandfather went to investigate, with Hanif trailing behind him, but the street at the bottom of his driveway was empty.

After lunch, we eavesdropped on my father and grandfather's conversation. They were in my grandfather's study, behind French doors that never closed properly, and we were hidden by heavy maroon curtains draped across the arch.

"Yasmin will stay in Pakistan." My father used my mother's Muslim name instead of Irene, her real name, as was his practice whenever he spoke to my grandfather, who never used Irene. "I'm not leaving again. She'll be fine. It may be martial law, but it's not war." And after a pause, he added, "If they throw me out, I'll find another job." It was obvious he was worried that his job was now at the mercy of the general.

All of us gathered around the black-and-white television for the general's nighttime address to the nation. We were joined by Hanif, who sat on the floor next to my chair, and except for swollen eyes that gave away he'd been crying, he was a miniature version of his father, with an ironed white shalwar kameez and crew cut to match. My father paid for Hanif's schooling, and in his presence I always remembered that this boy, named after a famous cricket player and much younger than me, had memorized his multiplication tables to nineteen before I'd mastered the twelves. I was uncomfortable sitting in a chair while he didn't, but as a rule, servants and their children didn't sit on an employer's furniture. And while I could have joined him on the floor, I didn't.

After months of drought, it was suddenly raining, sheets of water pouring in through the window screens before Yunis could close them. Thunder and lightning shook the grainy picture on the television screen. "I am a servant of God," General Zia said, before his words were lost on me because my Urdu was so poor and his impeccable.

The general was flanked by a huge embossed Holy Quran on his desk and a Pakistani flag with its white crescent moon above, as if bedecked in a private sky. As he spoke, the hint of a cleft lip peeking out from under his mustache and a finger jabbing in the air, I felt personally scolded. Hanif did, too, because he scooted farther back from the television the longer the scolding went on. I tried to imagine how the coup might affect me. Would my father lose his job? Would we move again? I was certain that the *coup*, already a household word, directed by the stern man peering at us from behind heavy black glasses, would have repercussions for all of us. The only thing left to chance was whether they would arrive that very night or sometime in the future.

In the three weeks before my mother returned home to Islamabad, the general decreed there would be no political activity and prohibited gatherings of more than five people in public spaces. Newspapers were marked by white columns, but in between sat thin strips of newsprint bland enough to pass a censor's scrutiny. One day Sadiq brought in a bundle of mail that included an envelope from my mother that had already been opened. When my father pulled out her letter and saw *Allahu Akbar* written in black marker over her loopy script, he asked, "What's this?" Sadiq kneeled down to study the letter in my father's hands, but in the end there was nothing to say.

On the day we picked her up from the airport, Prime Minister Bhutto, the man the general had overthrown, was indicted for the murder of a political opponent.

"Did he do it?" my mother asked my father.

"Of course not," he answered.

"Maybe the general isn't such a dimwit after all," my mother sighed.

My father said that the night before the coup, the prime minister had been a guest at the Independence Day celebrations of the American Embassy. While he stood near the swimming pool, an American official waved a tumbler of whiskey in his face and cried, "The party's over! The party's over!"

"The Americans knew?" my mother asked.

"Exactly," my father said. I didn't understand how my parents had arrived at that conclusion, but the most interesting detail in my father's story was the prime minister's location at the edge of the American Embassy swimming pool. Since I was familiar with it, I could easily imagine the scene with lights flickering on the water and poolside waiters rushing about with heavy trays. My parents continued talking, and as I left to find the letter that the censors had defaced, I held onto the detail of the swimming pool because, unlike what was happening in Pakistan, I could make sense of it.

Holding the letter, my mother rested her head against the back of the rocking chair and addressed my father.

"Your country," she said, not accusingly, but as if she were stating a simple fact, "has gone mad."

"You give me too much credit, my darling." My father smiled, his eyes masking his sadness. "It doesn't belong to me. There are eighty million of us, you know."

In truth, there were only three of us: Amir in Cairo; Lehla a week away from arriving in Syracuse, New York; and me. But that was only if you didn't count Sadiq, who did not sit on our furniture but was family nonetheless.

TWO

God was everywhere, but so was the general.

He was proving to be a fast worker when it came to the country, but when the telephone rang in the middle of the night, we learned just how seamlessly he'd reached into our lives. Like me, my parents must have thought something terrible had happened to Lehla or Amir. They were asleep in their bedroom, and I was barely awake, listening to Eddie Carapiet, the only English-music radio show in Pakistan. The fact that the show had evaded the general's censors made me more of a fan than ever.

There were three telephones on the table, but the short, shrill ring indicated that the call was coming in on our private line. We were forbidden to touch the other two telephones reserved for my father's use. The gray telephone was his office line, and the rarely used green one, the secret line, had been exclusively for the prime minister's calls but was now connected to the general's office. I couldn't remember the last time it had rung.

The receiver in my hand crackled with long-distance static, and the voice on the other end was unfamiliar. My father came up behind me and quickly took the receiver. He spoke Punjabi, told my mother it was Jamila, Sadiq's wife, and left to retrieve Sadiq from the servants' quarters.

"Something must have happened," my mother said worriedly, stating the obvious.

The nighttime pitch of howling jackals grew higher and longer, an eerily common sound as the animals crept closer to the city in search of food.

Sadiq arrived to take the call with the three of us watching over him. He turned his back and spoke softly, trying to carve out a bit of privacy. My father didn't take the hint and moved closer. Eventually Sadiq sank to a squat, his elbows on his knees, the telephone receiver pressed hard against his ear. In his chairmanlike way, my father *hmm*ed in agreement at various points and instructed Sadiq to ask questions of his wife, as if he had as much right to the conversation as Sadiq.

At that hour of the night, in a room filled with empty sofas and chairs, Sadiq's pose on the floor struck me as ridiculous. Jamila's voice carried to my mother and me, but we could not make sense of the Punjabi. Her tirade went on, her voice rising and falling, unable to settle on either anger or sadness. Sadiq sank deeper, uncomfortable with the news and our stares. Several minutes passed this way until my father took the phone and arranged a consensus between the two of them, and the conversation came to an abrupt end.

After Sadiq returned to the servants' quarters, my father recounted what he'd heard.

According to Jamila, who'd been with him when he learned the news, Hanif wept on hearing of the general deposing the prime minister, and overnight, a boy who'd had to be threatened to learn his prayers claimed his father's janamaz, prayer carpet, as his own. Now he spent more time on the janamaz than in school or on the cricket pitch.

My father asked, "You know that Hanif was named for a famous Pakistani batsman, right?"

He said that upon hearing the news of the prime minister's indict-
ment for the murder of a political opponent, Hanif had given away his
cricket bat. My father's grip tightened on the arms of his chair, and he
seethed that our great chief martial-law administrator's crimes extended
to destroying a young boy's love for cricket.

"How long has this been going on?" my mother asked, hopeful that
Hanif might yet come to his senses.

"Since the day of the coup!"

"While you and the girls were in Lahore? And Sadiq didn't notice
any of this—Hanif giving up cricket, praying all day—when he visited
his family afterwards?" asked my mother.

Sadiq had just returned from a weekend spent in Lahore with his
family. When we'd first arrived in Islamabad, my mother refused to hire
him until my father agreed to permit him to visit Lahore every third
weekend.

"How many times a day does he pray?"

"His mother says that he prays all the time," my father replied.

"The general would be pleased," my mother muttered, but her half
joke fell flat.

My father had directed Jamila to send Hanif to Islamabad. Though
Hanif always had a standing invitation, this would be his first visit. He
would arrive from Lahore in a few weeks, delivered by his uncle, Yunis.

We weren't certain of the exact ages of Sadiq's children. The daughters were young, one an infant, the other, two or three years old. My
mother guessed that Hanif was eight.

"Whatever it is, the boy is far too young to be distraught over the
country's politics," my father declared.

"Do children that young pay attention to the news?" my mother
wondered. No doubt, her measure of comparison was her own children,
which wasn't entirely fair, because the coup certainly had captured my
attention.

"I don't get it," I said, finally voicing my confusion over something everyone else seemed to have missed. "What's the connection between the prime minister, the general, and the janamaz?"

"She's quite right," my mother said. "It is worth thinking about."

Any mention of the general upset my father. He considered the general a traitor who had usurped power and was sure to ruin the country. He didn't say it often, but he also believed that the general had conspired with the Americans in a grab for power. He'd once stated as much: "Little men, *unelected* men, stand no chance without the hand of a greater power."

Ignoring us both, my father said, "Hanif is far too young to be plagued by such worries. Islamabad will be good for him." Then he promptly stood and left.

In his absence, my mother attempted an explanation. There was no question that Hanif loved the prime minister. She remembered hearing that as a toddler, he'd sat on his father's shoulders during an election rally, and it was likely he'd been taken with the prime minister ever since. With such excitement, what child wouldn't be? The obvious conclusion was that Hanif hated the general because of what he'd done to the prime minister. In this way, he was in good company, my mother said, raising an eyebrow and drawing a connection to my father and the rest of us. So Hanif spent all his time on his father's janamaz communing with God because, God knows, only He could set things right.

"You believe that?" I asked.

"We all have a right to our prayers." My mother shrugged.

My prayer was simple. I wanted God to grant me my immediate wish and let me go to sleep.

By then, the general had driven my father to Valium. During their first meeting a few weeks after the coup, my father lost control and couldn't stop his hands from trembling. Worse, the pounding blood in his head dulled his hearing and prevented him from conversing intelligently. The general's secretary made immediate inquiries into my father's competence, which made my father's heart beat even faster and more erratically than when he'd been in the general's presence.

"You must find a way to calm down, Javid!" my mother insisted.

"It's the strangest thing," he sputtered. "In person, the man is nothing like his finger-wagging television avatar. He is mild-mannered and calls *me* sir! No wonder he convinced the prime minister to appoint him army chief."

"The prime minister's mistake was underestimating the general's intelligence and assuming he wouldn't be a threat," my mother said.

Her criticism of the prime minister further upset my father and, finally, my mother suggested he try Valium before his next meeting with the general.

"Drugs?" my father said incredulously. "In front of my daughter, you are suggesting I use drugs?"

"Valium is not a drug, it's a sleeping aid," she started to say, before he cut her off.

"You want me to sleep through my meeting? Are you trying to get me fired?" His hands no longer trembled, but he was close to losing his temper.

She glared at him. My mother had once been a ballerina, but her slender frame could be intimidating when she was angry and leaned into her words. "I want you to *live*, Javid. That's all. And if you don't figure out a way to calm down in the man's presence, you are going to kill yourself."

Her outburst convinced my father. Fifteen minutes prior to all subsequent meetings with the general, my father swallowed half a Valium and stowed the other half in his pocket in case of an emergency. So it was that when my father returned from these meetings, he slept longer and more soundly than ever.

Not only did the general introduce pharmaceuticals into our home, he was responsible for altering vacation plans, too. We were expecting Amir and Lehla to visit us over the winter holidays, but Lehla's first semester at college had barely begun when my parents canceled her airplane reservations.

"There's no need to tempt fate," my mother explained.

"What?" I asked.

"*Pardon me*," she corrected.

"I don't understand."

"It's safer for your brother and sister to stay where they are than to visit this military dictatorship." She made it sound as if Lehla and Amir were planning to visit the general.

"But *we* live here, after all! And you're saying it's dangerous?"

Of course, nothing I said ever made a difference, and my parents stood their ground. But living in Pakistan meant living with the general because he was everywhere—in the newspapers, on television, on Hanif's mind, in our home, on my father's nerves. Worst of all was that the general's relentless invocation of God made him think he could compete with Him. He strived to be all knowing, but the difference was that he employed others to do his dirty work.

One afternoon shortly after the school year began, I arrived home to discover Sadiq and the chowkidar having a solemn conversation with a man on a parked motorcycle outside our gate. The visitor was dressed in a black shalwar kameez that blended in with his bike and was wearing leather gloves more suited to a chilly day. He pointed at me when I got off the school bus, and as I walked through the open gates, I tried not to be bothered by his gaze.

After my father returned from Lahore later that night, he explained that the motorcyclist worked for Pakistan's intelligence agency and was assigned to keep watch on our house. The man had given notice that he would stop by once or twice a month to collect information. Sadiq sought advice from my father on what to tell the intelligence officer in the future, and my father instructed him to convey whatever he liked about our dull lives. He believed that truth alone would rid us of the spy.

"We are reduced to being spied upon. My, how far we've come from Vienna." My mother stared in the window's direction, as if the city we'd left behind were within reach.

"I hate that man," said my father.

"You hate the spy?"

"The general, the spy, all of them!" my father replied, and his nostrils quivered as his voice rose.

"Did the general give specific orders to the intelligence officer to spy on our house?"

"What reason would he have for that? I've heard that all minister-level personnel are being monitored." My father was trying to assure us that we weren't being singled out, but in the next breath he boasted, "Don't forget that the prime minister appointed me. The general knows my loyalties."

My father kissed me good night and forbade me to speak to any stranger at our gate, motorcycle or not. I rolled my eyes, offended at his lack of trust in my good sense.

"Look at me, Aliya! I am serious. Do you understand?"

"Yes!" I groaned.

The next day my father promoted Sadiq from servant to WAPDA employee in order to protect him from the general's reach. He was proud at having outwitted the general: A WAPDA employee would keep his job even if my father were fired. "We have a responsibility to the man and his family," my father said, and I was struck by his overly developed sense of duty. My mother was relieved that the new arrangement changed nothing for our family. Sadiq's WAPDA duties were to serve us in our home as he always had.

~

In preparation for Hanif's visit, my mother rummaged through a trunk of clothes in the upstairs storeroom, coughing at the gas-like smell of shrunken mothballs. She did this once or twice a year, going through Lehla's old clothes, selecting items for which I might still have use. She also saved my clothes for Sadiq's family; one day his daughters would be old enough to inherit my party dresses, while Hanif might have use for sweaters and socks or jackets that had already been passed on from Amir to Lehla to me. Her frugality embarrassed me. While I didn't mind wearing my siblings' jackets, I drew a line at their socks. Further, why did Hanif, a boy, have to wear my old clothes? There was something wrong with that.

Apparently Sadiq and Hanif didn't think so. A few weeks after his mother's frantic telephone call, Hanif was on our lawn when I returned from school. I was barely inside our gate, the yellow school bus still rolling away, when he dribbled our soccer ball around me. He was barefoot and dressed in an old favorite, my red tracksuit that had belonged to Amir, which I had expressly asked my mother not to give to Hanif. The good news was that he wasn't on his father's janamaz, and when he passed the ball to me, I wondered if simply arriving in Islamabad had cured him.

"Kya haal hai?" I asked in Urdu, as this was the simple "How are you?"—impossible to bungle.

My schoolmates didn't mind my lack of Urdu facility, if they were even aware of it, but the reality was embarrassing in front of people like our servant's son. As a result, I'd never spoken much to him at my grandfather's house. If my Urdu were better, I might have ignored the fact that he was at least three years my junior and chatted with him. For fear of sounding like a fool, I didn't even try.

In the house, my mother was quizzing Sadiq about his day's work, and I was grateful Hanif was out of earshot. Were the books dusted? Were they dusted well? The carpets vacuumed? Underneath the bed, too? Windows washed? Copper polished? Her enthusiasm made me wonder if we were expecting guests. Their voices echoed along the corridor of our big house, and I missed Lehla and Amir, whose mere presence prevented echoes. I recalled what I'd heard my mother say to my father shortly after Lehla's departure.

"This is what we had children for? To scatter them across the world?"

My father was very sad. "In the end, it doesn't make a difference . . . if they are an hour or one day away from us."

Hanif had only been in Islamabad a few hours, but his mother probably felt the same way.

THREE

S chool was its own planet. The yellow school bus shuttling me back and forth every day was a lumbering satellite. Home and school were both in Islamabad, but it was almost impossible to conceive of them as part of the same galaxy. It was easier to think of them as parallel universes and pray they stayed that way.

The school's red-brick buildings, one classroom deep and one story tall, were octagons, each built around a courtyard. In the middle of each courtyard was a sunken concrete star, perhaps once intended to house a serious fountain but now a place where some of us ate lunch. The only other brick compound in Islamabad was the American Embassy. It was located in the diplomatic enclave, a far corner of Islamabad reserved for foreign embassies. For people like me, it was a place you could enter only if you were the guest of an American and, when asked, didn't admit to being Pakistani. No one told me this, but I somehow knew. Once when I'd been asked if I was a Pakistani by a marine manning the gate, I'd said, "Not really," and he'd let me in.

Any friends I made were from the parallel universe that was school. When we first moved to Islamabad, I made friends with a German girl whose father drove his family each summer in their green-and-white

Volkswagen bus from Islamabad to Frankfurt, making detours through Afghanistan and Iran and whatever else he felt like seeing that year. But later his company transferred him to South Africa, and I never saw her again.

Shortly after my sister left for Syracuse University, I met my new best friend, Lizzy. She was my age, blonde instead of brunette, the oldest instead of the youngest of three children. I never really understood why she wanted to be my friend, but she did, and so we were.

I met Lizzy for the first time in Dr. Moody's office. Dr. Moody was an orthodontist and the only dentist in all of Islamabad. None of his patients ever called him anything but Dr. Moody, a nickname he'd had for so long no one could remember him by any other name, so when the receptionist called with an appointment reminder, I was always confused why Dr. Mahmud was looking forward to seeing me for my next appointment. The dentist's waiting room was known in Islamabad for being one of the few places where Pakistani and American children ran into each other.

Dr. Moody's office wasn't far from my home. His street was lined with full-grown mango trees, and the one or two times my father accompanied me, he wondered aloud how mature trees had come to exist in such a young city. The office bungalow was wedged against the road, but there was an annex in the back where Dr. Moody lived with his family. The annex crawled upward from a shallow ravine. Once, when I sat there waiting for him for a long time, I thought the annex wound up the hill like the twisting staircases Amir used to build with his Legos.

Lizzy arrived in the waiting room with her mother, and my mother greeted them in a ritual of friendliness she reserved for other foreigners.

"How are you?" she asked, her Dutch accent as prominent as always.

When Lizzy's mother responded with an obvious American accent, I regretted wearing a shalwar kameez and tried to burrow deeper into the ample leather couch. The summer vacation had dragged by without my bothering to see my school friends or worrying about what I wore; now caught in the dentist's office in clothes I would never wear to school, I scolded myself for my carelessness.

Later, on the first day of school, Lizzy and I discovered we rode the same school bus, were in the same class, and had last names, Shah and Simon, that placed us in seats assigned next to each other. The first time she asked me where I was from, I told her Austria because I was born there. The second time, I told her Holland because that was where my mother was from. The last time, I confessed, "Pakistan, too."

"Which one is it?" she finally asked, clearly confused.

"All of them, actually," I replied, feeling caught in a lie, but now trying to tell the truth.

"That's so cool!" Lizzy said.

"Not really."

"I'm just from central New York," she said. "My dad is from Auburn, and my mom is from Skaneateles. My grandparents live in Cazenovia, and so do all my cousins."

"Are those cities close to each other?" All I knew of central New York was two facts: Lehla's university was in Syracuse, and the city sat next to a lake with an unpronounceable name, a lake that, as Lehla once wrote in a letter, contained mercury.

"Until I came to Islamabad, I'd never been out of New York state!"

"Really?" I had no idea how large New York state was, but the very idea of Lizzy only living in one country, much less a *state*, for all of her eleven or twelve years, struck me as unusual.

When she invited me home for dinner, her father, Mr. Simon, a big man who wore shorts at home and could balance his young twin sons on his shoulders, offered an emergency telephone number for Lehla in case she ever needed anything. "Maybe Lehla needs a place to stay for Thanksgiving? Or Christmas? Just let us know," he said, as if our families had known each other for a long time. I liked him right away, not only because he was friendly, but also because he pronounced my sister's name correctly, which was unusual for an American.

I took home news of Lehla's proximity to Lizzy's extended family in New York and Mr. Simon's offer.

"I see," my father said in a way that meant he would never think of it again.

"How kind," my mother said, because she worried about Lehla being so far away from home.

But my mother never asked the Simons for the telephone number, and I wondered if it was because of what the Americans were doing in Pakistan. No one knew what they were *really* doing since most of them were assumed to be spies and, as a rule, didn't advertise their work. But everyone knew they were everywhere. They drove cars with yellow CD64 license plates, announcing their American-ness, only to be outdone by the yellow CD62 license plates of the Russians, who all drove four-door tan sedans and therefore didn't really need the license plates to be identified. The CD64s and CD62s were at war with each other, a Cold War, whatever that meant, and their playground seemed to be Islamabad. Whatever the mystery of the Cold War, the license plate codes were easy to break: CD64 1 announced the ambassador; CD64 2, the deputy chief of mission; CD64 3, the military attaché, who was most definitely a spy; and on and on. Lizzy's parents' car was different. It was an AD64 car, which indicated her father worked for the USAID mission.

Lizzy's house might as well have been a hotel. There was heavy furniture everywhere, thick velvet drapes on the windows, even the big ones that faced a miniature orange grove in their garden, and there were matching twin beds in the children's rooms with identical sky-blue bedspreads and headboards holding rows of paperback books. Whenever I visited an American home, I was struck by how families moved in and out of the ready-made houses every few years, different fathers assigned to the same job. I'd been in Lizzy's house when Mr. Simon's predecessor lived there and his family hosted our class graduation party. The houses never seemed to belong to the people who lived in them. Despite the stray photograph or a finger painting, they were bare and impersonal, and, like a hotel, appeared in a permanent state of recently being occupied or about to be vacated.

After I'd been to Lizzy's house several times, I invited her to mine. It was a few days after my grandfather had arrived for one of his visits and shortly after Hanif had joined his father at our home in Islamabad. When Lizzy got to my house, Hanif was helping Sadiq work in the lawn, using a kitchen brush and dustpan to collect scattered leaves. From afar, their work was almost a dance, the barefoot boy squatting near his father, sweeping a brush in tiny half circles across the lawn, rising to move a few steps before doing it all over again.

Watching them unobserved from my bedroom window as I waited for Lizzy, I again tried to make sense of Hanif. In Lahore, he refused to go to school, spent all his time sitting on his janamaz and praying the prime minister would not be hanged by the general, who had decided robbers should have their hands chopped off. I, too, was worried about the prime minister, especially since I heard my parents claim that Dr. Moody had become his doctor and visited him in jail. Also, I had reason to worry about the general's behavior. At any moment, my father could be stripped of his job, and maybe we would have to move again. But what did the prime minister mean to Hanif? Why did he care so much? My father suspected it had to do with "Roti, kapra, aur makan!" the slogan of the prime minister's political party that convinced poor people, which meant almost everyone, to vote for him. Still, Hanif was only eight, or maybe nine, and my father's explanation seemed far-fetched.

After Lizzy arrived, she and I walked to the neighborhood park a few minutes away. We stopped at the unfinished house on the corner to skip up and down a concrete stairway that led nowhere. I shared what my father had told me, that the house was abandoned in midconstruction by a fleeing Bengali family during the 1971 war, but the possibility rattled us, so we hurried along. We were headed to the park to collect stones for a geology project in science class. The open space was dotted with cement benches and a playground structure with rust and red paint that made it look like it had never been used. It was almost dusk in November, and I was bitten by a mosquito.

"Aren't they all supposed to be dead by now?" I asked, annoyed, slapping at my shoulder where the mosquito was trapped in my shirt.

"It's not unusual for them to come out at dusk here," Lizzy replied authoritatively. "At least that's what Dad says." She carried my mother's vegetable basket, which was sagging with the weight of our stones. "My dad works with malaria."

"Why?"

"That's his job. What does your dad do?"

"When we lived in Vienna, he worked for the UN."

"Not anymore?" Lizzy asked.

UN employees weren't quite like Americans in Islamabad, but they had air conditioners in most rooms in their houses, frequently went on home leaves and vacations, and, generally, weren't Pakistanis. And they had yellow license plates on their cars that began with UN. I wondered how Lizzy could have missed all this. "Not anymore," I said.

"So what does he do now?" Lizzy said, kicking at the dry ground with her foot, trying to dislodge a small rock.

"He works for WAPDA, the Water and Power Development Authority." I didn't mention he was in charge, because I didn't want Lizzy to think that every time there was a problem with the electricity or water supply, it was his fault, even though maybe it was. I swatted at the mosquito now buzzing near my forehead. "Is there a lot of malaria here?" I asked, and the exaggerated wave of my hand could have been hinting at the whole country, almost a thousand miles south from the Margalla Hills to Karachi and the Arabian Sea.

"I think so."

"You need lots of water for malaria, right?"

"Standing water."

"Not much here, though," I said, jumping in place, a cloud of dust rising from my sneakers.

"Yup," Lizzy said. "He travels a lot."

"Mine does, too," I said and explained that my father commuted from Islamabad to Lahore for his job.

Together, Lizzy and I carried the vegetable basket, too heavy for either of us, to my house, where my visiting grandfather was cleaning his ears with my mother's cotton swabs in the mirror of the entryway.

"Assalamualaikum," I said. He kissed my forehead, his protruding front teeth leaving behind a dab of saliva, as usual. "This is my friend, Lizzy."

He smiled at her, and with the hand that wasn't holding a cotton swab, he reached to touch her head, a gesture he reserved for children, but Lizzy pulled away, maybe because she was scared to be touched by an old Pakistani man.

"This is my grandfather," I said, and Lizzy, white like her hair in the bright light of the foyer, blushed a deep pink with embarrassment.

The worst thing about school was the afternoon school bus rides. They were what I think made me most grateful for Lizzy. We sat next to each other every day, in the mornings and in the afternoons, our backpacks on the floor, where our feet kept them from sliding away. We always sat toward the middle of the bus. Lizzy could have sat anywhere, but she chose to sit with me, not in the front, where the youngest children sat, and not in the back, where the rowdiest boys planted themselves. They were relatively quiet in the mornings, but the bus could hardly contain their energy in the afternoons. By the time the bus neared the first turn in the dirt road that led from the school to Peshawar Road, the boys were at it. They cleared their throats, forced choppy coughs, and made unpleasant sucking noises. Eventually they puckered their lips and blew spit through the tight roll of their tongues and out the open windows. Hitting a pedestrian was worth one point, a bicyclist two points, and if the bicyclist lost his balance and fell, it was three points plus an extra turn. There was a lot of hooting and hollering and hand slapping, as if every afternoon the game and its rewards were being discovered anew. The bus driver, Pakistani like all our bus drivers, lacked the authority to put a stop to the games, and, anyway, he was no match for the boys.

I tried not to watch. Before Lizzy, I concentrated on the front windshield or on the aisle, where soda cans, pencils, and cookie crumbs rolled back and forth at different speeds. When we'd first moved to Pakistan, I was only six and sat close to the driver, from where I observed the boys through his rearview mirror. The accuracy of their spitting was frightening. Their targets, sometimes children, would jerk their heads sideways, trying to shake the spit from their faces rather than wipe it with their bare hands or a kurta sleeve. One time, suddenly brave, I'd turned in my seat to stare at the boys, daring them to single me out, but when they did—"whatchoolookinat?"—I tried to make myself as small as I could and faced the front for the rest of the ride.

I remembered the time Lehla asked my father if our driver, Mushtaq, could start picking us up from school. "What? You're too good for the bus, my darling?" he demanded, without asking her to explain. Even though the three of us had never discussed what happened on the bus, we all knew why she'd asked. If we'd spoken about it, it would have been as if the yellow school buses had driven right through our gates and parked in my home universe. The rides, the boys, the spittle, all of it would have been real and true, and we would have had to face the facts: Not one of us, not even my big brother who smoked cigarettes, had the courage to shout, "Stop it!" We were all cowards.

There were other reasons, far more difficult to admit, why I didn't tell my parents. A small part of me believed that Pakistanis deserved to be spit upon. I wasn't proud of this, of course, and I was horrified to imagine how my parents might react should they come to know. If my father had been told of the spitting boys, he would have taken us out of the school without another thought. The dreaded alternative, going to a Pakistani school, would have been worse. If I'd confided to my mother, she would have marched into the principal's office and made demands, and from that day on, everyone would have known me as the tattletale I was. All in all, it was easier to leave my parents in the dark.

During bus rides, Lizzy seemed as oblivious to the games as I pretended to be. We chatted about teachers and students, giggled about who wore what, and Lizzy, whose spot-on impersonations always had us in peals of laughter, mocked the boy in math class. "Why, the isosisillies triangle has two equal sides and two equal angles," she lisped, perfectly capturing his mispronunciation and Southern drawl.

Even with the distraction of Lizzy, though, it became harder to ignore the boys. At first, there had only been a few whispers about American involvement in the fate of the prime minister. But as the days passed and my parents and their friends talked about it more, the games in the back of the bus came into sharper focus.

One afternoon, not long after the prime minister's trial began and some time into Hanif's stay, the girl sitting behind us declared that Boot-toe (she, like most American children, couldn't pronounce *Bhutto*) deserved to be punished for rigging the elections. One of the boys gave up his turn in the spitting game to clarify. "What? You mean death?"

"What does Boot-toe expect?" the girl responded, shrugging her shoulders.

Lizzy rolled her eyes at the girl's remarks, picked up my hand, and played with the last of the unbroken glass bangles my grandfather had brought me from Lahore the previous summer. The glitter made roving polka dots of light bounce off the bus's ceiling.

The prime minister was about to die, but Sadiq was my biggest worry during those bus rides. What if he were hit by a ball of spit? He routinely rode his heavy black bicycle from one part of Islamabad to the other, doing chores for my parents that took him along our bus route. Over and over again, I imagined Hanif falling from Sadiq's handlebars, his slight shoulders hitting the road at the same time his father's did. Sadiq would wipe the spit from Hanif's cheek and from his own head with the back of his bare hand before picking up his bicycle and his son from the pavement of Embassy Road and heading home in the direction of the Margalla Hills.

"Call me tonight," Lizzy yelled from the bus window as I reached my driveway.

As always, Hanif was waiting for me on the lawn, running behind a soccer ball. He kicked the ball to me, but I missed the pass because I'd turned back to wave at Lizzy. The bus had already gone, and I was relieved to finally be home, safe from the spitting games.

During dinner, I told my father that children on the bus assumed the prime minister had rigged the elections. But what I really wanted to know from him was whether there was a connection between Prime Minister Bhutto's murder trial and the elections. My father concentrated on the second issue. Maybe there were overeager party members who had engaged in some hanky-panky during the elections to win the prime minister's favor, he reluctantly considered, but it was unlikely the prime minister knew what they were doing.

"So the elections were possibly rigged and now the prime minister is on trial for murder? And he's going to be put to death?" I asked, trying to put together what I'd heard on the bus that afternoon.

"Who knows?" my father replied, surprisingly circumspect. "The country's gone mad," he announced, sounding like my mother, who stayed quiet while he made her standard complaint about Pakistan. My mother instructed me to take out the garbage. "Doesn't Sadiq do that?" I asked. She told me to take it out immediately and imposed an earlier bedtime on me for asking the question.

I went the long way to the garbage bin through the servants' quarters, where I knew I shouldn't have been. Sadiq's bathroom door was open just a crack, and Hanif was reclined in a plastic tub my father had had installed for him. He was giggling continuously, like he was being tickled, while his father directed a steady stream of water on his soapy hair. It occurred to me that Hanif likely didn't have access to an unlimited supply of hot water, made possible in our house by the water boilers attached to every bathroom. Despite such luxury, I routinely ignored my mother's frequent reminders not to waste water with long showers.

I lingered near the bathroom and eavesdropped on Sadiq and Hanif. Even if my Urdu were fluent, I wouldn't have interrupted them, but I wanted to understand Hanif's devotion to the prime minister and to ask why he'd made the prime minister's sorrow his own.

I, on the other hand, had personal grievances against the prime minister. After all, he was the reason my father had decided to move us, against our will, to Islamabad. The country had just lost a war and half its territory, but the new leader used the defeat to rally expatriates like my father to return home to develop what was left of it. "It is my duty," my father had said. Now, many years later, I still blamed the prime minister. Whether it was reasonable or not, I held him personally responsible for my discomfort with what I was—half-and-half, mixed, Pakistani, whatever. I clung to the misplaced notion that if my father had not accepted the job as chairman of WAPDA, I could have gone on announcing I was from Pakistan in the safety of Vienna, and I would never have known what it meant to be Pakistani and neither, really, would anyone else.

The problem was, I knew the prime minister. That is to say, I knew his children, which was almost like knowing him personally. Two of them, much older than me, had attended my school when we first moved to Islamabad. They would arrive every morning in a sparkling black Mercedes. Their driver was outfitted like an embassy driver in a crisp white uniform with big silver buttons and a smart matching cap. A bodyguard sat in the front seat, and from my classroom window I thought I could make out a pistol belted to his stomach when he jumped out of his seat to open the car doors for the prime minister's children. The bodyguard didn't last long, though, and rumor had it this was because the prime minister's son, Shah, insisted on carrying his own pistol strapped to his calf. I often watched Shah play on the school soccer team with my brother, but I never saw a pistol on him. When Shah was graduating along with Amir, Begum Bhutto, the prime minister's elegant wife, was the guest speaker at my brother's commencement ceremony. I couldn't stop looking at this beautiful woman, tall like my mother and the only other person wearing a sari. I was staring so unabashedly, Lehla jabbed me with her elbow to make me stop. When the speech was over, we took our places in the receiving line and shook everyone's hand. Amir stood next to his friend Shah. My brother lifted me up and hugged me, the golden tassel on his pointy graduation hat tickling my nose. When he put me down, his friend did the same. "I'm going to marry you some day," Shah said and made us all laugh.

Hanif hadn't even known the prime minister. He'd never spoken to his children or watched his wife give a speech. What on earth made him feel so close to the man?

"Aliya! Aliya!" My mother was calling for me.

Lizzy was on the telephone.

"Liya?"

Leeyaa. I loved the way her nickname for me rolled off her tongue. The two syllables instead of three. It made me less myself, more a Lizzy or an Annie or a Chrissy, almost the name of a character in a book. It was a pity my parents hadn't thought to name me something so simple.

"You didn't call me like you said you would!" Lizzy was miffed, but her accusation didn't make me mad. No one had ever insisted on my friendship before.

FOUR

Thick white fog was the closest we had to snow in Islamabad, and that morning, fog closed the airport. Like snow, it amplified sounds, and when my father rang the kitchen buzzer to the servants' quarters, I had to cover my ears in my bedroom.

We were forbidden to use the buzzer. "We don't summon servants by pretending they are trained animals," my mother said.

"So what should we do?" Lehla once asked, caught with her finger on the buzzer.

"Use your voice and call him!"

"Because shouting is more dignified?" Lehla muttered, and she was punished for talking back.

My father miscalculated by thinking my mother would fail to notice the buzzer. I got up and cracked open my door to see what would happen, and in no time at all, my mother confronted him in the kitchen.

"I've asked you not to use the buzzer," she scolded.

"Don't be silly. That's what it's there for!" my father said at the same moment Sadiq appeared.

Because my father's flight to Lahore had been canceled, he intended to complete the journey by road. He had an important meeting at WAPDA headquarters at noon, which meant he had to leave within the next hour. He'd summoned Sadiq to offer Yunis and Hanif a ride and save them the scheduled bus journey the following day.

I walked in as Sadiq politely declined the offer.

My mother's Urdu was worse than mine, but she understood enough of the conversation to offer her thoughts.

"Please have them drive with sahib," she said. Although Sadiq understood her simple sentence, she insisted my father translate it. "Tell him the car is much safer than the flying coaches." She'd never been on the express buses that raced madly from city to city, but she was current on newspaper chronicles of their alarming accident rates.

Sadiq nodded in agreement but did not change his mind.

Yunis came to help with chores and also turned down my father's invitation.

"Oh, please!" said my mother, who had a soft spot for Yunis. He had converted to Christianity so that the woman he had wanted would marry him. My mother, who'd also converted to marry my father, made no secret of enjoying this story every time it was told, and it was the reason he was her favorite servant.

"How's the boy now?" my father asked, and Yunis's reply made him beam.

"What did he say?" I asked eagerly, and my father told us.

The previous night, Sadiq, Yunis, and Hanif were eating dinner, and Sadiq asked his son how he was doing. The boy replied that he was happy, and when Sadiq asked why, his response was surprising. He said, "The prime minister won't die. He'll live as long as I do!"

The adults ooohed and aaahed at Hanif's prediction, but I had no idea why they were taking him seriously. Had he had a dream? A vision? Why would that make his prediction come true? "How does *he* know the prime minister will live a long time?" I asked.

My father had already returned to his conversation with Yunis. From what I understood, Hanif no longer said his prayers more than five times a day, and he'd promised to go back to school.

"God willing, the boy will be fine," my father said.

"At least his mother will be happy," my mother sighed.

The reception on our Zenith radio was poor, and it delivered the BBC news headlines in incomprehensible bits and pieces.

"Did the announcer say Iran? Or Pakistan?" my mother asked, and in the short span of those two questions, my father's mood plummeted.

"What does it matter? Iran or Pakistan, it's never good news." The general's name, Zia-ul-Haq, filtered through the newscast, and my father added, "Especially when it refers to Cancel My Last Announcement."

"That's not funny," I grumbled.

My father was using the general's latest unflattering nickname, which shared an acronym, CMLA, with one of his titles, chief martial law administrator. It was supposed to be a joke, but there was nothing funny about it, because it was an accurate description of the man who was making my father—and the country—miserable. The general, in his CMLA incarnation, had broken several promises to the country, including holding elections ninety days after the coup. Worse, the Supreme Court had recently legitimized his martial law.

Before my father hugged us good-bye, my mother handed him a single Valium tablet.

"Do *not* forget to take it," she warned. "You can sleep on the drive home."

My father took it, even as he said the general was not expected to attend the meeting. "Just in case," he said.

Late in the afternoon, Sadiq asked my mother for permission to be excused from work for the evening.

"Kyun?" she asked, and in the Urdu-English pidgin that passed for communication in our household, she learned he wanted to buy his son a new pair of sneakers. She told him that since everything was more expensive in Islamabad, he should buy the shoes in Lahore, but he ignored her suggestion.

"Maybe Hanif is going to play cricket again and needs them as soon as he gets to Lahore," I suggested.

My mother complained that no one ever seemed to hear her. What she meant was that no one in Pakistan ever *listened* to her. Whenever it was convenient, people became deaf in her company. Her complaint was usually reserved for my father, but that evening Sadiq was also guilty.

She found her purse and tried to give money to Sadiq, who refused to take it. "He's deaf and stubborn!" she protested, grabbing a magazine and disappearing into her bedroom.

The airport reopened in the evening, and my father returned from Lahore by plane. The general hadn't been at the meeting, which accounted for my father's energy. He heated up the plate of food Sadiq had left for him in the refrigerator and made his own tea. We chatted a bit, but in no time my father was focused on preparing for work the following day.

The clang of metal on metal as our gate latch opened and closed was loud, but the latch took unexpectedly long to fall closed. A moment later, we heard a whispered, frantic exchange that included, "Sahib ko bulao," but it was impossible to tell if the speaker was Yunis, Sadiq, or the night chowkidar. My father looked up from the stack of unread reports and memos next to his dinner plate.

"Go and see who's there," he said.

I saw Sadiq and Yunis in the driveway, heading to the servants' quarters with the chowkidar following close behind. Sadiq was strangely unsteady on his feet. He wove from one side of the driveway to the next under the weight of what was in his arms. He was momentarily illuminated by the lighting and, suddenly, I recognized my favorite red tracksuit. Hanif's arms and legs swung limply on either side of Sadiq as he loosely cradled his son's body against his chest.

"Sadiq?" I called.

At the sound of my voice, the chowkidar spun around and barked, "Yahan nahin ana!" He ordered me to return to the house and get my father.

My father dropped a file of papers and hurried to investigate. I followed, but at the back door, he commanded me not to accompany him further. I waited until he couldn't see me and got a few steps closer to the servants' quarters before a muffled howl filled the night. It sounded like a jackal's cry, but I slowly realized that the wail was coming from our servants' quarters. My mother shouted for me to come back into the house, and I had no choice but to return.

When my father entered the lounge where we were waiting, his chin was on his chest and his hands were buried in his pockets. He moved carefully, knocked off balance by what he'd learned.

"What happened?" my mother asked. She hadn't bothered to turn on the overhead light, and the yellow glow from the copper sconce turned the three of us the same color.

His shoulders sagged, and he whispered, "The boy has died."

"What boy?" my mother asked.

"Hanif was killed in a hit-and-run accident."

"No, Hanif went with his father to the market to buy shoes," my mother explained.

My father said nothing and studied her. "You're wrong, Javid," she said, undeterred.

"Irene, the boy is lying on his father's bed, and he is dead." He'd given up his whisper; his voice was clear, his words horribly slow.

My mother jumped.

I didn't believe it either. "Are you sure?" I asked. When my father didn't respond, I clarified, "*How* can you be sure?"

Fifteen minutes later, when the doctor arrived to examine Hanif, I interrupted him. "Will Hanif be all right?"

The doctor, a family friend and my pediatrician, said, "I'm sorry. The boy has passed away." Silence spread around us like rapidly rising water, and I struggled not to fall. Then he added, "The city ought to do something about careless drivers. Light its streets. Hire traffic police. A number of things we could do that we don't." I found the phrase *passed away* absolutely inadequate for describing what had happened to Hanif.

I couldn't bear to be alone. I sat next to my father while he made more telephone calls than I could count to arrange to transport the body to Lahore the following day. Sometimes he spoke Urdu, sometimes Punjabi, and once in a while, English. My mother made me hot chocolate with special Dutch cocoa powder and brought me one of her pashmina shawls because I was cold.

My father revealed a few details. Sadiq, Hanif, and Yunis had gone to Aabpara Market to buy Hanif a new pair of sneakers, exactly as Sadiq had said they would. After purchasing the shoes, they didn't have enough money to return on the bus, so they walked home. At an intersection near Polyclinic, a car came out of nowhere and hit Hanif. The car sped away and Hanif was dead.

"It was as simple as that," my father said, taking off his reading glasses and rubbing the impression they left on his nose. "Here one moment, gone the next."

"Who did this?" my mother asked.

"Yunis says the license plate was yellow."

My mother gasped. "Foreign? My God, diplomats do whatever they want here!"

During another lull, when my father was not on the telephone, she asked, "Why didn't the driver stop, Jav?"

"Later," he replied.

"Why didn't the driver stop?" I repeated my mother's question, but the telephone rang again and he offered nothing more.

Eventually my parents persuaded me to return to my room. My father sat on the edge of my bed, something he hadn't done in a long time, and stroked my head until I closed my eyes and pretended to sleep.

Many times during the remainder of that night, while my parents bustled between the telephone and the servants' quarters, I fooled myself into believing Hanif was still alive. I heard his high-pitched chatter through the walls and the patter of hand-me-down slippers on his feet. The spraying water in the bathroom was his father drawing him a bath; the muted cries were his giggling. Through it all, he was wearing my brother's red tracksuit.

FIVE

Late February–March 1978

The morning after the accident, my yellow school bus and a mini-van appeared in front of the house at almost the same time. I was at the bus stop when the minivan drove through our gates to take Yunis, Sadiq, and what was left of Hanif to Lahore. I sat in the front seat of the unusually empty bus. The driver, accustomed to turning off the engine and waiting for me because I was always late, was slow to close the doors and continue the journey. I pressed my face to the window and concentrated on the activity in the driveway. The rear of the minivan was opening. Yunis and my father were straining to place the child's stiff body inside the van. I assumed Hanif was wrapped in my mother's best white sheets.

Lizzy did not get on the bus at her stop, and I wished she had so I could take my mind off the accident. I could not get Hanif out of my mind. He was a small boy, lean like Amir had once been, and over and over, I imagined his bones shattering from the impact of the car. I missed Amir and Lehla more than I ever had. I wished it had been me, instead of them, who'd escaped Islamabad so I wouldn't have been home for Hanif's death.

No one told me, but I knew exactly how he'd been killed. It was irrelevant that I hadn't been with Sadiq, Hanif, and Yunis on the walk home from Aabpara Market. I wasn't privy to the precise details, but I'd overheard things during the night. By the time morning came, the picture I'd formed in my imagination was so real I believed it to be true. Hanif tried on several pairs of shoes until he found the one that fit. It was the most expensive pair in the store, and that left his father without any money for bus fare, which was why they began walking home.

The streets were dark as they often were when WAPDA neglected to fix streetlights. Cars used their high beams, but the flood of light coming and going made things worse and sent the three scrambling off the shoulderless road every time a car passed. The men walked steadily, but Hanif, with his shorter legs, lagged behind. When they were halfway home, on an empty road and not paying as much attention as they should have, they were suddenly caught in blinding headlights. None of them could move to the side of the road quickly enough. The big car lost control and swerved toward them. Yunis, a few steps ahead of Hanif, shouted. Sadiq lunged toward him, but didn't reach Hanif until it was too late. In the long second between when the headlights fell on Hanif and when the car struck his son, Sadiq saw his face. Hanif didn't make the slightest sound. There was the thud of a body on steel, the burned rubber smell of brakes, the sound of the shoe box dropping to the side of the road.

Sadiq fell to the ground, crouching over Hanif, softly speaking to the crumpled body while Yunis focused on the car. He plowed his fist into the car's rear end, shattering a light and bruising his hand. When he tried to open the locked passenger door, the engine that had died with shrieking brakes came to life again.

"No!" he shouted, noting the diplomat's license plate, demanding the driver remain at the scene of the accident. The car lurched forward and disappeared, leaving in its wake a trail of dust and a dead little boy.

Yunis collected the shoe box from where it had fallen, and Sadiq gathered Hanif in his arms. Yunis suggested they call my father, but Sadiq said there was no need. Yunis hailed a taxi, which Sadiq refused. Sadiq walked along the road, Yunis close behind and at a loss to help. So it went until I saw Sadiq barely on his feet, weaving from side to side in our driveway with the chowkidar on his tail.

All day there were signs it was not a regular Thursday at school. Lizzy was only one of many absentees. Normally, school would not have been in session because of the midsemester recess, but a burst water main a month earlier forced the principal to close the school for repairs for two weeks, and since then all holidays had been rescinded. The empty buses and classrooms were a testament to how few people had bothered with the adjusted schedule, although I was surprised not to see Lizzy. She'd invited me to her house for dinner that night, and I worried that plans might have changed.

As empty as the school was, it was filled with more Pakistanis than I'd ever seen on the premises. This included the time when Begum Bhutto gave the commencement speech at Amir's graduation, and she'd been accompanied by a security detail of Pakistanis who crowded the oversized parking lot and filled the back halls of our auditorium. Despite repeated announcements, I'd forgotten that the morning marked the start of renovations to the brick walls surrounding the single-story school buildings. The parking lot was filled with trucks, worker crews, and their donkeys, lending the school the feel of a typical Islamabad street rather than the closeted American space it usually was. A caravan of donkeys strapped with jute bags carried piles of bricks from a truck to workers, who slapped cement on the bricks and set new rows on the walls. The work had been necessitated due to the construction of Islamabad's new railway station a few hundred yards from the school. Months earlier, I'd brought home a memo from the principal announcing the plan to increase by two feet the height of the walls around the school because the Pakistani government was reneging on its promise not to build in the area directly surrounding the school, and the dangers this created had school officials concerned. My mother thought such measures were absurd. "Why don't they go ahead and top off the walls with broken glass and barbed wire, too?" she'd asked my father who, as usual, wasn't listening.

I barely noticed the boys being marched into the principal's office for bumming cigarettes from construction workers. It was hard to think about anything but Hanif. Over the last few months, I'd passed him in the driveway, in the garden, in the kitchen, all the while barely speaking because I didn't know much Urdu. Had we ever exchanged more than casual greetings? I'd given him Amir's soccer ball and had intended to let him play with my basketball, but I didn't really want Hanif to touch it, because my father had bought the premium leather ball in some faraway place especially for me.

Sitting in math class, going through the motions of calculating angles and copying from my neighbor, who was much smarter than me, I could feel the shame set in. It starts at the tips of your ears and takes an eternity to curl around your earlobes, but after it does, it breaks loose and drowns you. It's like blushing, except it's not red, so no one can see it. Not sharing the basketball with Hanif was different from other things that made me feel shame: lifting coins from the pile on my father's dresser, stealing the precious European chocolate he brought back from his travels and giving it to my friends, the smell of caramelized onions in my house that bothered my American friends, and the reality I rarely thought about but which was true, that sometimes I wanted to be white or, at least, American.

I wished I had given Hanif my basketball.

As in the days when there had been three of us returning from school, today my mother was waiting for me at the kitchen table. She'd baked my favorite apple cake, but I wasn't hungry.

"How was school?"

I shrugged my shoulders. "Same."

"Are you all right?"

"Why wouldn't I be?" I said, daring her to bring up Hanif.

"I mean, are you really all right?" she said, persistent. "A terrible thing happened yesterday. Hanif . . . it might be a good idea to talk about it. If you'd like . . ."

"They started work on the school walls today," I said in a quick turnabout, changing the subject and momentarily declining to talk about Hanif with my mother.

"Not now, but when you're ready."

"When will Sadiq be back?" I relented.

"Your father has given him leave for as long as he needs. A few weeks, I would guess."

"That long?"

"After all, his son died yesterday, and . . ."

"Was killed," I corrected her. "His son was killed yesterday."

My mother, who hadn't moved since we sat down together, studied me. "It's good to talk about things when we are sad," she began, but I'd already tuned her out. There was nothing worse than being told how or what to feel when you recognized that grown-ups were hiding the truth.

"Did Daddy tell you why the driver left the scene?" I eventually asked.

"He doesn't know, my darling. He wasn't there."

It was true. He wasn't there, but I sensed he knew more than he was admitting.

Later, alone in my room, I thought it was odd how not having spoken much to Hanif bothered me more than being unable to communicate in Urdu with my own cousins, my father's sister's children in Karachi, whom I rarely saw. My father had tried. Before Amir and Lehla left for college, he'd insisted on Urdu lessons for all of us. But after Lehla went to America, he resigned himself to my disinterest and terminated Master sahib's lessons.

Remembering Master sahib, I considered for the first time what learning Urdu might mean, what it would feel like to walk into London Book Co. or A.M. Grocers in Kohsar Market and understand animated conversations or eavesdrop on hushed whispers. I wouldn't need to ask my father to translate the news, and I would read Urdu newspapers on my own. I would speak to our chowkidar or the motorcycle spy without hesitation. I would make my grandfather, who'd just been visiting, proud by reciting his favorite Urdu poetry. I would have cousins in the true sense of the word, rather than merely people who were related to me by blood.

Was this the time for me to learn Urdu? Wholly and perfectly, like I'd learned to knit cables on sweaters and stitch flowers in the corners of linen napkins or swish basketballs in our driveway hoop? The fact that my world had two universes would never change. But knowing the language would let me decide which universe I wanted to be in and when. Urdu would be the pole catapulting me to the other side if I ever needed to be there.

Just then, my mother knocked on the door to tell me Lizzy was on the telephone.

"Liya?" Lizzy said, sounding as if she'd caught a cold. "I'm sorry. You can't come for dinner tonight. I have the flu."

"Oh," I said, trying to hide my disappointment. "Feel better, OK? I missed you at school today."

"I'll call when I'm better." I was surprised when she hung up without asking me for the homework she'd missed, and I almost called her back.

Trying not to be too disappointed, I occupied myself with sorting through a pile of books on the bottom of my shelf. Some of them were mine, while others belonged to Lehla. I found my Urdu notebook and the first- and second-grade readers my father once selected for me in Lahore's famous Ferozsons bookstore. I couldn't help feeling there was something perverse about my sudden need to learn Urdu. After all, it had taken the death of Hanif, a boy I hardly knew and whose body I imagined still in the back of a rented minivan, to make me want to learn the language. I sharpened a pencil and slowly sketched shapes in the margins of graph paper in my math notebook. I would learn, I decided, without anyone's help. It would be my secret. I wasn't entirely sure why I wanted to keep it a secret, except that I suspected revealing it would somehow change how I was perceived. For example, would I still be half-and-half? I would tell my parents when I was ready. Maybe I'd wait until I could read an entire newspaper page, because that would really impress my father. After years in which my father had hoped we would learn, I would present the language to him fluently, as a gift, but only when I was ready.

Hours after my parents had gone to bed, I practiced words I already knew. *Pani* was water, *darvaza* was door, *bistar* was bed. But I couldn't conceive of stringing together those few simple words into a sentence to address Hanif. Water near the door got on the bed? What was *near* in Urdu? And *got*? What did they use for *on*? Before I fell asleep with my head on my desk, the letters began to dance in front of me. I tried to keep my eyes focused on them, determined not to let them slip away. I awoke in the middle of the night, after dreaming that Hanif was dribbling pani, darvaza, bistar like soccer balls on a cricket pitch. As I climbed into bed, pulling the blanket over my head to cover my ears, my head ached for Hanif, an eight-year-old boy who had worn my hand-me-downs, loved the prime minister, and who, all of a sudden, was dead.

SIX

March 1978

If my father hadn't bribed the officer at the Margalla Road police station who had filed the police report on Hanif's death, no one would have bothered to inform him of the conclusion. Yunis was right. The driver in the hit-and-run accident was a diplomat. And as a result of diplomatic immunity, no charges could be filed against the driver. He had killed someone, and he wasn't going to jail.

"What happens now?" I asked.

"Will his license at least be taken away?" my mother asked.

"Foreigners don't need licenses." My father dismissed her question.

"Too bad the general can't be bothered to decree anything useful. Like requiring diplomats to carry licenses or, better yet, funding traffic police."

At the mention of the general, my father muttered a curse, "Ulloo ka patha." It was his favorite curse—literally meaning "son of an owl," but in reality, impossible to translate into English. He remembered I was sitting beside him and quickly added, "This isn't a parking ticket, for God's sake! There ought to be consequences."

My mother smiled. "Do they give parking tickets in Pakistan?"

"The driver should be punished," my father said.

"But he won't be."

The accident increased my parents' paranoia about the blinding headlights of nighttime driving in Islamabad, and they reiterated the rule that forbade me to walk on the street at night. I didn't think it was the right time to reveal that Lehla and Amir had routinely broken the rule.

"Of course," I said.

A few weeks later, Sadiq returned from Lahore. I came upon him in the kitchen and was shocked to discover he'd shaved his head and grown a beard. I couldn't take my eyes off his head, which was white compared to the rest of him and in marked contrast with his straggly black beard. He cut me a piece of almond cake, my favorite dessert, because I'd never developed a taste for gajar halva and gulab jamun or any of the other Pakistani sweets that Lehla and Amir loved. I was halfway through my second piece when Sadiq put a steaming mug of milky tea next to me. He was waiting for me to finish so he could do my dishes, one of his final chores of the night.

"Aap ki biwee theek hain?" I asked if his wife was fine.

Sadiq paused but didn't look at me. He wasn't surprised that I'd asked about his family, but that I'd spoken a full sentence with all the words agreeing with one another. "Biwee theek?" is what I would have asked in the past.

"Haan jee," he answered in the affirmative.

"Aap ke larke ka bara afsos hua." I'm so sorry about your son. My father had coached me, but I wasn't confident I'd remembered correctly.

Sadiq didn't acknowledge me, sweeping imaginary crumbs from the table into his hand. I didn't move until, finally, he wondered aloud whether Master sahib, my old Urdu teacher, had recently come for a lesson. I shook my head.

Sadiq washed my dishes and put them away. He wrung out a wet cloth with hot water and wiped down the stovetop. Although it didn't need it, he ran a sponge over the plastic tablecloth and, looking for something more to do, began polishing the silver face of the Zenith radio.

"Tumhari biwee theek hai?" He repeated my question but modified it to reflect the informal case I remembered was reserved for servants, children, and friends.

Someone turned on the television in the family room, and the volume, accidentally set on high, startled us both. I guessed that the Khabarnama newscaster was reciting news that BBC had already reported. In its long-awaited decision, the Lahore High Court had awarded the death sentence to former Prime Minister Zulfikar Ali Bhutto in the Nawab Muhammad Ahmad Khan murder case.

Sadiq and I stayed where we were until I could repeat the question, Tumhari biwee theek hai? without errors. Then I joined my parents in the lounge and Sadiq returned to the servants' quarters. It disturbed me that he lived in the room where his son had lain dead.

By the next evening, Sadiq's shaved head was wrapped in a turban, in the past a look he only sported when he was ill.

"Are you sick?" my mother asked.

He wasn't, and from then on, the turban was part of his attire.

A few days later, the doorbell rang and a WAPDA messenger teased him about his new look before Sadiq waved him away. My father used a table knife to break open the red-wax seal on the manila envelope he was handed. He briefly peered inside before setting it aside to read later. I saw the envelope next on my father's bedside table, and its contents were spread like a fan on his lap. I'd stumbled in at the end of a conversation and caught my mother asking, "The driver thinks he can trade life for money?"

"What driver?" I fired.

My father shot me a look that silenced me, at least for a minute.

"What else can Sadiq do but accept the settlement?" my father asked wearily.

"We know that payment is wholly insufficient. The driver owes Sadiq an apology. In person."

I couldn't help myself. "Is this about Hanif? You know who killed him? Who's the driver?" I tried reaching for the single-spaced typewritten pages strewn on the bed. "Does it say who did it?"

My father gathered the papers in a single motion before I could grab them.

"Of course not," my mother replied, only bothering to answer my last question.

My father rose and slipped the pages back into the envelope.

"No use putting it off," he said and left.

"What's Daddy doing?"

"He's going to tell Sadiq about the settlement that we received in the mail for him today."

"Settlement?"

"It's a legal document drawn up by an embassy. In this case, the driver in the hit-and-run accident is taking responsibility for what he did and is offering a sum of money to compensate."

The only way to understand this was that the driver was paying off Sadiq for killing his son, so I said so.

"Well, because diplomats cannot be prosecuted, they sometimes make goodwill gestures—in the form of money—when they've broken the law."

"Sadiq's not going to be happy," I said.

"Indeed."

It occurred to me quickly. "Then you *do* know who the driver was!"

"Well," my mother said haltingly, ". . . yes, but there's no reason for you to know."

"You always think I'm too young to know important things. Hanif is *my* servant's son. If you know, why can't I?"

"Aliya! The identity of the driver doesn't matter. The important thing is that he acknowledged his crime."

"You said yourself he didn't apologize! What good is the acknowledgment?"

"It's *something*," my mother said, as if she'd just convinced herself.

"Money can't replace Hanif."

"True," she agreed, and I wasn't quite as angry.

Later, my mother told me that Sadiq hadn't wanted to accept the settlement. My father fought to persuade him that one day he might have use for the money. Although he finally did sign the settlement papers, I was proud of Sadiq. He was right to resist. Money couldn't take the place of Hanif, and, in the end, the only thing it did was help the driver feel less guilty. As far as I was concerned, the driver didn't deserve to feel the slightest bit better.

SEVEN

June 1978

When Lizzy finally returned to school after two full weeks, she didn't look like Lizzy. After recovering from what she said was the flu, she had dark circles under her sea-blue eyes and a sheet of gray across her face. If I hadn't been treated for dehydration at Polyclinic, Islamabad's government hospital, I wouldn't have believed you could miss so much school because of vomiting and diarrhea. I brought her up to date on school news, but I decided not to share what had happened to Hanif. It wasn't that I'd already forgotten him. Quite the contrary. But in the carefully structured compartments that comprised my life, there were specific places for everything, and I couldn't allow matters—even ones as sad and consuming as Hanif—to spill over from one into the other. Besides, Lizzy didn't know Hanif, who was dead, or Sadiq, who'd suddenly forgotten that tables were set with forks on the left side and knives on the right and that a napkin lay next to a plate, not wrapped around it.

In the months following her return to school, I could tell that Lizzy had changed. She hardly ate, offering me her Wonder Bread sandwiches before throwing them away. When my American classmates had first started bringing sandwiches made with newly available Wonder Bread from the commissary, I couldn't wait for a taste, but all it took was a single bite to want nothing more to do with the spongy bread. The best thing about Lizzy's appetite loss was that even when it slowly returned, she never regained an interest in sweets. I was the happy recipient of whatever desserts the Simons' cook packed for her, cupcakes and blueberry muffins made from powdered mixes, perfect squares of fudge, tiny packs of Junior Mints and candy corn. I never turned down the items that had made their magical way across half the world to the embassy's commissary, a mythical place to which all Pakistanis, half-and-half or not, were forbidden access. In exchange, Lizzy devoured Sadiq's samosas. They were my mother's ingenious method of using up leftovers and making us eat healthy, and instead of the standard spicy potato or keema filling, Sadiq filled the samosas with spoonfuls of saag or chhole. It didn't matter to Lizzy, because she didn't know that aloo saag or chhole weren't meant to be in samosas.

By June, when no one could decide whether the bus windows should stay open to let in the scorching breeze or closed to protect us from it, school was endless, especially my French class. French was the last hour of my school day, I wasn't good at it, and I didn't like the teacher. Mr. Duval was from Mauritius, but until I heard him speak for the first time, I thought he was Pakistani. He was almost as dark as my father, with deep brown eyes and extra-white teeth, but unlike my father, he was growing bald and kept what was left of his hair oiled and combed behind his ears. He spoke with an accent that was difficult to place, part British and part attempting to be something else, as if the way he talked could change who he was. He sported brightly colored ties that did not match his clothes and spoke in a faltering and timid voice. More often than not, he walked into our classroom after students had used the few minutes between classes to fill the blackboard with sketches of his paunchy belly. His eyes were the worst. There was something beggarly about them, something uneasy and defeated in the way they darted from one person to another and back again. We passed notes to one another during class about the stains in the armpits of his V-neck blue sweater, his graying nose hairs, and anything else that struck us as funny on a particular day. When he caught us, he never had the courage to send us to the principal's office. He probably worried about losing his job.

He spoke French hesitantly with an abundance of pauses and an annoying tendency to draw out even the shortest words, transforming a monosyllabic word into one with several syllables. It was exactly the way I spoke Urdu, so I knew his tricks. In the classroom, our laughter halted only once a week, on Wednesdays, when we prepared for the weekly quiz the following day. Instead of writing notes, we copied explanations for verb conjugations and Mr. Duval's own rhyming grammatical rules into our notebooks. It was the only time any of us asked questions, and in his eagerness for us to do well on the quizzes, he would provide us with the questions and, eventually, the answers.

One afternoon, I was slumped in my seat waiting for the end-of-class bell, aware that despite Mr. Duval's help, I'd done poorly on the quiz. He collected the tests and tapped them into a neat pile using the arm of my old student desk, which prevented me from getting up while everyone else left the classroom.

"You are not doing very well in the class," he finally said. "If you study for your quizzes, you will do better."

He didn't say anything I didn't already know, and I decided to be blunt. I told him I didn't like French, and it didn't make sense.

"But it is simple," he answered, genuinely surprised, "once you learn the rules. For one, the order of conjugation."

In the ceiling-to-floor window behind his shoulder, Lizzy was making faces, sticking out her tongue at him, scratching her armpits like a monkey, and blowing raspberries against the classroom window. Two or three other friends joined her. I'd done the very same things when we'd made fun of him together. "You don't even speak French," I mumbled disdainfully, suddenly brave, the words slipping from my mouth.

"Qu'avez-vous dits? What did you say? I am from Mauritius," he proclaimed, and the severity of his tone forced my gaze from the window to his face. "Do you know what we speak in Mauritius? French. French is the national language. French is my language." As if to prove his last sentence, he repeated himself in French, quickly and more loudly. "Je suis francophone."

He planted his hand on my desk, pulled up the sleeve of his stained sweater, and uncuffed his shirt. He brought his forearm close to my face, and I felt his arm hair against my chin.

"Because my skin is brown," he said quietly, as if he might be overheard, "you do not think I can speak French?"

A moment passed, and then another, before Mr. Duval moved. I could hear Lizzy and her friends giggling, but I followed his arm until it hung at his side, and the contrast between his white shirt cuff and his skin reminded me of my father. I was no longer sure he didn't speak French, and I was desperate with fear my father would discover my impertinence.

"You won't tell the principal, will you?" I pleaded.

Mr. Duval gripped my wrist until he pinched my skin.

"You are not one of them," he whispered, and let me go.

I rubbed the inside of my cheeks against my braces until they were raw. I wrapped my fingers around my wrist like a bangle and did not leave my desk until the color returned to my pinched skin and Mr. Duval finished tidying the classroom.

Lizzy had tired of waiting, but we caught up with each other walking to the bus.

"Liya! What did evil-Dooval want?" Lizzy asked.

"Not much," I mumbled. When Lizzy continued to look at me expectantly, I added, "To go over my test, that's all. I didn't do so well."

"Did you see his sweat puddles today?" Lizzy said derisively.

I had, like everybody else. But Mr. Duval no longer seemed stupid, and his armpits were no longer funny. I nodded and got on the bus.

When the principal called home, he didn't mention the scene with Mr. Duval but told my mother he was concerned about my performance in French class. My attendance at the school was contingent on outstanding academic performance, he noted, and added that my French marks fell far short of excellence. When my mother repeated the conversation to me and I didn't offer an explanation, much less an apology, she resorted to her common refrain. Attending the American School of Islamabad was a privilege, not a right.

I hated the reminder. My mother had once told me that a year's tuition was more than my father's annual salary, and we could afford the school only because of our scholarships. While my mother went on to express her disappointment in my French marks, I wondered if there were any Pakistanis who did not need scholarships. The prime minister's children?

Starting that evening, I was forced to spend half an hour with my mother, my French homework spread out on the dining room table. Having learned French when she was a child, she could conjugate any verb without thinking, while I couldn't remember how to conjugate the easiest ones.

"You must learn other languages," my mother said patiently, launching into yet another favorite refrain, "for not everyone will speak yours."

I sighed, but I was grateful for her concern. I was even more grateful that Mr. Duval hadn't told the principal what had happened between us.

Alone in the room I'd once shared with my sister, I could still feel the pressure of Mr. Duval's hand on my wrist. Dinner, my mother's version of nasi goreng, churned in my stomach, and I'd already stood up a few times thinking I'd have to make a dash for the toilet. "You are not one of them." Mr. Duval's final words echoed inside my head until, all strung together, they became my only thought.

I was *not* one of them. I was not American. I didn't look like them, and try as I might, the details of trying to pass for one were exhausting.

Every day they included a whole host of things, such as wearing jeans, which I worked hard at not calling *denims*, copying their accent, staying away from British words my parents used, like *fetch* for *get* and *senior to* instead of *older than*, and saying things like *That's cool!* and *What's happening?* I even pretended to be aware of what my classmates discussed, including movies they saw on home leaves in America or houseboats they stayed in while visiting Indian Kashmir, where my Pakistani passport would never have allowed me to go. I recalled one Halloween when a trick-or-treater, the son of an American teacher, stepped into my house while Sadiq was cooking biryani and wrinkled his nose with distaste. While I put my mother's carefully wrapped meringue cookies in his bag, he said, "Your house smells like Pakistan." My parents drove a car with black license plates, not the yellow ones sporting special codes of numbers that announced their foreign embassy and rank. My mother packed my lunches in oversized yellow paper bags from the fruit market, not the brown paper ones that could be purchased in packets of fifty or one hundred at the American commissary.

The afternoon I put my name on a list to join the Girl Scouts, my mother received an apologetic telephone call from the troop leader claiming Pakistanis were not allowed in her group, but there was a local equivalent if I was still interested. Then there was the evening I was invited for the first time to the movies at the American Embassy with Lehla and one of her friends. The young American man collecting the tickets looked us over from head to toe before indicating Pakistanis were not permitted in the movie theater. But he finally allowed us to pass after putting his face to mine, his breath in my ear, and chuckling, not unkindly, "You're not really one, are you?" I'd been delighted at first, but if passing for white was what I wanted, why did my gleeful reaction trouble me when we got home? Lehla said to forget about it because the point was, we got to see the movie.

Being white is nice, I thought. *It's blonde bangs falling away from your forehead with the toss of your head. It's slathering baby oil on your skin to make it turn golden in the sun. It's wearing blue jeans that sit on your hips and flare to the floor. It's the steering wheel being on the wrong side in a car with yellow license plates. It's eating Pringles and Twinkies and Wonder Bread flown into Islamabad from America. It's knowing what prime rib is and how bagels are made. It's having a cook who makes cinnamon rolls. It's wearing clothes advertised in magazines and using catalogs to buy underwear. It's knowing the best lines in* The Spy Who Loved Me *and all the verses in "Staying Alive." It's not having to remember to spell* color *without the* u. *It's ordering donuts at United Bakery or poking at the pomegranates in Covered Market without ever thinking of lowering your voice. It's knowing who you are because you look like people in magazines.*

But the most important thing was also the simplest. Being white is not being half-and-half. It's being whole. And knowing it.

My mother looked like one of them, but she was not, really. Being married to my father had made her brown, though, of course, you couldn't tell by looking.

Although it was too late to do well in French, the principal's warning made me worry about getting good grades in other classes. So I convinced Lizzy to join me in a complicated science project that involved mosquitoes and malaria, and we asked the help of her father, who was an expert on the subject and who promised us colorful brochures and real mosquito larvae.

I couldn't think of Lizzy's mother as anything but *Anne Simon* because that's how she'd introduced herself, as if we could be on a first-name basis. Although I called her Mrs. Simon, she was *Anne Simon* inside my head. The resemblance between Lizzy and her mother was astonishing. Aside from their blue eyes and white-blonde hair, they both spoke softly, as if they were concerned their words might intrude on others. I'd also recently noticed they shared half-moon shadows under their eyes, bruises almost, and I was surprised I'd missed the likeness earlier. When we went to Lizzy's house to start work on the project, Anne Simon was hard at work on her sewing machine, holding folds of material and guiding hems into white-lace curtains she intended to hang throughout the house.

Mr. Simon was sitting on the other side of the sofa, and laid out on the cocktail table in front of him were Polaroid photographs documenting a work trip to Kabul through the Khyber Pass, from which he'd only just returned. We sat with him for a moment and he pointed at a few photographs, giving us the names of towns and exclaiming on what a beautiful country Afghanistan was.

My mother had raised her eyebrows when I'd told her he was going on the trip. There had recently been a coup in Afghanistan, but instead of removing a prime minister from office, as our general had, the king had been removed, and according to the BBC newscaster, a Marxist-Leninist government had been installed. "Is it safe for Americans working on malaria projects to be there?" my mother had wondered aloud, but my father, back from Lahore, was preoccupied with a new electricity or water crisis in the country and hadn't responded.

Several cardboard boxes were stacked against the bare white wall across Anne Simon's sewing room. One of the boxes was open, and I peeked inside. I saw piles of white shirts, miniature versions of the white ones my father used to wear to the office until the government changed the dress code a year or two earlier and demanded citizens give up Western shirts for Pakistani clothes. More garments lay draped on the backs of chairs and scattered on other surfaces. Although the clothes were sewn in different fabrics and colors, they all appeared the same size. I touched a flannel shirt hanging on the back of a chair and drew my fingers over the careful stitching on the pockets.

"You made these for the twins?" I asked Anne Simon, referring to Lizzy's brothers, who were still a year away from beginning school.

"They're much too big for the boys," she answered as the two identical beings, four years old, pranced into the room clutching plastic train tracks. "I made them for a women's charity group. The clothes we make go to kids who need them."

"They're all the same size, right?" I asked, but Anne Simon was being called to the telephone. She was the embassy nurse, and according to Lizzy, she was always being called at home for advice. While Lizzy ordered cookies and soda for us from the kitchen, I held one of the shirts up to the light. The white cotton suddenly resembled a child's torso, Hanif's size, and I quickly put it down.

We finally opened our notebooks and began to write up notes for our malaria project. Mr. Simon gave us an illustrated poster that chronicled the life of a mosquito and a map of the world that depicted the countries most prone to be plagued with them. He promised to get us mosquito larvae to display as part of our presentation as soon as he had the time.

Anne Simon was going to the embassy to see a friend and suggested that Lizzy and I go along and have an early dinner in the embassy dining room. "How would you like a cheeseburger?" she asked me.

I accepted the invitation immediately and without asking for my parents' permission or informing them. I had good reason not to tell them, because recently my father had forbidden me to go to the American Embassy and had cautioned me against speaking to Americans about Pakistani politics entirely. He'd explained that the growing tension around whether the prime minister would or wouldn't be hanged, along with concerns that the Americans were conspiring with the general to hang him, made the situation volatile. Neither my mother nor I thought this fair. She also thought it was pointless. "She goes to their school, rides their yellow buses. What on earth difference could it make?"

Before the driver picked us up, Lizzy and I sat in front of the mirror on her grown-up dressing table, dabbing Vaseline on our eyelashes and Anne Simon's powdered rouge on our cheeks. As different as we looked, Lizzy's alabaster against my olive skin, our bodies were virtual replicas of each other's. We both wore stretch bras over budding breasts, and unlike many of our classmates, neither of us slouched inside our clothes to hide them. Lizzy opened her closet and I selected a worn pair of jeans that hugged my waist as though they were mine. She told me I could keep them, because with the weight she'd lost with the flu, she didn't know when they would fit her again. I copied Lizzy and tied my shirt in a knot around my waist and gathered my elbow-length hair into a high ponytail with Lizzy's purple ribbon. Right before we left, Anne Simon said, "You're both gorgeous," and I was thrilled at the word, *gor-geous*, as if Lizzy's mom couldn't see the miniature railway tracks on our teeth.

The car smelled new. Lizzy explained that Mr. Simon had bought it as a gift for the family right before they moved to Islamabad. He'd presented it to Anne Simon with a pink ribbon rising from the belly of the car and tied into a bow on the roof.

"So the car was shipped here?" I asked.

"From Virginia," Lizzy answered, and I wasn't surprised, knowing this was done all the time. Still, the car was so big.

"Mom doesn't like it, though. She says it's too much. She calls it 'The Extravagance' when Dad isn't around. Don't you, Mom?"

The steering wheel, of course, was on the wrong side of the car, on the left instead of the right; never mind that cars in Pakistan were driven on the opposite side of the road. There were traces of clear plastic covering the leather armrest and around the window where they had not been completely removed. The backseat was so wide that with each of us sitting against opposite doors, there was space for two or three more people. The driver switched on the cassette player, and the sound of an American disc jockey in a faraway city filled the car.

"My friend sends me tapes," Lizzy said, as a weekly countdown of popular music hits in her hometown began.

A woman's voice filled the car, and the driver turned up the volume. "Touch me in the morning," she sang, and I wondered if he understood the words.

"Who's that?" I asked.

"Diana Ross," Lizzy replied, assuming the name would mean something to me. "She's really good," she added. My musical knowledge was limited to the music program on Pakistani radio and didn't yet include Diana Ross.

Tapes like Lizzy's were a regular component of school events, including parties, the lead-up to pep rallies, and school assemblies, so it wasn't the first time I'd heard one. On those occasions, the disc jockeys' voices seemed particularly alien to me, but during the extrasmooth drive in Lizzy's plush car on a too-wide road, there was nothing extraordinary about the voices on the radio or the advertisements for Dr Pepper or the electronically controlled windows and melon-sized speedometer. It was only when the disc jockey announced the day of the week and read the weather report that I remembered he spoke of a life thousands of miles away, where Lehla lived and snow arrived in October and people needed reminders about snow tires.

As we rode on Constitution Avenue, past the showy but empty new president's building, "The Extravagance" seemed at home on the only eight-lane roadway in the city until the empty expanse abruptly ended one short mile later, and the driver turned onto the single-lane road to the diplomatic enclave. The big white car drove through the gates of the US Embassy, and I tried not to be nervous. Security was tight, and I'd heard Americans were discouraged from bringing Pakistanis to the compound. But the guard at the gate did not so much as look up from his post before he waved us through the checkpoint.

The lights were bright in the dining room, and as I followed Lizzy to a corner table, I felt conspicuous in my tight jeans and knotted shirt, although I was dressed no differently than Lizzy. The dining room was filled with my classmates, many of whom greeted us, but I worried I was being regarded as a Pakistani rather than Lizzy's friend. I shook my bangs, the ones I'd badgered my mother into cutting for me to match Lizzy's, and brushed them back from my eyes with a gesture I hoped would make people think I was oblivious to them. I was not, however.

The waiter greeted Lizzy by name and nodded at me. He took her order first, and when he'd written it on his pad, he turned to me.

"Aap ko kya chahiye?" he said, asking for my order.

I was startled he spoke in Urdu and that he'd done so with such certainty, dismissing who I was with, the clothes I was wearing, and the light streaks in my chestnut hair that apparently made me look less Pakistani. I considered pretending not to understand him. I raised my head from the menu and studied the man attending to me, trapped by the contradictions of my life—the brown and white, the Dutch and Pakistani, the English and Urdu, the belonging and not. My instinct was to respond in English, but as I was about to stammer out my order, I reconsidered. The hours I'd spent in my room learning Urdu vocabulary words and practicing verb conjugation came to me, along with the memory of the years I'd fortified myself so I wouldn't have to learn from Master sahib. Pretending my hesitation was due to indecision, I fumbled for the words, and although flustered, in the end, I spoke them.

"Ek . . . uh . . . grilled cheese, aur . . . aloo fries, and uh . . . thanda pani baraf ke baghair." I'd not intended to ask for a glass of water without ice, but I did because it was one of the few phrases I could speak fluently in Urdu. Besides, I hated the American fascination for ice.

The waiter took my order without comment.

"I often forget you're Pakistani," Lizzy said.

I laughed. It felt odd to speak Urdu, even the broken variety I'd attempted. I imagined people at nearby tables looking at me, but more than that, I was astonished I'd been persuaded by a waiter to own up to that part of myself.

For the rest of the evening, we talked about the new boy in our class, the sister of another friend who'd been expelled from school by the principal for the brick of hash he found in her locker, and other gossip.

When Anne Simon was finished with her appointment, the driver took us home and drove into the carport, where my parents' beige Toyota Corolla was dwarfed by the Simons' still-new American car.

Immediately upon entering my house, I smelled the chicken tikka masala I loved, the chili tickling my nose, and greeted my parents, who were sitting down to dinner.

"Come, join us," my father said, pulling out my chair as my mother gave me a once-over.

"I ate already. At Lizzy's house," I lied.

"Those aren't your jeans." My mother slapped her hand against the table as she sometimes did to command attention and asked, "Don't you have clothes of your own?"

"I do," I said.

"Then wear them!" she barked.

I turned to my father for support, but he was looking elsewhere in the special way he had for making us believe he was in a different room.

The next morning, out of earshot of my parents, I made light of Sadiq's creative table setting.

"Have you forgotten? Forks on the left, knives on the right."

"*You* have forgotten!" Sadiq exclaimed. "Left is this side, and right is that side," he said, correcting my Urdu, in which I'd confused the words for *left* and *right*. "You knew this, correct?"

I giggled at my mistake. "But why are you setting the table like that? You're making my mother . . ." I struggled to find the least disrespectful word for *crazy* and my mother in the same sentence before I gave up and said plainly, "pagal," crazy.

Sadiq shook his head disapprovingly, and I was sorry for what I'd said. "Begum sahib samajhdar hain," he declared. He made me repeat the word for *wise*, samajhdar, three times before shaking out the orange dustcloth and turning his attention to my parents' bookshelves.

Alone at the correctly set table, I was left to mull over Sadiq's declaration that my mother was wise.

EIGHT

November–December 1978

O ne morning my father sat down to breakfast and discovered utensils, plates, and napkins in a mess that did not pass for a table setting. As if Sadiq's dereliction finally required action, he fired the mali, our ancient gardener, and put Sadiq in charge of the garden. This was in keeping with one of his favorite assumptions, that a healthy dose of fresh air was certain to mend things, like when he'd fixed Lehla's poor grades by demanding she join the field hockey team.

Unfortunately, Sadiq was so ill-equipped as a gardener, he did not know where to start. When asked which task he should tackle first, my father, who knew nothing about gardens, waved in the direction of the gardening tools and told him to prune the rosebushes. In the evening, when my mother saw the rosebushes pruned in full bloom, she admonished both Sadiq and my father. In the end, she hid the gardening shears and suggested my father limit his suggestions to water and electricity.

One Friday, Lizzy and I were sitting in the sun on the upstairs veranda, which offered a perfect view of Sadiq crouched among the ruined rosebushes, pulling weeds from the flower beds, his turban slipping from his head. Lizzy sat there aiming for a one-day winter tan, and I was simply happy for the warmth. We were supposed to be hard at work on a science project for which I'd enlisted my father's help. We'd planned on making a conduction kit, but instead of supplying the parts, my father's secretary assigned an office engineer to the job, and we'd been sent a hand-powered electric generator that we could never have built on our own.

"Wow! Even my dad didn't do our assignment for us!" Lizzy exclaimed. I didn't expect to feel proud, but I did.

We'd spent the afternoon relaxing rather than writing the notes that were required to pretend we'd designed and built the science project. We'd been to the kitchen a few times already, snacking from a fruit tart my mother hoped Lizzy would like. I could hear my father on the telephone, issuing instructions to manage the latest WAPDA crisis that had shut down the electricity supply to half of Rawalpindi. My father arranged to visit the site as soon as he could.

"Your father works on Fridays?" Lizzy asked, and her question surprised me because my father always worked, so I replied, "Doesn't yours?"

My mother had left for her monthly get-together with her few Dutch friends in Islamabad. My grandfather was visiting again, but I hadn't seen him all afternoon, which meant he was taking a long nap in Amir's room.

At first the afternoon was quiet, much as it was every Friday after Jumma prayers, and then suddenly it wasn't.

The gate latch lifted and fell, and our weekend chowkidar, a short and fat man, carelessly swung open the gate, which caught with a loud clang on the metal hook that held it in place. Although it was unusual not to have been told we were expecting company, I didn't pay much attention to the visitors. But when they grew louder, Lizzy and I hung over the railing and observed the driveway teeming with men. Our view was better than the chowkidar's, and we noticed another long line of men heading into our driveway.

As if on cue, my father stuck his head onto the veranda and told us to stay where we were.

"Who are all those people?" I asked.

"My employees have come to talk to me."

"Does this happen often?" Lizzy asked, and I shook my head in the negative.

The next time we looked down, my father was jogging alongside the column of people in our driveway to where the growing crowd had encircled our Toyota Corolla. The men had begun chanting, but I couldn't decipher their words. Much to my surprise, my father hopped onto the hood of the car, and then jumped onto its roof. I gasped, "*What* is he doing?"

"Oooh!" Lizzy said, impressed.

In a gesture I knew well, my father extended his arms as he did when he was overflowing with generosity. "Welcome, welcome!" he shouted, as if he'd been expecting them all afternoon. "Thank you for coming," he started.

The first few sentences of his improvised speech were drowned by the speeding motorcade of black Mercedes and police cars on Margalla Road. The blinking lights and blaring sirens suggested the general was in town, and evidently he was unconcerned that his decree limiting gatherings to fewer than five people was being broken in our driveway.

"What's he saying? What's he saying?" Lizzy asked, jumping up and down excitedly, returning my attention to my father.

The truth was that I could not understand what my father was saying. Like an idiot, I repeated the English words scattered in his speech. Once in a while I strung them together with some Urdu words I understood.

"He's saying, 'You are important to Water Power Development Authority.'"

"Your father is the boss of WAPDA?" Lizzy asked, and I was taken aback that she remembered the words that formed the acronym for my father's office.

"Yes," I said, forced to be honest.

"What did he just say?" Lizzy asked again.

Rather than admit I had no idea, I made it up. "He's saying that without his workers, the streets would be black at night, offices would be dark during the day, radios would be silent . . . Something like that."

While my father spoke, I considered him as I would a stranger. He was an excellent public speaker, at ease in the crowd and unperturbed by their demands. I knew he'd been on his college's debating team, and I could see why he'd won medals. The effect he had on the crowd was palpable, and it seemed to me that the longer he spoke, the more success he had in diminishing his employees' concerns. I thought of the prime minister, known for his oratory skills, and wondered what it would have been like to be in a crowd when he shouted his famous slogan "Roti, kapra, aur makan!"

"What is he saying now?" Lizzy asked.

"My Urdu isn't fluent, you know," I finally confessed. "I *think* they are asking my dad for a pay raise." It was only a guess, but why else would angry employees descend on our house?

Just then, my father stumbled on his words. I thought I knew the phrase he was attempting because government officials commonly used it on Khabarnama, the evening newscast. "In this nation of ours," he said, and like a scratched record, he repeated it three or four times. He'd lost his train of thought, and I was mortified for him. But out of the corner of my eye, I saw the reason for the interruption: My grandfather was suddenly upon the scene. Everyone said my grandfather was deaf, but he constantly proved us wrong, and the fact that the noise had awakened him was yet another example.

My grandfather started down the stairs, clasping his hands above his head in greeting. He was tall and thin, and one might have expected him to fade into the crowd, but when he stepped into our driveway, people moved aside as he wove between them and made his way to my father.

After the moment's reprieve granted by my grandfather's arrival, my father found his voice with even more confidence than before.

"What's he saying?!" Lizzy cried a few minutes later.

His speech was coming to an end, and I suddenly recalled what he'd once said when asked to explain why he'd moved us to Pakistan. "When your country calls on you, you fall on your knees ready to deliver whatever it needs!" Lizzy was satisfied, and since my invented translation was something he'd once said, I didn't feel too bad about the lie.

My father and grandfather led the men in a final chant, "WAPDA zindabad!" As impressive as the solidarity was, I doubted my father had the power to keep any of the promises he'd made. The general's grip was unforgiving, and pay raises wouldn't be arranged without his permission.

"Was this a demonstration?" Lizzy asked.

"Demonstration of what?" I said.

"You know . . . a protest."

"I guess," I said.

"It's my first one!"

"Me, too!" and we bumped hips to confirm our thrill. Demonstration or not, my father's employees had provided me with more excitement than I'd ever seen in Islamabad.

Lizzy and I waited on the veranda until the men, one by one and then altogether, exited the gates. Our chowkidar stood watch proudly with his rifle at his side, as if to suggest that since he'd initially allowed them all in, he therefore had the sole power to send them away.

My father named the event by the time my mother came home: Our house had been the scene of a mini-royit. My father, like most Pakistanis, routinely transposed the *io* in English words into *oi*, which resulted in an *oy* sound. So as far as he was concerned, a mini-royit was exactly what had happened. Unlike other instances when my father's mispronunciations embarrassed me (*violent* was *voylent*, for example), neither my mother nor I bothered correcting him this time. Listening to my father describe the Friday incident convinced me that the event needed its own word.

"Riot?" my mother asked in disbelief, because our house was exactly as it had been when she left.

"*Mini*-royit, my darling, *mini*-royit!" my father said, insistent.

As far as I was concerned, my father was exaggerating. Real riots resulted in trampled lawns, burning tires, and broken windows, among other things. Riots happened in Iran and were documented on the BBC, as they'd been recently when one million Iranians took to the streets to protest the Shah's rule.

"And where were the girls when this was going on?" my mother asked in alarm.

"Upstairs," my father said, waving at the ceiling.

"Weren't you afraid?" my mother asked me.

"Oh, no," I replied truthfully.

"I can't even trust you to keep my daughter and her friend safe while I have a cup of coffee with friends."

"But they *are* safe!"

"Really, Mama, we were fine!"

She turned back to my father. "Can you imagine the story Lizzy will tell her parents? Her best friend's house is the scene of a mini-royit, and she and her friend had front row seats! I'll be surprised if the Simons ever let her come here again."

"That should be the least of their worries," my father muttered, and I had no idea what he meant.

I was the last person to have seen Sadiq that day, and when it was time for dinner, my mother realized he'd left without permission and had not made preparations for the meal. She cooked dinner and served us a nonspicy version of chicken cutlets, a step above the grilled cheese sandwiches she might have served if my grandfather hadn't been visiting. The only topic of conversation was the mini-royit.

"Did you give them what they wanted?" my mother finally asked.

"Of course not. I can't promise them money. I don't pay them. The government does," my father replied.

"Semantics, no? As far as your WAPDA employees are concerned, you are the government!"

"I don't have control over the money."

"You should pay them more," my mother said, dismissing my father's last remark. "I bet the electricity supply would be more reliable if you did."

My grandfather guffawed, and a few grains of half-chewed rice fell to the tablecloth near my glass.

"Thanks, Yasmin," my father said, using my mother's Muslim name, which is what he did when she made him mad.

"Subhan'Allah," she said, a phrase she reserved for being called Yasmin and, as in this case, usually a preface for anger. "This is what you left your UN job for? A country where the prime minister is sentenced to hang and people don't take to the streets? But your employees see fit to riot in our garden while our daughter and her friend watch from the veranda?"

My father's silence made my mother angrier. For the most part, she was a good sport about living in Pakistan, but sometimes she lost patience, and evidently the mini-royit had sapped her reserves. She launched a tirade on what was wrong with my father's country. I squirmed in my seat, uncomfortable that she was going on in front of my grandfather.

Before long, she was caught up in denouncing Pakistan's unpredictability. "A democratically elected government one day, a military regime the next; the prime minister in the national assembly one day, on death row the next; a dapper prime minister in suit and tie one day, a Nazi-like uniformed general in charge the next." She took a breath, and my grandfather nodded as if in agreement, even though he could not have heard all she said. "A quiet house one Friday afternoon, a mini-royit in it the next! This place is as far away as you can get from Vienna—where buses and trains run on time, sugar and flour are not rationed, and grocery stores carry the same goods from one day to the next." She glared at my father and continued, "Not to mention, in Vienna the city's water and electricity supply is a simple fact of life!"

No one knew what to say until my father figured it out.

"Pakistan has Vienna beat in one way," he said.

"And what would that be?" my mother asked.

"Chowkidars! We have more chowkidars here than we know what to do with!"

My mother thought his comment so absurd, she paused before stammering, "And that's a good thing?"

My father informed us that he'd fired our weekend chowkidar, and starting the following night we would have two nighttime chowkidars who would spend their shifts walking rounds.

"Is that really necessary?"

"Probably not. But government regulations require two chowkidars once security is breached in an official's home."

My mother had a point. Pakistan *was* unpredictable; anything could happen here. There were strict regulations for a minor security breach in an official's driveway, but a general could do what he wanted with a prime minister. Rather than stay at the table, I asked my grandfather if I could be excused. Surprisingly, he heard me, said yes, and left with me.

~

At breakfast, Sadiq reported that in his absence the previous evening, the motorcycle spy had paid a visit. The new chowkidar didn't know what to tell him, so he suggested a return visit the following day. Since they had time to prepare, was there anything specific my father wanted the man to know?

"God help us," my father quipped. "Everyone in the neighborhood knows there was a mini-royit at our house yesterday, yet the spy comes to us for information."

Sadiq's appearance that morning was unsettling. His forehead had grown wider, and his eyes were bulging. No one commented, but he had shaved his eyebrows.

"What did you tell Sadiq?" my mother asked.

"The truth, of course. What else is there?"

"Spies aren't supposed to let people know they're being spied upon, right?" I asked.

My father threw his head back with laughter. "Good point, sweetheart."

"This *is* Pakistan, after all," my mother said and shrugged.

Unlike the previous evening, she was calm and matter-of-fact, and she was right.

NINE

I was home alone but it didn't feel like it. The footsteps of two nighttime chowkidars making rounds from dusk to dawn made sure of that. I had learned to fall asleep to their booted feet hitting the pavement at precise intervals, *click-click*, like a ticking clock. A rifle slung across his shoulder, each of the guards circled the house in opposite directions, and the words they exchanged when they met up every eight minutes were absorbed into my dreams about school. *Bismillah. Allahu Akbar*, said Mr. Duval in French class in my sleep.

My father was serious about making sure the chowkidars did their jobs. He could control the light in the chowkidars' hut using a button, and the men had to respond by clicking a switch that ignited a light in the bedroom. It was my father's way of making sure the chowkidars weren't sleeping, at least when there was electricity. Once my father instituted this ritual, my mother swapped sides of the bed with him. She insisted that since my father had chosen to play games, the bulb should flicker in his face, and she was right. All this upheaval was because of the *mini-royit*. Lehla was lucky to be away in America, because it wouldn't have been easy to sneak out of the house at night with two chowkidars on patrol.

Every so often, my parents were invited to the American Embassy, and this night they were attending a reception there. They received invitations to the embassy because of my father's job, yet I couldn't help thinking it also had to do with the fact that he had a foreign wife, and the three of us children were students at the American School. Inviting my father was like inviting the least Pakistani Pakistani. My father and mother, it seemed, gave themselves permission to go to the forbidden place.

Sadiq had finished his work for the night and was in his room, probably listening to a cricket match. I was playing with the television, switching it back and forth between the country's two channels, adjusting and readjusting the volume and sharpness of the picture, as if that act provided me with more options. In any case, television was hardly worth watching. The general had recently decreed that the news on one of the country's two channels be delivered in Arabic. He didn't understand that saying your prayers in Arabic five times a day did not mean you could understand an Arabic newscast. The other station was showing an intermediate hour-long Holy Quran lesson featuring a stern religious scholar behind a bare desk. Finally, it was time for an episode of *CHiPs*, an American television show about the adventures of policemen on motorcycles, but it had been so heavily censored, I couldn't follow it.

The general had ruined everything. In order to pass censors, television shows like *CHiPs* were sliced into spastic panoramas with incomprehensible plots. Women newscasters adopted new hairstyles to accommodate the dupattas covering their heads and began each broadcast with "Bismillah-ir-rahman-ir-raheem." Even my grandfather, who spent countless hours sitting on his prayer rug, was outraged. "In the name of God, the merciful and compassionate!" he sputtered sarcastically in English, confident that God had nothing to do with the news that was being read.

Across from where I sat with the television was my mother's antique walnut desk, the only object in the house from her childhood that had made the journey from Europe to Islamabad when we moved from Vienna. Hidden underneath letters from Amir, electricity bills, and invitations, I found what I was looking for. After memorizing its exact location, I carried it to the sofa where I had a view of the gate and the driveway. I undid the red tie string and pulled out a typewritten statement from the legal affairs officer at the American Embassy.

The facts spoke for themselves. On Wednesday, 22 February 1978, ten minutes after ten at night, on the corner of Embassy and Majlis Roads, Sadiq's son, Hanif, approximately nine years old, was struck and killed by a hit-and-run driver. The white luxury sedan was registered in the name of a USAID official. Rather than face what could have been a hostile, possibly violent reaction from the two adults with the boy, the driver returned home and, following procedure, immediately reported the accident to the chief security officer of the American Embassy.

The last page of the document outlined the terms of the settlement and included four signatures. Sadiq's name appeared in Urdu with my father's next to it. I scanned the next name quickly, unprepared for it to be significant. But when I realized how familiar it was, I read it again more slowly. The blue signature looked like practice words in a cursive-handwriting workbook, tall and even letters leaning to the right. The last signature belonged to Mr. Simon, the designated witness.

Anne Simon. It took me a moment to connect the name with Lizzy's mother. Perhaps there was another Anne Simon in Islamabad married to a different Mr. Simon. Then I began recalling details. Lizzy's mysterious illness which kept her out of school for two weeks, and when she'd returned, her lack of appetite, the shadows under her eyes, deep and dark like bruises . . . and the same expression on her mother's face.

Further along, the settlement indicated Sadiq would receive 50,000 rupees as compensation for his son's life. Did Anne Simon know what that amount of money could buy? Did I? Did Sadiq? A car, maybe, but Sadiq couldn't drive. A tiny farm somewhere, but Sadiq wasn't a farmer and he couldn't suddenly become one, because, after all, he had to look after us. I settled on the idea that the money might buy him a new house with cement walls to keep out rats and a roof thick enough to ward off the monsoons in the rundown quarters of Lahore. Perhaps the sum would buy him running cold and hot water. A lorry rumbled on the road and shook the windows of the living room, reminding me that my parents might soon be home. I carefully returned the papers to the envelope and buried it between Amir's latest letters and my mother's silver-embossed stationery.

For the next hour, I wandered around the empty house, up and down the steps, in and out of Amir's bedroom, through the kitchen, around the living room, into the front hall, in a series of circles that would have made anyone dizzy. I wanted to eject what was in my head, like a sixty-minute cassette from Amir's tape recorder, but I couldn't stop the refrain. Instead, the sheer repetition of *Anne Simon was the driver* lodged further and further into my consciousness. I finally stopped in my parents' bedroom long enough for their formal smells, Old Spice and Chanel N° 5, to distract me.

I sat on my father's side of the bed, and although I'd never done it before, I pressed the new light switch, waiting a few moments for the flickering lightbulb to respond.

Suddenly Sadiq appeared, asking me if everything was all right.

"Why?"

"Are you testing the chowkidars?"

I took too long to answer, trying to reconcile the information in the settlement with the man standing in front of me.

"It's too early for them to be asleep," Sadiq teased, but his missing eyebrows took away the joy from his half smile. When I didn't respond, he asked, "Can I get you something? You want some water?"

"What's the word for when two people agree on something?"

"They settle on something?"

"Yes. Something like that."

"Samjhauta karna." He repeated it twice, and as was his habit, did not stop drilling me until I had said it perfectly and used it in a sentence.

"The agreement between them was wrong," I stated.

"Not a good sentence. But it's good enough for tonight. If you need another word, don't bother the chowkidars, ask me."

"OK," I said.

"Good night?" Sadiq asked.

"Good night," I confirmed.

A few hours later, while I sat in the armchair in their bedroom, my parents discussed one of the guests at the reception, a middle-aged Pakistani executive of an oil company. He was famous for carrying a narrow flask of whiskey in his breast pocket wherever he went. At the American Embassy, where alcohol was abundantly available, he'd been seen drinking from his flask in plain sight of the host.

"What a disgrace," my father said.

My mother then mentioned a man who'd pretended to speak in an official capacity and claimed that the exposure of her midriff was un-Islamic. She'd been so annoyed by his comments, she pushed her sari farther down below her waist and walked away.

"Please tell me you didn't do that," my father said.

"But I did!" my mother replied. She didn't look up because she was busy expertly unwrapping her sari into perfect folds of pink silk as if she'd worn saris all her life.

My father asked me if I knew an Iranian boy, Humayun, in our high school.

"Humayun? I think so," I said, finally recalling a skinny teenager who reminded me of Amir. "I think that's his name. I don't really know him, though. He's much older than me. Why?"

"We heard that yesterday he and his family left for the US in the middle of the night."

"Why would they do that?" I asked.

"His father must have been appointed to the Iranian embassy by the Shah, and they fled because of Khomeini," my father suggested.

"His father was SAVAK," my mother said, quickly getting to the point.

"The spy agency?" I asked, displaying knowledge I'd recently gained from the radio, secretly thrilled that Islamabad, the quiet, sleepy city where nothing ever happened, suddenly housed Iranian spies fleeing in the middle of the night. The thought of spies in Islamabad set my mind wandering. I knew they weren't *Get Smart*–type spies (one of the many television shows canceled by the general), but more likely, boring people who studied what they saw and reported back—to whom exactly, I didn't know. There had to be multiple bosses, because the one thing I knew for certain was that all the spies running around Islamabad were not on the same side.

"What's the license plate number for Iranians?" I asked, as if the two digits had some relevance to what was being discussed.

I was pointlessly trying to make conversation, but neither of my parents answered me. My father walked to the bathroom to brush his teeth while my mother was carefully hanging her sari in her closet, alongside the rest of her colorful collection. Their silence made me worry that they'd detected a change in me and magically concluded that I'd read the settlement papers. But as I was glad to see, my parents were not mind readers, and I was almost disappointed when they behaved normally with me. It meant I would have to keep the shocking information to myself, and I wasn't very good with secrets.

The last thing I wanted to do was to retreat to my room, preoccupied with my fresh discovery, so when my father came out of the bathroom, I tried to start another conversation.

"Humayun's family went to America because the Americans are friendly with the Iranians?" I asked.

"*Were* friendly," my father corrected me. He explained that the Shah of Iran and the United States had been close friends for many years, ever since the United States had engineered a coup d'état against Prime Minister Mossadegh, an elected ruler of Iran, and replaced him with the Shah. Now that Ayatollah Khomeini had returned to Iran, the United States was rightfully worried.

"Why did the Americans get rid of Mossadegh?" I asked, and it rang both true and peculiar to refer to a country and a prime minister like chess pieces.

My father embarked on a long explanation that didn't make sense to me, having to do with colonialism and American and British oil interests. He mentioned a different country, Guatemala, where Americans had also directed a coup and ousted another leader for different reasons. As he went on, my mind wandered back to the settlement papers I'd just discovered, and a parallel began to form in my mind. With the hit-and-run accident on an Islamabad street, Anne Simon had behaved in her personal life the way American governments behaved in the world, doing whatever they wanted, without, for the most part, suffering any consequences.

"Let her go to sleep, Javid," my mother interrupted. "It's late."

As I was leaving the bedroom, I tested my resolve at keeping my secret and asked whether there had been any Americans at the reception.

"Of course, sweetheart," my mother replied. "It was at the American Embassy!"

"Who?" I demanded.

Between them, my parents recited a list of my schoolmates' parents, and I was glad the Simons were not mentioned.

Getting ready for bed, I felt guilty about having accepted rides and having had the Simons' driver bring me back from Lizzy's house in the white Buick. Sadiq was a servant, not a friend, yet I felt I'd betrayed him. I vowed never again to accept rides from the Simons or wear Lizzy's jeans. I puzzled over how I would react to Lizzy when I saw her next. *Your mother killed our servant's son*, I imagined myself saying, and I doubted I had the courage ever to utter such an accusation.

When the noises of Sadiq's routine stopped—his prayers had been said, the toilet flushed, the door bolted—and the new chowkidars were on their third or fourth circuit outside my window, I sat on the floor of my bedroom with my Urdu readers spread around me. In one, a picture of a young girl stared up at me, and I was reminded of Lizzy's face in the weeks following the accident. Her face had been as lifeless as the girl's in the book. Was it possible? Did Lizzy know what her mother had done? Had she lied about getting the flu, about the lining of her stomach being flushed down the toilet? I wasn't angry with her, though. Who knows how I would have behaved if my mother had been driving that car?

Before I climbed into bed, my head a jumble of Sadiq, Hanif, Anne Simon, and Lizzy, I was overcome with a strange feeling. The world was closing in on me, settling into the small cracks of my life, inhabiting them and widening them. Until then, my life had been neatly divided. In the mornings and evenings, there were my parents, and before they moved away, Amir and Lehla, and in the hours tucked safely in between, there was my other universe, the school. But knowing who'd killed Hanif made the spaces in my life fall into one another like collapsing sand tunnels. It would be impossible to separate them, reshape them, and restore them to the way they had been. I was alarmed. I closed my eyes to the image of Hanif's faded photograph on the ledge above the kitchen sink. The bony fingers that held the cricket bat, the shy smile for the camera were as real as if Hanif were in the room with me. I tried my very best not to think of Anne Simon's white Buick crashing into him.

TEN

Early March 1979

On Sunday, the first day of the school week, I was quiet when I saw Lizzy. "What's wrong?" she asked, but of course, I couldn't tell her.

"I don't know. Maybe I'm getting the flu."

"I hope not. It's awful."

"Really?"

"Remember when I had it last year?"

"Is that what was wrong with you?"

"Leeeeeya!" Lizzy said, and when she said her nickname for me all drawn out like that, I almost felt like someone else.

I locked eyes with her and slowly asked, "Did your mother have the flu at the same time you did?" Lizzy looked puzzled, and I almost blurted out *Or did she just kill Hanif with the Buick and run away from the scene?*

"Why? Is your mom sick, too?"

"Never mind." I quickly ended the conversation. "I don't feel well, that's all."

A few days later, my mother dropped me off at Lizzy's house. I hadn't wanted to go, but she had answered the telephone when Lizzy called to ask me over, and because I always wanted to go, she told Lizzy she would drive me. I couldn't refuse the invitation and make my mother suspicious.

I noticed things about Lizzy's house that I hadn't noticed before. It smelled like the plastic covering in the white Buick. It sounded like humming air conditioners permanently set on fan mode. Lizzy's twin brothers' finger paintings on the wall looked like posters that made the house seem less rather than more personal, and the newly framed black-and-white photographs of central New York might as well have been pulled from a calendar. When Anne Simon said, "Happy to see you, honey," I felt as if we were trapped in a movie.

Lizzy must have sensed I was distracted and immediately engaged me in her new crochet project.

"I don't want to knit like my mom." She held up matching purple finger puppets and told me, "Crocheting isn't so bad."

"Try it," she said, almost stabbing herself with the curved end of the needle as she began her instructions. After an hour, our legs were tangled in unspooled wool, and I wasn't quite as obsessed by the image of Anne Simon behind the wheel of the Buick.

Soon Lizzy was telling me about great blizzards in her hometown of Cazenovia that left behind snowdrifts tall enough to bury stop signs. She pointed to a black-and-white photograph hanging on the wall and told me it was the old barn her grandparents had spent ten years renovating as their home. It sat on the banks of Cazenovia Lake, close to Lehla's university, with farmland stretching over lazy slopes in all directions, as far as you could see. Lizzy described the barn's rounded roof, ceiling beams in the kitchen and dining room, and the second-story walkway that circled the open space in the middle of the house.

"There's a hole in the middle of the house?" I asked, and Lizzy giggled, "Yup."

"Aren't beams supposed to be hidden?" I said, without saying *like houses here.*

"Grandpa says the exposed wood connects him to the land."

At first, I tried to picture the barn, but even if Sadiq's settlement papers hadn't been vying for my attention, I wouldn't have been able to manage. In my mind, all grandparents' houses looked like my grandfather's Five Queen's Road in Lahore. All I could do was apply my memory of his house to the image of a green meadow near a lake. The contrast of Five Queen's Road, brimming with flying cockroaches, large black ants, and the noises of bicycle vendors, set against the placid background Lizzy described didn't leave much room for comparison. As a rule, I tried not to be envious of all she had (prime rib, chocolate chip cookies, endless air-conditioning), but I wasn't always successful. My grandfather had finally moved into a new, clean house my father had built for him in Lahore, and although I'd yet to see it finished, I knew I'd prefer Lizzy's grandparents' renovated barn to his nondescript box.

It was a Friday afternoon, and like Sadiq, the Simons' servants were off duty. We ventured into the kitchen, where Anne Simon opened a floor-to-ceiling cupboard lined with bags of Hershey's Kisses, tubes of Pringles, boxes of leftover Valentine's Day chocolates, canisters of what looked like liquid cheese, and many other items I did not recognize.

"Help yourself, honey," she said, inviting me to make a selection from shelves of goods never to be found in a Pakistani store.

"What are these?" I asked, pointing to large, brightly colored plastic bottles on the floor.

"Detergent," she answered, and I pictured the white bags of powder my mother bought at the bazaar for our washing machine.

I knew Anne Simon was just back from her daily walk, but I asked her, "Did you just get back from a drive?" The only reason I asked was out of loyalty to Sadiq. The question required me to picture her in the white Buick and forced me to remember Hanif. That way, the injustice of what she'd done stayed vivid.

"Oh, no," she answered. "I'm just back from my walk. The city really is beautiful."

She wore two sweaters underneath a pashmina shawl, which was casually draped around her shoulders. I wondered how the guilt over what she'd done hadn't managed to affect her appearance. In fact, her face seemed fuller and her hair thicker. Regardless, Anne Simon was what she'd called Lizzy and me: *gorgeous.* But she was gorgeous in a blonde-and-blue-eyed-*Glamour*-magazine kind of way, which I could never be with my dark eyes and hair.

"Aren't you hot?" I couldn't help asking. Lizzy and I were both wearing embroidered kurtas that Mr. Simon had brought us the last time he was in Kabul, and our sleeves were rolled up as far as they would go.

"Honestly? I was never cold until I moved here," Anne Simon answered.

"That's not true, Mom. Did you forget about the snow already?" Lizzy said. She was emptying a bag of pretzels into a large bowl.

"My mother says the exact same thing! She says it's the size of the houses and the large windows that make them so difficult to heat," I said.

It was early evening when my mother came to get me. The streetlights hadn't yet been lit, but in the growing twilight, I could still make out the vague shape of a turbaned man crossing Anne Simon's street. I studied him as my mother turned onto Embassy Road, and his face came into view: It was Sadiq. My skin tingled and my ears rang like they did when I was afraid, but my mother continued to drive calmly, either not having seen Sadiq or pretending not to.

What was he doing there? I thought I knew his Friday routine. Shouldn't he have been at the mosque or listening to a cricket match? Lying on his charpai thinking of his son? Expecting him to be at the mosque or holding a radio or lying on a charpai was easier than acknowledging what was happening. Sadiq had been plucking the hair from his face and maybe from his head, as well. He was gradually discarding parts of himself. Maybe one day we wouldn't even recognize him.

In my panic, I could only see one explanation for Sadiq's presence. He, like me, knew Anne Simon had killed Hanif. That he might have known all along no longer seemed strange. He'd seen the white Buick swerve toward the edge of the road. Although it had been dark, Sadiq wouldn't have required any details about Anne Simon's appearance. Hair color, skin color, accent, clothing were all beside the point. The Simons drove the only white Buick in Islamabad, and disregarding the license plate, this fact alone would have made Anne Simon easy to identify. She had just finished her walk. She always went on her Friday walks at the same time. There could be no doubt. Sadiq had to have been waiting for her.

A few minutes later, our car passed the intersection where Hanif had died, the identifying street name painted on the blue background of a typical Islamabad knee-high concrete street sign. Could Sadiq hurt Anne Simon? I tried to picture him approaching her with a cricket bat, calling her a murderer, wishing her dead, but I couldn't imagine it. All I could imagine were his haunted eyes following her down the street. Suddenly the burden of knowing what I should not have became too much to bear.

"You know what? There are rumors in school about Lizzy's mother," I said, although there weren't.

"Yes?" my mother asked blandly.

"They say she was in a hit-and-run accident and killed someone. She was driving home late one night and went off the road and hit a child."

The driver racing toward us had his high beams on, and my mother flicked hers in response.

"You think it could be true?" When she didn't answer me, I leaped to the heart of the matter. "Do you think Anne Simon could have been the one to kill Hanif?"

I could tell my mother was carefully weighing what to say, which was unusual because she generally said whatever thought came first.

"I suppose . . . it could be true," she finally replied and didn't speak again until we were home.

Later, as she put the kettle on to boil and absentmindedly rinsed a teapot with hot water, my mother asked, "Did you girls have fun this afternoon?"

"What?" I asked, even though my mother always objected to this *American* monosyllabic response.

My mother pulled a chair from the table and faced me.

"Yes. In answer to your earlier question, in fact, I do know. The driver was Lizzy's mother."

Although I already knew this, spoken aloud the truth had terrifying substance.

"Anne Simon," I whispered.

The teapot spout sent wisps of steam in vague curls above the table, and I put my hand over my mug so my mother couldn't pour my tea. She said that when she discovered the driver was Anne Simon, she couldn't tell me. "She's the mother of your closest friend. It wouldn't have been fair to either of you. It was her mother who was driving the car, not Lizzy. It was Sadiq's son who was killed, not Amir. God forbid. What happened has nothing to do with you girls."

I had the impression that my mother was intent on trying to explain Anne Simon's actions to herself as much as to me. "It was late. She was alone in the car. She was new to Islamabad." As if she'd rehearsed an explanation, my mother speculated that Anne Simon had been afraid, as any woman would be at that time of night on a dark road, alone with two strange men, one who was the father of the child she'd just killed. My mother pointed out that Anne Simon's blonde hair would always have drawn attention in Pakistan, even on a dark night. In a few months in Islamabad, Anne Simon's brilliant blue eyes and blonde hair would have garnered the usual catcalls from men at the bazaars.

"Don't forget," my mother added, "she's never been outside America before." In Pakistan, everything—the men, the food, the heat, the smells, the sounds—would all be new to her. Perhaps Sadiq and Yunis had screamed at her, pounded their fists on her car, or tried to open the door and drag her out. What had happened was an accident, my mother insisted. Anne Simon had not meant to kill Hanif. When she saw him lying crushed at the side of the road, it must have taken all her strength not to get out of the car and rush to help the boy any way she could. "Remember, she's a nurse," my mother pointed out and ended by saying that by the time it occurred to Anne Simon to get out of the car, Hanif was probably already dead.

"What if he wasn't?"

"Well, we don't know." My mother paused. "Who knows? Maybe she wasn't alone in the car. Lizzy or the twins could have been with her."

"What?!" I exclaimed.

"Anne Simon is a mother," my mother concluded. "Her first responsibility is to her children and then to herself. Even if Lizzy was not in the car, her children were her responsibility. If she got out of the car and put herself in the hands of two angry men, she might have been harmed, either beaten or killed."

"Sadiq would never have killed her! Yunis either!" I didn't know if it was the absurdity of my mother's suggestion or that it was a valid possibility that was making me nauseous.

"Then what would her children do?" My mother continued as if she hadn't heard me. "Her children are her primary responsibility." She claimed that safety was the least that parental responsibility entailed and, in what must have been a moment of sheer terror, it was probably the most Anne Simon had to offer.

"And then there's the other issue." My mother changed the subject a bit tentatively. "Who knows exactly what Anne Simon's husband does for the Americans?"

"He's a malaria expert."

"No, what he *really* does."

"The CD64s and the CD62s, you mean?" It was much easier to announce license plate numbers than to ask the obvious question. What *did* all the Americans and Russians actually do in Islamabad? A moment later, I tired of codes and lies. "Is Mr. Simon CIA?" I demanded.

"Oh, I'm not saying that. But if he has a sensitive job, more sensitive than being a malaria expert, let's say, it would explain why Anne Simon left the scene as she did. Having a husband who's CIA might make a wife worry more."

"He *is* a malaria expert, you know. He helped us with our science project on mosquitoes. He knows everything there is to know about them."

"Of course he's a malaria expert. It's just, well, he travels to Afghanistan quite often. Didn't he go a few weeks ago after the American ambassador was assassinated?"

Some weeks earlier on Valentine's Day, after we'd heard on the BBC that the American ambassador in Kabul had been murdered, Mr. Simon traveled to Kabul. I now regretted sharing that information with my mother. "So what if he travels to Kabul for work?"

"I'm just saying . . . You know, the Afghan government isn't friendly toward Americans anymore. It is Communist now . . ."

"And you?" I demanded. "Would you have driven away?" My mother concentrated as hard as she could, and I bit my lip while waiting for her answer.

"I don't know, darling. I can't say. I'd like to think I would have stopped to help, driven them to the hospital, maybe. But who's to say what might have happened?"

When I went to my room, I lay fully dressed on the bed. Alongside the image of a dead Hanif wrapped in my mother's best white sheets, I saw Anne Simon at the helm of a new Buick with a steering wheel on the wrong side of the car. Although I did not believe it myself, I pictured Lizzy next to her mother, both caught up in the horrible event. I wanted to believe that if Lizzy had been in the car, Anne Simon might not have fled. As for me, I resolved never to learn to drive.

Sadiq knocked on my door a few mornings later and asked to dust the bookshelves. The Urdu dailies were spread out in front of me, and as I did each day, I forced myself to read one complete column. I read aloud with Sadiq in my room, and my parents at the other end of the house. Since I made more mistakes than usual, I expected Sadiq to correct my pronunciation. But when he allowed me to read uninterrupted from beginning to end, I asked him what was wrong. He told me he could no longer correct my Urdu while I read from newspapers because he'd forsaken them altogether.

"Forsaken?" I repeated, unfamiliar with the Urdu word.

"Given them up," Sadiq explained.

"You're joking."

"No."

"You've stopped reading newspapers?"

Sadiq said what was written about in newspapers had nothing to do with him.

"Nothing?"

"Not one thing," Sadiq said slowly and emphatically.

"Not even this?" I asked, pointing to the day's headline: "The Supreme Court Upholds Bhutto's Death Sentence."

"Not even that."

"Achha, achha," I said, OK, OK, quickly ending the exchange. But strangely, our conversation was slightly comforting. Sadiq seemed almost normal, if you didn't look at his missing eyebrows. He no longer seemed like a person who might attack Lizzy's mother; he almost seemed like a father again.

"Do you still miss Hanif?" I asked.

"Of course," Sadiq said, surprised at the mention of his son.

"You didn't see him very often because you lived in Islamabad and he lived in Lahore," I remarked. "How old would he be now?"

"Nine."

"We were three years apart—I'm older."

Sadiq pulled a few paperbacks from the shelves and slapped them together. With the way Sadiq and my mother constantly cleaned the house, I doubted there was any dust to remove.

"The police never found the person who hit him?"

Sadiq hesitated. "Not that I know," he said. He sounded so sad, I didn't even mind that he was lying.

"It's not fair, is it?" I said, but rather than engage me in the obvious, he directed my attention back to the newspaper I was reading.

Our private lessons continued and I became fluent enough in Urdu to be able to admit to him that I'd seen him on the corner of Lizzy's street, but I said nothing. Much, much later, I wondered what difference it would have made if I had.

"Try not to let the accident affect your friendship with Lizzy." My mother continued our conversation the next time we were alone. "She's always welcome here. Remember, she didn't have . . ."

". . . anything to do with it?" I finished her sentence.

"It wouldn't be right to share this information with her."

"It's not like she doesn't already know." I challenged her.

"We don't know. She might not. In any case, it isn't your place to tell her."

"Of course not," I answered, painfully aware of how difficult it was to keep the secret.

"Do you think Sadiq knows who the driver was?" I asked. I'd read the settlement papers and seen his signature, so of course he knew. But I hadn't told my mother I'd read the papers, and I wanted to hear how she would respond.

"I doubt it," my mother said.

"Because I thought I saw him on Embassy Road yesterday when you picked me up."

"Really?" I couldn't distinguish whether her surprise was real or concocted.

"Wearing a pagri," I said, using the Urdu word Sadiq had taught me.

"Pagri?" my mother asked.

"Turban."

"It's odd how people wrap their heads here sometimes, you know, when they're not feeling well," my mother suggested. "Listen. I've given you a lot of information that must have come as a shock to you. It's a lot to think about. Try not to worry so much or jump to conclusions. The person with the pagri? I'm sure it wasn't Sadiq."

"It *must* have been someone else," I said forcefully, hoping for the miracle that would make this true.

"Must. Have. Been," my mother agreed, pausing between each word as if she wanted it to be true even more than I did.

ELEVEN

Late March 1979

No one stood a chance against my mother's baking. She transformed Pakistan's yellow-orange buffalo-milk butter and coarsely ground sugar into mouthwatering goodies. After Amir and Lehla went to college, my mother baked less often, so I was always thrilled when visitors provided a reason.

Uncle Imtiaz and my father had been friends since before Pakistan's independence from the British. I knew their tales of participating in mass rallies and surviving the summer of Partition in 1947. "We aren't brothers, but we might as well be," Uncle Imtiaz had said. They had many things in common: studying abroad, marrying foreigners, and returning to serve their country. He visited us more frequently as the political situation worsened, bringing my father news that was censored at his newspaper. It was hard to believe that Uncle Imtiaz once hated the prime minister. He'd held him responsible for the 1971 war between East and West Pakistan because he'd refused to do the right thing and concede defeat to the East Pakistani political party that had won a majority in the polls. However, after the coup, you would have thought Uncle Imtiaz had always been the prime minister's best friend.

That afternoon, my mother outdid herself by baking a flourless choc-olate almond torte, a plate of linzer schnitten packed with raspberry jam, and my favorite, horseshoe vanillekipferl dusted with powdered sugar. My father returned from a meeting a few minutes before Uncle Imtiaz was expected and insisted on supplementing the desserts with store-bought samosas and chutneys. My mother was annoyed and did her best to be patient with him. A few days earlier, the Supreme Court had upheld the prime minister's death sentence, and my father's mood had not recovered.

Uncle Imtiaz arrived with a bottle hidden in a paper bag. When alcohol was declared illegal in Pakistan, he became my mother's sup-plier. Since my mother was a foreigner, she was eligible to legally buy a monthly quota at a hotel, but she refused to do so. Even though my father did not drink, she said she would not give people a reason to gossip that the wife of the WAPDA chairman bought alcohol for him. It was understood that either Uncle Imtiaz gave my mother his wife's monthly quota, or he bought the alcohol on the black market, where servants sold their foreign employers' liquor.

Uncle Imtiaz was barely inside the house before he demanded a shot of bourbon. When my mother said she didn't have any, he pulled a bottle of bourbon from the paper bag and dropped it into her hands. There was almost always bourbon in our house because my mother required it to make her own vanilla essence for baking. "Just kidding. Whiskey, please. Join me."

"You know I don't drink it," she protested.

"Why not? Ah, yes. You prefer sherry. The drink of the colonizer."

"The English?" Apparently my mother knew who Uncle Imtiaz was talking about, because she'd guessed correctly.

"Even my wife doesn't like sherry, and she's English!"

"Are you saying I behave like I'm English?" my mother asked.

"No, no. You're from *Nederlands*," Uncle Imtiaz said, pronounc-ing the only Dutch word he knew and laughing so loud he was almost bellowing.

"Tell me something, Imtiaz," my father said. "Sherry is to the English as what is to the Americans?" His question was nothing short of a riddle.

It took Uncle Imtiaz only a moment to follow my father's analogy. "You mean, if sherry signifies the English, what drink represents the Americans? I don't know. Martinis? Do you have gin? Vermouth?" he asked my mother, knowing full well she had neither.

"You're lucky I offer you anything to drink at all," she replied, still mildly offended. My mother had double standards. She was allowed to draw comparisons between Pakistan and Europe whenever she liked because she was Dutch, but she did not appreciate others pointing out she was foreign. True to form, she replied, "I am not English."

"True . . ." Uncle Imtiaz started, but stopped after glancing at me.

"You'll really upset me if you say anything about my children," my mother warned.

"Why would I do that?" he said and winked at me. "You know I would never tease your children. Only you. It's the price you pay for having married this man."

My father was still contemplating Uncle Imtiaz's response. "Martinis are made from gin and vermouth?"

"But what difference is it to you? You don't drink anyway."

"It's important to know the enemy," my father said. I hated it when I had no idea what adults were saying.

"Since you wouldn't know the difference between vermouth and sherry, how does this help you?"

"Don't take me for a fool. That's their mistake," my father said, and I sat up. Suddenly there was no mistaking his reference. His eyes were squinted, his lips drawn, and his head was slowly shaking. I'd solved part of the riddle. He was talking about the Americans.

"Indeed," Uncle Imtiaz said, suddenly angry. "Just because we've been colonized by the British doesn't mean we're about to allow the Americans another go at it."

"The Americans underestimate us," my mother said, and it was sad that she thought it necessary to announce she was in the same camp as my father and Uncle Imtiaz.

Uncle Imtiaz leaned in toward my father. He'd just begun working for *The Muslim*, a new daily, and spoke with authority on lots of things. I'd heard my father say that in order to keep his job, he could only write as the censors allowed, so he spread the real news by talking.

"I've heard the Americans have given the go-ahead," Uncle Imtiaz said. It wasn't the first time he'd suggested the Americans were supporting the prime minister's death sentence.

"The general can't do it," my father insisted, as they contemplated the Supreme Court's recent rejection of the prime minister's appeal. "There will be royits in the street if they hang the prime minister."

"What are you talking about?" Uncle Imtiaz said. "That fool of a general can do whatever he bloody well wishes. For men like him, medals pinned to their shoulders put stars in their eyes, and they go blind. Mark my words, he's going to kill him."

His fury was frightening.

He added, "Not that our prime minister is an angel, you understand."

"Perhaps the Saudis will do something," my father said, but he didn't sound hopeful.

"They've been sitting on their asses for the last twenty months. Why would they do something now?"

"The British have sent warnings to the general," my father said instead.

"You see, no world leader *believes* it can happen. Therefore, none of them are doing much of anything."

"What's Dr. Moody got to say?" my father asked, and my stomach somersaulted. My dentist was the only person granted access to the prime minister in his death cell.

"They're such bastards!" Uncle Imtiaz went on, making the prime minister's jailers, the army, and the general the subjects of his invective. "The prime minister's gums are covered in abscesses. Puss drools from his mouth. The stink is unbearable. He hasn't been able to eat in weeks. They don't let him see his wife or give him fresh clothes . . ."

I couldn't bear to listen anymore. I left to serve myself pastries, but standing in front of a table heaped with my mother's confections, I realized I wasn't hungry. As their conversation continued nearby, I felt the end of something drawing near, not the world or our lives but something equally real. It was coming in hops and skips, half steps even, but like the next BBC newscast, it was definitely coming.

"Aap ko kya chahiye?" Sadiq asked if he could get me anything, supposing I required more to satisfy me than what was on the table. He was barefoot; as always, he'd left his sandals at the edge of the large Bukhara carpet in the dining room.

I waited until he looked at me again, and then I said in Urdu, "What happened to Hanif's sneakers?" I whispered so no one else could hear.

My question didn't seem to surprise him, and he responded as if Hanif's sneakers were on his mind as well. The sneakers were in Lahore with his wife.

"Yunis picked them up, right?"

"Yes," he said. It was just like I'd imagined. Hanif's sneakers had fallen to the side of the road, and Yunis had picked them up. "Eat something," he added.

I shook my head and looked out of the window at the lawn where Hanif had dribbled a soccer ball. His prediction had been a mystery. *The prime minister would not die. He would live a life as long as the boy lived.* No longer. Just as Hanif had foretold, he was gone, and the prime minister would soon follow.

I wished we'd never moved to Pakistan and, very specifically, that my father did not work for the general.

No one was hungry at dinner. I couldn't understand why I was required to be there, and I regretted turning down Lizzy's dinner invitation. In the last day or two, my father had almost stopped speaking during meals, and given how much he'd conversed with Uncle Imtiaz, I didn't expect him to say anything. My mother hated his silences more than anyone, and she was determined to change the situation.

"If there's one thing I know, it's that leaders behave every bit as badly as your worst fear," my mother began.

"Do you think they'll do it?" she asked when Sadiq, his head wrapped in a soiled pagri that needed to be adjusted, brought in the food.

"When?" she asked while Sadiq refilled the water glasses, and she ignored the splash of water on the tablecloth.

"Do you know," she said to me as I loaded butter and sugar on a chapati that I didn't even want, "that the Nazis didn't hang their victims?" Comparing the general to the Nazis was a stretch, and I turned to my father, but he wasn't listening.

My mother's rising frustration with the dinner silence filled the space until the large, airy room was claustrophobic, and I couldn't breathe.

"Your country isn't even civilized!"

My father didn't so much as look at her. He tilted his head in the direction of the kitchen, where a newscaster announced through static that Iran had proclaimed itself an Islamic republic.

"The general and his men. They'll be remembered as the animals that they are." My mother punctuated her final pronouncement with a loud sigh, and Sadiq came to ask if she needed anything.

"Your country," my mother had said.

Half-and-half that I was, I wondered what, if anything, might make it mine.

TWELVE

4 April 1979

The morning shouldn't have been so quiet. I'd missed the unwelcome sounds from the servants' quarters, including Sadiq's urine streaming into the toilet and the clinking of a cheap teakettle on his single-burner stove. Closer to my bedroom, I'd been oblivious to the drone of my parents' radio and the aroma of my mother's first cup of coffee.

I drew open my curtains, and my quiet world went perfectly still, as if frozen in a camera frame. My father and Sadiq were at the far end of the driveway. My father was in his pajamas that had long since lost their color, but he refused to throw them away. As always, Sadiq was dressed in an ironed white shalwar and kurta, his head wrapped in a pagri. They wore identical sandals, with wide leather straps crisscrossing from toe to ankle. The men opened their arms at the same time and fell into an embrace. They locked together, their shoulders shaking in almost heaves, but neither emitted a sound. It took me several moments to understand what I was seeing. I'd never seen my father cry, much less imagined it, yet there he was, weeping, in the arms of our servant.

After a while, Sadiq pulled himself out of the embrace and wiped his face. He and my father slowly returned to the house, and I pulled the curtains closed, wishing to erase what I'd seen.

Some minutes later, I found Sadiq alone in the kitchen, his glazed eyes rimmed with red.

"Kya hua hai?" I asked him.

Although the radio was off, he pointed to it.

"Kya?" I asked, just as my father entered the room.

"The prime minister was hanged this morning," my father answered. His words took a long time to get to me because they weren't meant to go together.

"He's dead?"

"Murdered," he replied.

Noose and all, it had finally happened.

"Qatal kar diya," Sadiq said, and *murdered* became an accidental vocabulary lesson.

"Qatal kar diya," I repeated. I stumbled on the *r*, but Sadiq didn't comment because he was helping me keep my secret of learning Urdu from my father.

My father peered at the radio, his brow wrinkled with concern. Sadiq's bald head was wrapped, his face was missing eyebrows, the glass pitcher was full of freshly squeezed orange juice, and from another part of the house, my mother was calling for my father. The prime minister was dead and nothing had changed.

"Where is he now?" I asked my father.

"Buried."

"Where?"

"Larkana."

A few years earlier, Amir had gone to Larkana, the prime minister's ancestral village, on a school trip, because Shah, the prime minister's son, had invited his graduating class to the prime minister's estate. Now his village had also become his burial site.

"Was Shah there?" I asked. Despite the solemn circumstances, I recalled that long ago, the prime minister's son had jokingly promised to marry me.

My father tapped the radio's speaker. "The children weren't allowed to attend, and neither was Begum Bhutto."

"The radio said so?"

I took a step or two closer to my father, who was bent over the counter tuning the radio, and leaned against him. For a moment, his fingers stopped playing with the dial. I couldn't imagine waking up to the news that my father was dead. Would it make a difference to know he'd died in his sleep rather than having been hanged in a jail? Would it matter to me not to be present when his body was lowered into a grave? The sunflower garden on my mother's new plastic tablecloth blurred as I tried not to cry.

"Allah ki marzi," Sadiq whispered out of nowhere. When my father returned the phrase, *It is God's will*, the call and response sounded like a secret conversation.

More than a year had passed since Hanif's death, and for all I knew his body had decomposed. But I pictured him intact, lying next to the dead prime minister of Dr. Moody's descriptions, who would have had a broken neck that must have flopped this way and that when the hangman removed the noose. In reality, of course, the two bodies were nowhere near each other. The prime minister's was in Larkana, and Hanif's was in Lahore, but death was the same everywhere.

"Where's Hanif buried?" I asked my father, who asked Sadiq the question in Urdu.

"Miani Sahib," Sadiq said, just as the toaster popped, and he left the kitchen with toast meant for me. I tried to imagine Hanif in what even I knew was the biggest, most overcrowded graveyard in Lahore, if not the world.

My father continued to listen to more news, this time in English on Voice of America. "In Pakistan today, authorities announced . . ."

"Hanif was right! Remember?" I recalled out loud. "He said, 'The prime minister will live a life as long—'"

"Smart little boy," my father interrupted me.

"But he didn't *really* know the prime minister was going to die so soon, did he? Hanif thought the prime minister would live as long as he did, and since Hanif was so young, that was supposed to be for a very long time!" I had to admit that the irony of Hanif's words was striking.

My father didn't answer. Instead, he pulled me in a bear hug and squeezed until I couldn't breathe anymore. It was a relief, because my mind, like my body, felt all out of air and I couldn't think anymore.

At first I was lucky, and no one in the house noticed I was an hour late for school. My father couldn't find his favorite vest, and after my mother discovered it twisted and tangled at the bottom of a stack of unfolded clean laundry, she unknotted it and ironed it without comment. The old washing machine made loud banging noises that brought Sadiq and my mother running from different directions. Sadiq wrung out the wet laundry and hung it to dry on the clothesline my mother could see from the kitchen. When the telephone rang, I could tell it was my grandfather calling from Lahore. My father shouted into the mouthpiece as he always did when he spoke to him, as if the volume helped my grandfather hear better. I didn't need to know Punjabi to understand my father was discussing current events. I was lingering over my one last bite of toast and sip of tea when I heard the school bus at the gate. Because my parents were in listening range, I reverted to my old Urdu-English speech and sent Sadiq to tell the bus driver I wouldn't be coming. I hadn't asked my parents for permission to stay home, but they didn't protest. It was only a little while later, when my father was about to leave for Lahore, that my mother realized I wasn't in school.

"You missed the bus! Hurry up and get ready for school," she said, rushing into my room, where I was lying in bed. "Nu!" she said—Now! in Dutch—ignoring my pleas to stay home.

I did not want to go, because how much more humiliating could it be to attend an American school on the day the CIA fathers of my classmates had sanctioned the hanging of my country's prime minister? Who knew if they really had, but at that moment, with the momentous news of his hanging and rumors of American involvement, I was angry and it was easy to blame the most powerful nation on earth.

My father appeared at my mother's side. "You must go," he said.

"I don't want to."

"You will go because you will not give anyone the pleasure of knowing that you don't want to go," my father said, his calm tone failing to soften the finality of his words. Although my father didn't spell out his reasoning, I knew he wanted me to go because it was important not to seem unwilling to show up at the American School on such a day.

"No one cares whether I'm there or not!" Really, who would notice besides Lizzy? Mr. Duval, maybe. It wasn't as if a special roll call would be called to count the number of Pakistanis attending school.

"We care."

"I'll drive her," my mother offered.

"No, let the driver take her. People will be very angry about the prime minister, and the streets won't be safe now," my father warned her.

"There are going to be royits, and you're sending me to school?" I pressed on.

"Aliya!" my mother chided me.

"You're going, and that's that," my father insisted. Almost immediately, he called for Sadiq to notify the driver. When Sadiq came running, the sleeve of his kurta clung to his forearm, where a reddish-brown stain had set, and I wondered why I hadn't noticed it before.

In the safety of my father's official car, through the tinted windows in which the city sped by, the day was no different than any other. Bicyclists, buses, and cars wove in and out of lanes, children walked to school holding hands, shopkeepers rolled up their shutters. Mushtaq, the driver, didn't say much, and we neared the American School of Islamabad before he initiated our habitual license plate game. When we passed a car with a diplomatic plate, we quizzed each other on the country that corresponded with the number. Mushtaq had memorized them all.

"You think there are more CD62s or CD64s on the road?" I asked him that morning.

"Too many Russians, too many Americans," Mushtaq joked before finding a CD49 on the road. "You know that one," he urged. I always remembered too late that CD49 belonged to the Philippines.

I was two hours late to school, but when I arrived, the first thing I did was buy a 7UP I didn't want from the snack bar in order to further delay the start of my school day. I managed only a few sips before returning the bottle to the cashier, who insisted on refunding my money. I worried I'd been spotted by teachers and decided I had no choice but to get a late pass.

"It's not like you to be late, honey," the secretary said while she marked my attendance in the school roster book, as her husband, the principal, watched from his office.

I started across the quad again on my way to class, but I paused halfway across, plopping down in the sunken concrete star and allowing the burning heat radiating from it to overwhelm me. A low hum from above broke the silence. I stared at an airplane crawling across the endlessly blue sky, and I pretended it was a military transport airplane transporting the prime minister southwest to his grave.

The Pakistani field hockey coach, Mr. Farid, called out my name. He was always friendly, because for years Lehla had been the captain of the team. When he smiled, I covered my eyes to protect them from the glare of his perfectly white teeth.

He waved his hand toward the sky as if he'd read my thoughts. "Maybe they're flying him home."

"He was buried before the sun came up," I corrected him.

"You're late," he said, gesturing at the pink late pass in my hand and sitting down beside me. When I didn't move, he said, "I don't want to be here either. You couldn't stay home?"

"My parents wouldn't let me," I replied.

"Mine neither," Mr. Farid teased me as the bell rang announcing the fourth period of the day. I took my usual seat in science class next to Lizzy, and I sat through the entire hour ignoring every word that was said. No one mentioned the news, but it didn't have to be spoken out loud. The prime minister's death was like having another person standing in the cafeteria line with us or blocking the basketball during gym.

"Are you OK?" Lizzy finally asked when school was over and we were walking to the buses.

"Why? Because the prime minister was hanged today?" I replied, and just like that I violated my father's request that I not talk about politics.

Lizzy was confused before she finally said, "No, because you didn't take notes in any of the classes."

"I didn't need to today, that's all," I said as I spotted a beige, nondescript sedan with the unmistakable black license plates of a local vehicle. Unlike the drivers of other waiting cars, who wore uniforms and sported caps embroidered with embassy insignia, Mushtaq stood beside our car wearing a wrinkled shalwar kameez and simple sandals. I was confused to see Sadiq in the passenger seat, for I could not recall him ever being on the school premises. But at that specific moment, more than being alarmed at his unexpected presence, I was relieved that I would be spared the afternoon's spitting games.

"You're not taking the bus?" Lizzy asked me.

"I've got an appointment with Dr. Moody." I lied about an orthodontist appointment because I didn't want to give Lizzy a ride home. For that day, at least, it was important to me to keep my school life separate from my home life, and no matter what, Lizzy was my school life, and my father's official car belonged to my home life.

"Today? Didn't we schedule appointments at the same time next week?"

"Emergency appointment. A bracket broke," I said, touching my braces and continuing to lie.

I remembered the last time I'd seen Dr. Moody. The electricity had been out, and he'd pumped the foot pedal with great effort to adjust the chair's height. Slipping on plastic gloves, he'd run his forefinger over my braces and I almost bit him trying to swallow. "It's all right," he'd reassured me kindly. I suddenly wondered if Dr. Moody had said that to the prime minister when he examined his abscesses for the last time.

"Liya! Call me later, OK?" Lizzy yelled from the bus steps.

Mushtaq locked the car doors. He drove slowly through the open gates, where a uniformed guard sat dozing on a chair, his arms crossed at his waist and an unloaded rifle propped between his legs. Sadiq didn't say a word, so I practiced Urdu numbers with Mushtaq, and by the time we reached the first bend in the dirt road, he had me adding two digits. Normally, doing math in Urdu was too difficult for me, but that day I was happy to be distracted from life beyond the car windows.

My father was wrong. Perhaps people were angry, but they hadn't gathered in the streets or anywhere else to demonstrate against the general. There were no royits, not even mini ones like the one at my home. If countries could be people, Land of the Pure was standing tall, wrapped in a green-and-white sari-flag, no midriff or cleavage showing, not a hair out of place. She'd hardly noticed she'd been violated.

THIRTEEN

Late April–May 1979

I stood across the street from my house, waiting for the school bus, wishing I'd worn different clothes. For one thing, it was so hot that my underwear was sticking. For another, I was wearing a red sundress that Anne Simon had made for me, and I was embarrassed that my shoulders were bare. The hemline was shorter than it had been, and the elastic bodice was tighter than when I'd tried it on at Lizzy's house. My father hadn't helped my confidence when I'd kissed him good-bye, and he'd casually remarked that my dress was too short. I'd appreciated my mother's irritated "For goodness' sake, Javid!" but standing on the street as bicyclists and pedestrians went by, I worried he was right.

Waves of heat rose from the asphalt and the road appeared to move. I shifted from foot to foot in my sandals, impatient for the bus to arrive. A man began to walk up the hill, and from the moment he appeared, he stayed directly in my line of sight. The closer he came, the more space he seemed to fill, and eventually, the bottom of the hill disappeared behind his immense form. His clothes hung loosely on his body, as if they were meant for an even heavier, larger man. I couldn't tear my eyes off him, although I knew I should. As he neared, I could see folds of his baggy shalwar pooled on his sandals. He was fidgeting with his shirt or trying to retie the string of his shalwar. Now he was close enough for me to see he'd tucked the bottom of his shirt in his armpit and was using both his hands to play with the fabric of his shalwar. Suddenly he dropped the shalwar and surprisingly kept the pants from falling to the ground. His hands were buried in the mass of dark hair between his legs, rubbing the layers of skin from side to side and up and down. Without warning, his pace became urgent until he stumbled and let out an uncontrolled groan. He was so close to me that I could see there were gray hairs on his unshaven face.

"Amrikan," he said. His voice was rough, but not loud.

Sweat rolled down my back, and all at once hundreds of pins pricked my scalp. I crossed the road without looking and grabbed the gate. I didn't dare turn around and couldn't know for sure if he was following me, but there was an unfamiliar smell hanging in the air, and it made me certain he could have touched me with his dirty hands if he'd only tried.

I fled down the long driveway past my father's empty office car and almost ran into Mushtaq and Sadiq, who were chatting away. Rushing into the house, I collided with my mother, who scolded me for leaving a mess in my room. Gripped by fear, I rummaged through my desk, pretending to have forgotten something, burying my flushed face in a drawer. A minute later, Sadiq came in to tell me the bus was waiting, and he picked up my book bag. He slung it across his shoulder as if he were going to school and lifted the heavy latch I'd had trouble with and easily swung open the gate. The man had vanished. All that waited was the big yellow school bus.

I regretted not changing my clothes. In my bedroom, panic rising in my chest, my mother a few steps away scolding me, I hadn't even thought of doing so. Now I yanked the elastic bodice higher than it was supposed to go and slipped my book bag onto my back. Lizzy was wearing a sundress identical to mine and didn't seem the least bit uncomfortable.

During English, my first class of the day, she passed me a note. *What's wrong?*

I held onto it but didn't answer until science, two classes later. *Have you ever seen a man's genitals?* It was the first time in my life I'd used the word *genitals* in a sentence, and I'd scrawled it on the back of an old lab report that I almost didn't give to Lizzy for fear the teacher would catch me and read it.

You mean, not my brothers'?

I nodded. The teacher misinterpreted it as interest in the class, and asked me the next question, which I could not answer.

Not your brothers', I wrote back. *Or your Dad's.*

No. Have you?

This morning.

What happened?

Broaching the incident, however cursorily, on a crinkled piece of paper, made it possible to describe some details later when I could talk to Lizzy.

"His pants were down, and he wasn't wearing underwear. He was holding his, you know . . ." I started to say but stopped.

"No! Masturbating?"

"I guess," I said, wishing away the word.

"Gross."

"Gross," I agreed, although I felt shame, not disgust.

"Should you tell someone?" Lizzy asked.

"Who?"

"I don't know. Your mom or dad?"

"My dad?" I said, shocked, recalling his comment about my dress, which seemed a warning now.

"Your mom, then?"

"No way," I said and ended the discussion.

Lizzy was my best friend, but the whole time we spoke, I couldn't share the most terrible part of the incident with her: He had called me

Amrikan. Lizzy was American, I was not, and although I sometimes envied her because of it, the possibility that someone else assumed I was American suddenly horrified me. The word, *Amrikan*, was hurled at me like an abuse, a curse, and I wondered if the way I felt—small and dirty—was how regular bicyclists and pedestrians felt when they were hit with a spitball from the yellow school bus. Being labeled American also made me think of the prime minister, dead now, who'd yelled about Americans, calling them elephants in a long-ago speech, and I wondered where I fit in.

Every morning after that, I waited for the bus from inside the safety of our latched gate. Instead of staring at the hill until the bus appeared, I learned to recognize the sound of the engine and the opening and closing of the bus doors a street away. I would sit with my back to the gate on the edge of a low retaining wall, taking care not to look at anyone who passed by. I saw the man again only when he crept into my dreams and forced me to relive the shame of his accusation. I never told anyone about the taunt, not even my mother when she came to check on me one night after I'd cried out in my sleep.

"What was the dream about?"

"Nothing," I declared.

"*Nothing* doesn't wake you from sleep, Aliya," my mother said skeptically.

In my dream I had argued with the man.

"Amrikan," he had cursed me.

"I am *not*!" I wanted to shout in Urdu, but I always woke up before I finished the sentence, and I hated him all the more because I was cheated of completing my thought.

As time went on, I admitted to myself that the shame I felt at his curse was because there might have been some truth to it. What was I, anyway? Half Pakistani? Half Dutch? Half Austrian? And did my accent, the generic one American schools cultivated, make me part American, regardless of my protests?

Standing on the street—sundress tight on my budding chest, my knees and shoulders bare—what had I been thinking?

On Friday, without a bus to catch, I sat at a kitchen table strewn with egg-stained dishes, opened jam and honey jars, and empty glasses rimmed with the dried fragments of orange juice. I was eating a paratha, a Friday treat I looked forward to all week. I was wearing jeans and one of Amir's old sweatshirts that was far too big for me and far too heavy for the hot day. Until Sadiq entered the kitchen, I had been preoccupied with what had happened earlier in the week. He'd wound a black-and-white pagri on his head and his clothes were ironed, but my first impression was that he was lopsided. I puzzled over this oddity as he moved about the kitchen. Was one eyebrow growing faster than the other? When had he shaved his eyebrows, anyway? Why was only one sleeve rolled up? Sadiq switched off the radio, which I hadn't even realized was on, the background of newscasts and analysis nothing more than a stale hum these days.

I felt the presence of Sadiq's secret fill a corner of the kitchen until the fact that he was spying on Anne Simon inhabited the entire room. I was always aware of the secret when I was alone with him, but it was unavoidable in a different way that morning, and I felt compelled to put an end to it. I ran to retrieve my new English-to-Urdu dictionary, opened it in front of Sadiq, who was watching a boiling pot of pasta. I found the entry for *secret*, pointed to the Urdu equivalent, *raaz*, and used it in my question.

"Do you have a secret?"

"Do *you* have a secret?" he promptly countered, correcting my chronic misuse of the formal tense in his presence, replacing the respectful *aap* with the informal *tum*.

We studied each other, equally intent on eliciting a response when my mother burst into the kitchen and admonished Sadiq for overcooking the pasta.

"What are we going to do with you?" she demanded, while removing the pot from the burner. A few droplets of boiling water splashed on the dictionary. "A kitchen is no place for books," she added, glaring at me.

Sadiq got to work scrubbing spinach leaves in the sink, furiously scattering water in all directions. A little while later, I returned to the kitchen with my dictionary lodged under my arm, and Sadiq was drying the spinach leaf by leaf with a kitchen towel.

"I have a secret," I said again. "Do you?"

Sadiq narrowed his eyes into slits that matched the thin lines of his new eyebrows.

"No," he said with conviction, and for that single moment it didn't matter that I knew otherwise.

It was hard to invite Lizzy to my house after I'd read the settlement papers, but after discovering Sadiq loitering on Anne Simon's street, it was almost impossible. I tried to keep in mind my mother's words, specifically that what had happened had nothing to do with Lizzy and me or our friendship. I didn't know how long he'd been spying on her or how much he'd seen, but he knew Lizzy was Anne Simon's daughter. How could Sadiq see Lizzy as anyone other than Anne Simon's daughter? Inviting Lizzy home meant betraying Sadiq, pure and simple. Also, I was worried for Anne Simon and Lizzy. Not that I thought Sadiq would ever do anything to harm them, but because spying on Anne Simon made it seem he *could*. I made up all sorts of excuses not to invite Lizzy over, and the few times I did, I made sure it was during one of Sadiq's infrequent absences. Even then, it was excruciating because all my energy was spent worrying Sadiq might suddenly appear.

During one of her visits, when it was still cool, I asked Lizzy if she was warm enough so many times, she asked me to stop.

"Why wouldn't I be?" she'd said, pointing to her chaddar on the back of the chair, assuring me she would put it on if she were not.

"This isn't like your house, that's all," I feebly answered.

"Right. This is a real house," Lizzy answered a little wistfully, which made me like her even more.

During her visits, I watched my mother closely, eager to see if she had difficulty hiding what we knew. She was always friendly, driving to United Bakery to pick up a sampling of Pakistani croissants and donuts, and making sure bottles of 7UP were in the refrigerator before Lizzy arrived. "If there's anything you'd like, just let me know," she would tell Lizzy. Then she would ask about the twins and Anne Simon, once drawing out details from Lizzy about her grandparents' town in upstate New York. "Cazenovia," Lizzy said, and my mother tried the word, counting the syllables with her fingers. "Five!" she exclaimed before inquiring, "And how close is that to Lehla in Syracuse?"

I was much more comfortable spending time with Lizzy at her house. One Friday afternoon she taught me to make Rice Krispie Treats. We emptied a jar of marshmallow creme and several cups of Rice Krispies into a pan with melted butter and took turns stirring the mixture. While we waited for the treats to set, Lizzy's mother returned from her walk drenched in sweat and poured herself a tall glass of ice water.

"I love your country, Liya, I really do. The mountains, the people, the city, the food . . . But you'd think the men have never seen a blonde before!"

"Before you?" Lizzy asked.

I giggled to hide my discomfort.

"They think you're beautiful, Mom," Lizzy said and winked at me. She wrapped her arms around her mother, and she was right, her mother was beautiful.

Anne Simon drank her water and smiled broadly. She picked at the empty jar of marshmallow creme and half joked that she couldn't exercise without feeling watched. Take today, for example, when there was a man in a turban lying under a tree, pretending to take a nap, and he was in exactly the same position when she left for her walk as when she returned. His gaze followed her all the way up the street and, forty-five minutes later, all the way back.

"He's probably a neighbor's servant, because I've seen him there before," she said.

Dread washed over me as I remembered it was Friday, and the full impact of her words registered. That very moment, not a few hundred yards away, Sadiq was lying underneath a tree on 87th Street in order to spy on Anne Simon. The thought was excruciating. I hardly heard myself as I asked, "Did he say anything?"

"Oh, no. People here just *look* at me funny," Anne Simon explained.

"Well, you are blonde *and* more funny-looking than usual today!" Lizzy teased.

Lizzy and her mother exchanged a few more sentences before Anne Simon left to take a shower. I tried to focus on Lizzy so she wouldn't notice anything, but it was impossible. Having given up waiting for the Rice Krispie Treats to set, Lizzy ran a knife along the pan.

"Wait a minute, Liya! You didn't take offense to what my mom said, did you?" Lizzy asked.

"What?"

"You know, when she said she liked your country, except that people looked at her weird."

"No," I said, but I didn't say anything more, and very quickly it was awkward between us again.

"Are you OK?" Lizzy finally asked, her voice low, although we were the only ones in the room.

I nodded my head vigorously, but it was hard to speak.

"Oh my God!" Lizzy finally stammered. "*He* wasn't there this morning, was he?"

"No!" I almost shouted, wishing she hadn't brought up the man at the bus stop, but finding my voice again. I looked for him whenever I left the house, whether it was a school day or not, and earlier, when my mother had backed out of the driveway, was no exception. He hadn't been there.

"I still think you should tell your mom or dad about him. Did you?"

"No."

Lizzy said that the next time we made Rice Krispie Treats, we would add M&M'S. I considered the possibility a waste of the special chocolate candies, but I kept that to myself. After a bit, I admitted that the encounter with the man had been scary.

"What if he'd touched you?" Lizzy asked.

"Yuck!" we cried in unison, wrinkling our noses and scrunching up our faces in disgust.

I wondered if the two of us, together, could keep the man—or anything worse that might yet happen—safely at bay.

In May, during the last month of the school year, Lizzy told me her mother was pregnant. She said she'd wanted to tell me much earlier, but her mother made her promise she wouldn't. Anne Simon was a nurse, but she was superstitious and concerned that if the news were publicized, something might go wrong with her pregnancy. Lizzy rolled her eyes at this, and we burst into laughter. "She's pregnant!" we exclaimed through uncontrollable giggles, as if this fact were hysterical on its own.

I'd noticed Anne Simon was different. Her chest and stomach were ample curves, her face was fuller and pressed into a smile, but the possibility of pregnancy hadn't occurred to me. *Mothers became pregnant?* While obvious, the prospect was unsettling. It made me imagine my own mother swollen with a baby, and I wondered what Amir, so many years older than me, had thought when she was carrying me. I sympathized with Lizzy. The thought of your own mother growing a huge belly was repugnant, and this was saying nothing about the unacknowledged reality of conception. A diagram detailing the process was taped to the blackboard in our health class that year, and now my best friend's mother was walking proof of the end result.

I couldn't tell Lizzy what I really thought. The transformation of Anne Simon on 87th Street was not so different from the transformation of Sadiq in my home. Both of them were fundamentally changing. The contradiction, that one human being was expanding while the other was fading away, was obvious. While Sadiq disappeared, shaved his hair and eyebrows, Anne Simon grew breasts and a belly. Anne Simon was making a new life, even though she'd run away from what was left of another life on a dark night only a year earlier. Anne Simon wasn't suffering and Sadiq was. It wasn't fair.

The very day that Lizzy shared the news, I told my mother.

"Really? She's expecting?" my mother said. "Doesn't she already have three children?"

"Is there a limit to how many she should have?" I was surprised at my defensiveness.

"Of course not," she said, ignoring my rudeness. "I was just saying . . . When is the baby due?"

"August."

"August? She's been expecting all this time and you didn't know until now?"

"I guess not. I didn't think of it much. She looked like she was getting fat, that's all," I replied, wishing my mother said *pregnant*, like everyone else, rather than *expecting*, which didn't sound like proper English.

"You do have a bit of growing up to do, don't you?" she chuckled. "When in August?"

"I don't know. The beginning maybe?" I didn't know why I withheld the date.

"It's good news for Anne Simon," my mother said. "She's been through a terrible time, and the baby will be a happy distraction for her."

"Sadiq doesn't have anything to distract him. Maybe he could visit his family in Lahore more often."

When my mother raised her eyebrows, I knew she was noting my loyalty to Sadiq. She'd told me once I was the most loyal of her children and that when I grew up I needed to be careful other people didn't take advantage of me.

"Maybe you could talk to Daddy. We could give Sadiq another train ticket to Lahore. Or maybe he would go by bus? He might feel better if he could get away for some time. And he could stay with his family longer." It was suddenly important to engineer a scheme for Sadiq to leave Islamabad, if only for a while. I was terrified he was spending every Friday afternoon on the corner of Anne Simon's street. *Did he already know she was pregnant?*

"It's not always possible to fix things," my mother cautioned, unaware of my primary concern. "Sadiq might never feel better, my darling. But I'll talk to Daddy. It's worth a try."

My mother kept her word, but some days later, when my father gave him another train ticket and strongly suggested he return home to his wife for a break, Sadiq refused. He slapped his palm over the train ticket without looking at it and slid it the length of the kitchen counter back to my father before leaving the room.

"That man!" my father complained after Sadiq had gone. "I have half a mind to fire him."

"No, you don't," my mother replied. "You just don't like it when people don't do what you want them to."

"You could have been more gentle, asked instead of commanded," I offered.

"What do you know?" my father snapped, losing patience with us, as was his habit since the prime minister's hanging. "You people think you know everything. Besides, he works for me!"

131

"And I thought he worked for me!" my mother tried to joke, but he pretended not to hear her.

My father flicked open the afternoon newspaper in one deliberate stroke and hid behind the same old news: The general decreed this and the general decreed that. All anyone ever hoped when picking up the paper was that General Zia had run out of things to decree, but that hadn't happened yet. I conjured up the sight of my father holding a newspaper strewn with white empty columns, the way it had been in the days following the coup. Because journalists like Uncle Imtiaz eventually figured out what the censors would and wouldn't allow, my father's head was buried in newsprint that covered every inch of the paper and bled on his fingers. I wished he'd been staring into empty pages so I could have laughed out loud at him, even if I agreed that he, not my mother, was Sadiq's principal employer.

But searching for humor didn't lighten the moment. My parents were angry, Sadiq was sad, and Anne Simon was pregnant. As for me, I had a sneaking suspicion nothing good would come of any of this. I tugged on my ponytail, sucking on the insides of my cheeks until I could feel the imprint of my braces, and left the room as if it were just another day.

What choice was there, anyway?

FOURTEEN

June 1979

I'd been rude to my mother—with something I had no memory of saying—and so she forbade me to spend the afternoon with Lizzy. As a result, I was stuck at home enduring one of her more creative punishments: organizing a year's worth of magazines in chronological order. Had she been reasonable, she would have admitted the enterprise was silly, but as it stood, she retired with a book to her bedroom and left me to the tiresome task.

I found the glossy postcard wedged in the bottom of the copper magazine tub. It featured an artist's rendition of Islamabad's Shah Faisal Mosque, a spaceship-like building under construction, complete with minarets as tall as the Margalla Hills. Written in March of the previous year and addressed to Yunis at my grandfather's house in Lahore, it had never been sent. I assumed it had become separated from a pile of outgoing mail placed on the neighboring table and had never made it to the post office.

Between Sadiq's lessons and my speculation, I was able to piece together most of his cramped message:

After Hanif's death, Sadiq expected the Margalla Hills to crumble. Day after day, he awoke with surprise to find the hills still standing.

Every morning the sky was blue, and all day long it screamed in his head. God Almighty had nerve, and as magnificent as it was, His world remained unchanged. Perhaps this was the miracle that was God, but Sadiq could have done without it. *Insha'Allah, I'll see you soon*, Sadiq had written in the end.

By the time I finished, my mouth was paper dry and I couldn't breathe. Although I was alone in the room, I felt caught in the act of intruding. In the seconds it took to read the postcard, I'd traveled to the most private places in Sadiq's mind and learned things I had no business knowing. I was ashamed of what I'd done and regretted I could not take back my actions. I quickly tucked the postcard inside the pages of the nearest magazine and hid it at the bottom of a stack of *The Economist* magazines.

And yet Sadiq's message fascinated me. I couldn't imagine sharing that much of myself with my brother or even my sister. And the depth of what Sadiq conveyed was stunning; who would have thought that our servant had such powerful thoughts? That he recorded them? That he was angry with God? That there was a relationship between grief and the hills across the street? I had nothing as painful or personal to share with anybody. Perhaps this was the secret that separated children from adults.

The next time Sadiq spoke to me, I saw crumbling mountains and screaming blue and could not answer him.

"Aliya?"

"Not now," I answered dismissively.

My mother caught me walking away. I didn't doubt her when she said that unless I apologized immediately, she would impose punishments that would occupy me for a week. "Yes, Mama," I said and controlled my tone.

~

My grandfather was in Islamabad again, this time for a cataract operation, and he took to treating Sadiq like his personal servant. He wanted his shoes polished every day, regardless of whether it was necessary. He insisted his shalwar kameez be starched and pressed, and if this had been done the day before, he hung the suit on a curtain rod for inspection in the morning before dressing. He drank only boiling hot tea, and on the first day of his visit, when Sadiq presented him with tea that did not meet this standard, he refused to drink it.

"You don't drink lukewarm tea. Why should I?" my grandfather demanded in his usual whisper.

By the time Sadiq returned to pour freshly brewed tea in a teacup he'd boiled in water and removed with tongs, Amir Shah had changed his mind.

"Pani," he instructed Sadiq, ignoring the steaming tea placed in front of him. When my grandfather began to interfere with the way the household was run, my mother tried speaking with him, but it made no difference. He said Sadiq had become a lazy, useless good-for-nothing because my father had allowed it. Hard work was the only remedy for grieving and furthermore, Sadiq did not keep the house clean enough.

We were astounded by my grandfather's newfound appreciation for cleanliness, and Amir and Lehla, too, would not have believed it. In Lahore, the three of us had always fought over who would sleep on his living room sofa, farthest from the black ants that ruled his home. But suddenly, during this latest visit to our home, my grandfather's cleanliness standards had become tyrannical. He may have lost his hearing, suffered damage to his vocal cords, and been struck half-blind with cataracts, but there was nothing wrong with his ability to issue commands.

On the day my grandfather had his second cataract operation, we returned from the hospital just as Sadiq was putting down the telephone receiver.

"How is Jamila?" my father inquired, guessing he'd been speaking to his wife.

"I don't know," Sadiq said, and the vacant look in his eyes worried me.

"What do you mean?"

"She wasn't home."

"Out this late? Where was she? Is everything all right?"

Sadiq studied my father as if his question, *Is everything all right?* did not make sense.

"A birthday party," Sadiq said, and I knew it was a lie.

"Listen, now that my father is here with us, why don't you send Jamila and the children to Yunis? He can help look after them." It was an old suggestion. Despite Sadiq's visits to Lahore, my mother could never reconcile herself with separating Sadiq from his family. Over the years, there had been long discussions about various possibilities, among them a scenario in which Jamila and the children lived in my grandfather's house.

"She won't do it."

"I'll send Yunis to check on her when I'm in Lahore tomorrow," my father told him.

"No need," Sadiq protested.

"It's *my* need," my father said, rejecting Sadiq's thought. "I want to make sure she's fine."

Beginning the next day, every time my father went to Lahore, sometimes as often as five times a week, Yunis dutifully rode his bicycle the few miles to Jamila's home to confirm that she and the children were fine. The next weekend, my father learned from Yunis that Sadiq and Jamila had stopped speaking to each other. When my father pried and asked why, Sadiq simply confirmed that they were no longer speaking.

"How on earth is this possible?" my father complained to my mother.

"I'm not sure," my mother said.

"The parents have lost a child. Shouldn't they be supporting each other?"

"It's the distance. Maybe you should send Sadiq back to Lahore."

"And what if they don't speak to each other once he gets there?"

I kept it to myself, but I could explain what had gone wrong between Sadiq and Jamila. After all this time, the pain and sorrow recorded in an unsent postcard had burned a hole between them.

The next morning, Sadiq did not come to work. My father took a bottle of aspirin and went to check on him. When he returned, he said Sadiq had caught his thumb in a car door and lost his nail.

"Should we take him to the doctor?" my mother asked.

"Let me . . ."

"You treat the man like a baby," my grandfather whispered indignantly. "The more you spoil Sadiq, the longer he'll take to recover. You're the first VIP to deliver aspirin to a servant's room." My grandfather coughed, the consecutive sentences taxing his perpetually dry throat.

"Let's get you some water," my father said, in order not to contradict his father.

"He takes advantage of you," my grandfather insisted.

My mother could not contain herself. "It's not possible for a person with no power to take advantage of a person with all the power. He's the servant, for God's sake."

"So? By now, you should understand that *they* are the exploiting class!" my grandfather guffawed.

My mother stared at my grandfather in disbelief, speechless only for a second before she was reduced to saying, "That's ridiculous!"

"Dada abba," I said weakly. My grandfather didn't hear me, so I took his hand. "Let's sit in the sun," I said, and he allowed me to lead him to the upstairs veranda.

My mother wasn't good at keeping secrets. She finally told my father that we'd seen Sadiq at the corner of 87th Street several weeks earlier. They called me into their bedroom and made me sit on the rocking chair.

My father looked at me sternly and said, "I understand that you know Anne Simon was the driver?"

"The driver?" I said with dread, trying to buy time.

"You know she does. We just talked about this!" my mother complained.

"Please answer me," my father said.

"Yes, I know."

"How did you find out?"

"From people at school," I lied easily.

"Did Sadiq see you on Anne Simon's street?"

I tried to remember. "I don't think so."

"Think?!" my father said, suddenly raising his voice and looking at my mother. "No one is doing any *thinking* here. If Sadiq is caught on her street, he could be thrown in jail. We're responsible for him. A servant . . . my God, *my* servant! What will people say? Stalking a woman . . . an American! Why didn't you tell me?" My father was more worried about his job than Sadiq.

"He's not stalking her," my mother said.

"How do you know?"

"He's here most of the time!" my mother exclaimed.

"*Most* of the time. Who knows about the rest of the time?"

His question hung between us until my mother gave up and said, "You're right," and my father calmed down.

I expected my father to fire Sadiq. Instead, he forbade him from ever returning to 87th Street. If he was ever caught there again, he would lose his job. There would be no second chances. On Fridays, Sadiq would accompany my father to Jumma prayers. Afterward they would return together to the house. Sadiq had Friday afternoons off, but he could not leave the premises unless he was in the company of someone such as my father.

"Daddy's putting Sadiq under house arrest?" I asked my mother. She was in the pantry opening and closing tin containers of flour and sugar, sounds that augured well for dessert that evening.

"For now," my mother said, as if restricting a servant's movement was acceptable.

In the morning, Sadiq burned my toast and then my egg but served them to me anyway because he knew I wouldn't complain.

"What's this?" I asked when I added my plate to the stack of dirty ones in the sink and pointed to the brown butter in the frying pan.

"Makhan," Sadiq simply said, butter.

He was wrong, and I corrected him. But I was required to whisper so my father, who was sitting at the table reading the newspaper, wouldn't hear my Urdu. "This is the butter that burned when you were frying my egg and making my toast."

"What did you say?" my father asked, and I knew he'd caught part of what I'd said.

"Makhan," I said. "I *do* know the Urdu word for butter, thank you very much."

He let me get away with speaking to him like that because he was preoccupied, and my mother, thank goodness, wasn't there to notice.

FIFTEEN

June–Early July 1979

I spent as much time as I could with Lizzy, but not at the American Embassy, which I was boycotting since the prime minister's hanging. I turned down invitations for movies, lunches, tennis tournaments, and a children's scavenger hunt, part of a special Thank God It's Thursday! sponsored by marines, which I especially wanted to attend. I'd made the decision independently of my father's decree. I'd grown increasingly uncomfortable watching movies or swimming with my classmates in the compound. I didn't know if their fathers were spies or if they had done anything to conspire against my country, but each time the embassy guard waved me through the gates, my Pakistani half surfaced and made me want to flee from the grounds.

Lizzy's home was a different matter. I began to accept all of her invitations, but without reciprocating. My house not being air-conditioned was just an excuse; in truth, I didn't want to remind Sadiq of my friendship with her. I couldn't do anything about spitballs flying out of the yellow school buses, but I could spare Sadiq this. My mother, on the other hand, argued that my failure to return Lizzy's generosity was bad manners, and she finally persuaded me to compromise. She wouldn't demand I invite

Lizzy to our house, but I could take her to the Islamabad Club, the only exclusive Pakistani club in the city.

The enormous swimming pool was so impressive, even the Americans talked about it. The high-diving board was one of a kind in the city, and Lizzy, who dreamed of becoming an Olympic diver, loved to jump up and down on it before performing flawless swan dives and somersaults and flips, which despite countless hours of instruction, I could never learn to duplicate. But that was only once a week, on Thursdays, her only completely free day, when Mushtaq drove us to the Islamabad Club and we spent the day lathering baby oil on our skin, wearing identical Thai batik bikinis Anne Simon had ordered for us. "You're so lucky! You tan so well," Lizzy would say when we compared our tan lines and she was forced to apply sunscreen to her sunburned body. While my skin darkened to the same shade as my father's, Lizzy's hair grew lighter, until my mother described it as platinum blonde, a color most women only achieved with hair dye. Lizzy helped the sun along with frequent applications of lemon juice, which her cook squeezed and bottled for her on Thursday mornings. She was more than glad to share her lemon juice with me, but it did nothing for my brown hair except turn it into a sticky mess. I was relieved to rinse it out in the chlorinated pool.

I spent lazy June afternoons at Lizzy's house several days a week, air conditioners whirring in every room, including the kitchen. Every so often, Anne Simon, who'd given up her job as a nurse to spend more time with her children and to get ready for the baby, joined us in the den, where her sewing machine sat on a table, the floor around it littered with scraps of fabric and threadless wooden spools. The five-year-old twins were forbidden from playing there, but they tried anyway, knocking things off the table that were immediately retrieved by servants. Anne Simon gave the staff instructions in English, but when I visited, she asked me to translate complicated orders into Urdu. I was pleased to do so.

The coffee table had been moved flush against a wall and was now piled with stacks of gray crates that had contained gallon jugs of milk flown from America to the commissary in Islamabad. Peeking through the crates were baby clothes: tiny cotton jumpers, hats and shirts, miniature pants with belt loops, bibs stitched from multiple fabrics and lined with plastic, crocheted white sweaters, cream booties, and blue hats threaded with satin-ribbon ties. I picked up a green-and-white pair of what we called Kabul socks, woolen slipper socks covered with a geometric-diamond design. When Lehla brought me back a pair from a school trip to Kabul a few years earlier, my mother had stitched leather soles to help me better manage our slippery marble floors.

"How old will the baby be when it walks?" I asked Anne Simon.

"A year maybe. Lizzy walked in twelve months, the twins in ten. Who knows when this little guy will be ready?"

"You know it's a boy?"

"Mom *thinks* she knows," Lizzy said playfully.

"Well, carrying the baby in the front like I am usually means it's a boy. That's what people say. But you girls wouldn't know that!"

"Is that what nurses say?"

"Nurses are people! What do you think?" Anne Simon asked, standing tall and turning in place.

"You were fat with the twins!" Lizzy said.

"What was it you used to say? 'Your belly is high as the sky.' Remember? Look. I'm only fat in the front," Anne Simon said, as if this were something that interested us.

"If she's right, you're getting another brother," I said to Lizzy later, a plate of warm sugar cookies in front of us and a cold glass of genuine American milk in my hand. Lizzy was attacking a bowl of freshly popped and buttered popcorn. "Do you mind if it's a boy?"

"I don't know," Lizzy replied. "A baby is a baby. I guess a girl might be nice. My dad wants a girl, but I don't really care."

"He does? Why?" I asked, licking my fingers, stained green and pink from the warm cookie's melting sugar sprinkles.

"I don't know. It's his first child."

I didn't know what Lizzy meant until she told me that her real father had died of a heart attack in his sleep when she was seven and the twins had just been born, and that the man she called Dad was really her stepfather. Her mother had met Mr. Simon when he was recovering from an emergency appendectomy in the hospital where she worked as a nurse. Lizzy didn't mind calling him Dad. She barely remembered her real father and didn't think about him very much. "Do you think that's strange?"

"I don't know," I said, trying to imagine my father dying and not remembering him. "Why didn't you tell me earlier?"

"I don't think about it a lot." Picking up a toy-sized wooden sailboat I'd never noticed from the bed's headboard, she said, "My real father was a carpenter, and he had a shop in Cazenovia. He made this for me."

I touched the sail, a rough piece of cotton, and ran my fingers over the weave. "It even floats!" Lizzy said.

"Did you try it out on the lake by your grandparents'?"

"Yes. I've never been to any other lakes."

"I thought there were tons where you're from."

"There are. I just never saw them. My real father was always working. I don't know how many he ever saw."

"He wasn't a big traveler?" I asked, and Lizzy nodded.

"But Dad has been posted everywhere," Lizzy said proudly. "He was in Iran before he met Mom. He's lived in Cambodia, too. And somewhere in Africa . . . Addis Ababa, maybe. Kabul, also, but I don't know when."

"All those countries have malaria problems?"

Just then, Anne Simon called us for dinner. Mr. Simon had come home early from office. He'd changed into jeans and a white polo shirt that made him look younger than his age. I liked his casualness, a stark contrast to my father, who was known to wear suits at home. Anne Simon explained that the dinner was prime rib, and after checking with her that it wasn't pork, I began to eat. I'd never tasted meat so tender.

"Do you like it?" Mr. Simon asked. "My mother sent it to us from her farm in New York. By the way, Aliya, how's your sister doing at Syracuse University?"

"She loves it there so much she isn't coming home this summer." I smiled without checking with my tongue if I had prime rib stuck in my braces. "How did the meat get here? Without going bad, I mean."

"Dry ice," he replied. "It came in the diplomatic pouch, so it was pretty quick." The term *diplomatic pouch* was a mystery to me. All I knew was it allowed Americans to receive mail very quickly.

"Were you the malaria specialist in all the other countries you were posted in?" Lizzy suddenly asked. When Mr. Simon looked confused, she glanced at me and added, "We were just wondering."

"I work on public-health projects specific to countries."

"It's malaria here, right?" I asked.

"Yes, mostly malaria," Mr. Simon replied before Anne Simon noticed the twins playing with their food and told them to stop.

I was curious about Mr. Simon's job in the way that I was curious about what all Americans were really doing in Pakistan. But I was further intrigued upon learning he'd been to many places, maybe even more than my father, who traveled all the time. When my father returned from Lahore that night, I asked him about Mr. Simon's job.

"I don't know exactly. Didn't you say he was a malaria specialist?"

"He's lived in a lot of countries. Cambodia, Ethiopia, Afghanistan, and Iran, too."

My father looked up from the newspaper and over the frames of his glasses.

"When you join the foreign service or USAID, you're posted to many different countries during your career."

"What do you think he does?"

"Isn't he a health specialist or something?"

"Malaria expert."

"Well, he's been to a lot of important places. He's probably in Islamabad because the ambassador wants him here," my father said.

"So the ambassador is also interested in malaria?" I'd never heard of an ambassador interested in illnesses, and after a few minutes, I became suspicious, as the prime minister had in his famous elephant speech in the parliament right before he was deposed. "Who were the elephants the prime minister was talking about?" I asked my father. Mr. Simon, a nice man who asked about Lehla and shared prime rib with me, couldn't have been an elephant.

My father, irritated at my last question, didn't respond directly. "It was a metaphor," he said. "An approximation. The prime minister didn't mean it literally. He was referring to various foreigners and their interests interfering in the politics of the country."

"A lot of Americans know each other from before," I offered. I was making my own observation as I had heard classmates remind each other they were in first grade together at an earlier posting, or their fathers once lived on the same base in California or Virginia for a short while. "In fact, the new principal who's coming to my school is a friend of Mr. Simon's. They knew each other in Iran." I'd learned about the new principal at dinner, when Mr. Simon gave the news to Anne Simon.

My father, not displaying much interest, shook his head in a way that meant he was finished listening.

"Is Mr. Simon CIA?" I asked, repeating the question I'd once presented to my mother, and was immediately rewarded with my father's attention.

Without much reflection, he said, "He very well could be."

"What do you think? Does Mr. Simon interfere in the politics of our country?"

"Come on, darling!" he exclaimed impatiently.

"His wife did," I said, "with Hanif."

"It was an accident," he insisted. "It's a scandal how badly the roads are lit. God forbid, it could have been your mother behind the wheel. And, by the way, that doesn't qualify as interference in the country's affairs. Maybe family affairs."

Overlooking the distinction, I asked, "Would Mama have gone to jail? Even though she's a foreigner, she wouldn't have had diplomatic immunity, right?"

"Of course not! Only diplomats have diplomatic immunity, and obviously we're not diplomats. Go on now, I have work to do," he said, waving me away.

But I wasn't finished. I wanted to ask him what sum of money my mother would have had to pay if she had been the driver, but I didn't want to risk revealing I'd read the settlement papers. Instead, I attempted my own calculations. If an American was charged 50,000 rupees for the offense, would a Pakistani be charged the same amount? But my mother wasn't a Pakistani. Would she count as a foreigner? What about Lehla? If Lehla ran over an American child in New York, what would her penalty be? Jail time? A fine? How much? More than what Lizzy's mother had been fined for Hanif's death? In the end, I lost my way in the calculations and was no closer to understanding the methods or reasons of compensating death.

"What was Anne Simon's punishment?" I asked.

My father put down his reading glasses and was clearly struggling to be patient. "The lawyers took care of it."

"Sadiq had a lawyer?"

"Lawyers took care of it," he repeated. He picked up a pen and began to scribble on the papers in his hand.

I left the room. My father hadn't lied to me, and I appreciated that. I knew Sadiq did not have a lawyer because my father witnessed his signature on the settlement papers. Anne Simon must have had more than one lawyer.

In the hall, I met Sadiq carrying a heavy brass tray as he made his way to collect empty teacups from the cocktail table. My grandfather had given my parents the antique tray he'd bought in the Old City of Lahore. I suddenly wondered what kept Sadiq in my parents' home. After what had happened, why didn't he leave Islamabad and return to be with his family in Lahore?

"You don't want to go to Lahore," I said, halfway between fact and question.

"My work is here," Sadiq responded.

"In this house?" I demanded.

Sadiq slowly blinked his eyes in a private nod of agreement. I allowed the gesture to register, doing my best to believe him. His work was in my father's house, not on the corner of Lizzy's street, or anywhere else.

"Manzur," I said, uttering the Urdu word he'd taught me, *agreed*, as if it was a pact between us.

He left the room reciting a nursery rhyme to which I only knew the first few lines. "Ek tha larka Tot Batot, Nam tha uska Mir Salot . . ." *There once was a boy Tot Batot, His name was Mir Salot . . .*

The words fell safely into place like a metronome.

I decided to believe Sadiq. His work was in my father's house. I wouldn't worry about Anne Simon going on walks and Sadiq spying on her. Besides, he was under house arrest, which is why it was a Friday and Sadiq was safely home with us.

I didn't imagine Anne Simon going on walks with a baby in her arms, because August, like Lehla's highways, was far, far away.

SIXTEEN

Mid-July 1979

M y grandfather would never have admitted it, but it was true: Lahore stank, and Islamabad did not. Arriving at Lahore airport was like landing in the belly of an olfactory machine. Dung, charcoal, onions, sweat, garbage, sewage, oranges, and diesel fumes. For the first few minutes on the tarmac and during the car ride home, it was difficult to breathe.

It was the first time I'd visited my grandfather in his new boxlike house, made uglier by wrought iron grills installed across the windows for security. It was ironic because Shadman, the district to which my grandfather had moved, was once a sprawling jail, leveled long ago to make room for a residential area. Yet, here was the jail, coming to life again in my grandfather's windows. The mosque across the street made me think my grandfather would have been safe without grills. Who burglarizes a home within sight of one of God's houses?

After giving me a tour, my grandfather deposited me in the kitchen, then hurried to his new study, already a mess, to listen to the radio news. I waited while Yunis prepared my favorite Lahore lassi, the special one he'd been making for me ever since I could remember. Just as Yunis handed me my glass filled to the brim with the delicious mix of mangoes, yogurt, and shaved ice, the house shook with such shrill shrieks of microphone feedback that I spilled the drink.

"Allah!" Yunis said, using God's name in vain to complain about the noise and the pool of orange near my feet.

"Allahu Akbar, Allahu Akbar." The muezzin's call to prayer became decipherable. The microphone shot the muezzin's voice into the kitchen, shaking the single-pane windows and the wooden cabinets and making the teak door between the kitchen and dining room swing slightly back and forth.

"Is the azaan always this loud here?" I shouted in Urdu to Yunis. "How can you sleep in the morning?"

"Our general doesn't think we should be sleeping," he joked. "We should all be praying on a janamaz!" Yunis laughed hard and I joined him. Since he was Christian, I'd never pictured him on a janamaz.

My grandfather suddenly threw open the intricately carved front doors. The bolt slammed into the wall, where it had already left countless marks. He stood on the front stoop, waving a flexed palm in a threatening gesture at the mosque across the street. The azaan grew louder.

All across the country, in small and large cities alike, the call to prayer was heard five times a day. The only exception was my school, where not even the slightest echo had ever been heard. But my ears had never been assaulted by an azaan like this, an azaan so extraordinary that it sent my deaf grandfather into a rage.

From the kitchen, I could see the neighborhood mosque behind my grandfather in the doorway. My father had used it, and anything else he could think of, to persuade my grandfather to leave Five Queen's Road for a new home in Shadman. "You'll hardly have to walk across the street for Jumma prayers," I remembered my father saying. For years, my grandfather had fought my father "tooth and nail," as my father was fond of saying, to stay in Five Queen's Road, the utterly dilapidated remnant of a home in which my father had grown up. My grandfather only acquiesced when a violent monsoon season flooded the house and made it uninhabitable once and for all.

Later that night, as my grandfather and I watched Indian newscasts on the black-and-white television, I asked him, "Where do you go for Jumma prayers?" He put his face close to mine to hear me better, and I tried not to notice that his dentures were too white for a man his age.

"No need to go anywhere," he whispered.

"Because the azaan is so loud?" I asked.

"Your parents give *me* hearing aids, but *you* will be deaf in a month if you stay here." He left the room for a moment, and after returning, dropped a set of earplugs in my hand, instructing me to use them when I slept, or else, he warned, "You won't get any sleep in Lahore!"

The television showed grainy images of India's Prime Minister Morarji Desai, American President Jimmy Carter, and the new president of Iraq. While the formal Urdu of television newscasts was difficult for me to follow, I caught almost every word that night. The former president of Iraq had resigned and a new leader, Saddam Hussein, had just been appointed to take his place.

I jumped up and stood in front of my grandfather, obscuring his view.

"Can you keep a secret? I speak Urdu now," I announced proudly and translated what I'd just said into Urdu to prove the point.

"You always did," he pointed out kindly, although he was lying.

I didn't argue with my grandfather but made him promise not to mention to my father what I'd confessed. I still wasn't ready to tell him.

I spent the night tossing in bed with my window closed, the ancient air conditioner dripping water on the floor instead of blowing cold air. Along with everyone else in Lahore, I awoke to the clamor of competing azaans, a mess of unsynchronized calls ricocheting across the city. I pushed my earplugs deeper into my ears, and while they didn't muffle the muezzins, they kept out the sounds of the rising city at dawn—bicycle bells, shrill calls of vendors, car horns—and eventually allowed me to sleep again.

My first few days were spent the way my Lahore visits always began. I went to Ferozsons bookstore on Mall Road, where my grandfather let me select whatever books I wanted. Next, my grandfather took me on our standard tour of Lahore's sights in his battered Toyota Corolla. He drove through red lights as if they were green and proclaimed that cataract surgery had given him perfect vision. We visited the Shalimar Gardens, where the dozens of fountains in shallow pools of water actually worked that summer. We managed a longer visit than usual to the Lahore Fort, where I learned that the wide walkways were designed for elephants and that the tulips painted on the tiles came from Central Asia, not my mother's Holland, as I'd assumed. Then we went to the Old City, where we rode in a tonga and ate chicken tikka and naan prepared right in front of us. From the rows of tiny stalls that sold thin glass bangles of every color and design, I picked out dozens of bangles, including green ones with gold glitter, maroon ones braided with silver, and plain purple ones. The shop owner slipped two dozen of the most beautiful glass bangles I'd ever seen over my wrist without breaking a single one. My grandfather instructed him to put together an identical set for Lehla, and because I asked, he bought another set for Lizzy.

As we drove, my grandfather, normally reserved with words, offered running commentary on the inferiority of Islamabad, "the village," as compared to Lahore. Its restrictions, such as no rickshaws or tongas on the streets, forever separated it from the rest of the country. Filled with foreigners and laid out in a grid with broad avenues and numbered sectors that served no purpose, the place was insufferable. Constitution Avenue was a national disgrace: six wasted lanes that rarely saw more than a few cars and, worse, was named after a document that was suspended, amended, and abrogated so many times it had come to mean nothing, especially under the new general. My grandfather went on to mock the Presidency, a futuristic palace with secret underground chambers meant for god-knows-what. He repeated a rumor that city planners had imported Japanese trees to line the streets. "As if what grows in Japan has any chance of thriving at the foot of the Himalayan mountains!" he said.

I didn't care much about Islamabad one way or another, but I finally asked, "What did the city ever do to you?"

"*Village*," he corrected me. "It gave me the general!" He was right. The country's leaders ruled from Islamabad, but the army's headquarters, from where the general ruled, were in Rawalpindi. Not to mention that the general had been born in what was now India, but it was best not to argue such fine points with my grandfather.

One afternoon, just as Yunis was about to serve a lunch of aloo saag (which was the only way I agreed to eat spinach), my grandfather answered the front door to find Sadiq standing on the stoop. After looking him up and down and poking an index finger into his scrawny chest as if to confirm his presence, my grandfather whispered, "None of you can stay away from Lahore!"

Sadiq's arrival was completely unexpected. My father had charged him with looking after the household in Islamabad while my mother and I were away. Instead, my father reported that the following day, on a Sunday evening not one week into my visit, he returned from a long workday to find Sadiq missing. I was standing next to the telephone when he rang, but Sadiq got to it first.

"What are you doing there?" my father demanded, the shock in his voice booming through the static-filled line.

"Nothing," Sadiq replied blandly.

"Nothing? I thought something happened to you." When Sadiq neither apologized nor offered an explanation, my father became furious. "If it weren't for my wife, I'd let you go. First you forget how to set the table and make my tea. Then you go off to . . ."

Sadiq moved the receiver away from his ear and covered the earpiece with his hand to protect me from my father's tirade.

"Give it to me!" I ordered him. Sadiq held the receiver beyond my reach, my father's words safely muffled by his hand until Yunis came to see what was happening and took it from him.

"My brother is not well," Yunis pleaded with my father.

"I'm losing my mind!" I could hear my father shout.

"Sir," Yunis said, with a seriousness appropriate to the statement he was about to make. "*He* has lost his mind."

Sadiq had taught me the Urdu words for *lost his mind*, but it still took me a moment before I comprehended what had been said. Had Sadiq been showing signs of a man who'd lost his mind? If so, had he lost it in the exact place and at the precise moment Anne Simon had run over Hanif? Or had he been losing it bit by bit since then? Was grief wearing him out, grinding him away, leaving a dustlike trail behind his shrinking body? The last possibility comforted me, if only for a crazy second in which I imagined chasing him with a butterfly net, catching scattered pieces of his mind and safely returning them to him.

"Put him on the telephone!" my father shouted to Yunis, who grimaced but did not obey. Suddenly my grandfather appeared, wrested the telephone from Yunis, and dropped it back in the cradle.

Within hours, my father arrived in Lahore to deal with Sadiq in person. He entered my grandfather's house, closely followed by a WAPDA driver who was struggling to carry his two briefcases and keep up with him at the same time.

"How are you?" my father asked no one in particular, then went right to the kitchen where Sadiq had relegated himself for the day. I intercepted the WAPDA driver and instructed him to leave my father's baggage by the front door.

"You left without telling me," I heard my father say. "Why?" He was met with silence, except for Yunis, who had barely begun to defend his brother when my father ordered him to be quiet. "You left without telling me," my father repeated with even more gravity, as if there were no crime more serious than leaving without informing someone.

Later in the evening, my father sank into the sofa and, because my grandfather was not in the room, put his feet up on the coffee table. "What can you do with these people?" he asked me, although it wasn't really a question at all. Sadiq brought us our tea and stirred three spoonfuls of sugar into my special oversized teacup.

"You take that much sugar?" my father said.

"We're visiting Dada," I answered, as if in my grandfather's house, my father should know better than to offer comments about my sugar intake. Luckily, he was so preoccupied with Sadiq, he dropped the subject.

"How's your wife?" he asked Sadiq. "Your daughters? Do they need anything?"

"No," Sadiq said in a monotone.

"Where are they?" my father asked.

"Home."

"Why aren't you there?"

Sadiq froze, but I knew he wanted nothing more than to sprint to the kitchen away from my father's interrogation.

"Well, now that you're in Lahore, you should be with your family." My father made it sound like a reasonable suggestion, seeming to forget that Sadiq and Jamila weren't on speaking terms.

Sadiq slowly shook his head, but my mother's absence made my father less careful and more stubborn, so he pressed on without tempering his words. "Why not? They are your family."

"I don't have a family anymore," Sadiq mumbled. He left the room and soon we heard him heading for the mosque across the street, where the muezzin was fiddling with the microphone before calling the azaan.

With Sadiq gone, my father directed his lecture at Yunis. He told Yunis tragedies struck all sorts of people in all walks of life, but, God willing, they found the courage to survive and continue to be responsible to their families. "You're his brother. Explain this to him," my father insisted.

"Pardon?" Yunis said, unable to hear my father through the roar of the beginning phrases of the azaan.

"Goddamnit!" my father said, breaking into a single English curse, only to immediately revert to Urdu. "What's that bloody noise?"

My father didn't curse often, but when he did, his anger had the rhythm of Urdu curse words, not the ones I heard on the bus, but curse words all the same—haramzada, ulloo ka patha—but I'd never heard him say *goddamnit* before.

"It's the azaan," I said. My father appeared surprised that I'd followed his Urdu or, more likely, that I should think he really required an answer.

"What *is* this?" my father said, waving in the air as if the wailing muezzin's "Ashahadu an la illaha illallah" was something he could touch. Just then, my grandfather appeared in the hallway on his way to his study.

"It's the mosque," my grandfather whispered curtly. "Remember, you bribed me with it to get me to live here?"

His second sentence was lost on my father, who'd already headed for the bathroom to wash before offering his prayers. He never missed them in his father's house.

"I'll deal with this situation later," my father said mainly to himself, which was fine because no one believed he had any idea of what to do.

As always, the azaan ended with "La illaha illallah." There is no God but God. The last line was my favorite. Even with all the muezzins across Lahore shouting it through microphones at slightly staggered times, the melody of that last line hovered in the air, gentler than the lines that had preceded it. The entire azaan once had sounded like that final line, before the amplification of the general, his loudspeakers, and microphones. My mother told us that when she visited Pakistan for the first time, she fell in love with the azaan. The melody of music and prayer five times a day! Things were different now. I'd seen her cover her ears when the din began. Was that blasphemy? My father didn't always say his prayers five times a day, and did sometimes say *goddamnit* or worse. Was that blasphemy? It didn't really matter because he was responsible for my mother's conversion to Islam, and as a result had a seat reserved for him in heaven.

Heaven . . . where, hopefully, Hanif was.

I hadn't realized how much I'd worried about Sadiq staying behind in Islamabad until the sight of him in Lahore flooded me with relief. He'd been forbidden to go to Embassy Road, but who knew what he was up to when my mother and I weren't in Islamabad? The first time I was alone with him in my grandfather's kitchen, I asked why he'd decided to come to Lahore.

Instead of answering me, he said, "For months, you people give me train tickets to Lahore. Now I'm here and it's a problem. Whose fault is that?"

"Daddy's." I shrugged. "How long did the train take?"

"Four hundred twenty minutes," Sadiq said, testing my knowledge of numbers.

"Seven hours!" I said triumphantly, having long since learned to count in the hundreds.

"Please don't be so angry with Sadiq," I pleaded with my father later over a dinner interrupted by work-related telephone calls. "After all, he lost his son," I added, copying an expression adults used to talk about death.

"The child is dead, not misplaced," my father countered.

"Do you have to be this angry with him?"

"You let me worry about him. You worry about yourself. Yunis!" my father called, and in a second, Yunis was standing in front of him, ready to receive instructions. Yunis would continue to visit Jamila every day. If there was anything she or the children needed, he was to report it to my father.

"I could always tell Sadiq," Yunis suggested.

"That would only be helpful if the two of them were talking again. Are they?"

Yunis shook his head and smiled, but his smile was very sad.

One morning, two days before I was to return to Islamabad and one day after my father had left, I woke up in what seemed to be an empty house. I couldn't have been alone, but it was unusually quiet. After a breakfast of Yunis's special halva and pooris that was left on the dining room table for me, I carried my dishes to the kitchen. The kitchen was an oven, regardless of the time of day or whether cooking had begun. I put my head in the freezer looking for ice cubes, but found only freezer snow that scraped and numbed my fingertips. My grandfather had told me there were plastic ice trays somewhere in the kitchen, and that morning I decided to finally look for them.

I began in the far corner of the kitchen, methodically searching each cabinet. I went through shelves of glasses, plates, pots, and pans, without finding the ice trays. I rummaged through the cabinet where Yunis stored the various flours he used for chapatis, parathas, and pooris, and found squeezed between the flour bags, brand-new hearing aids—still in their original boxes—that my father had bought my grandfather. In another cabinet, I discovered plastic food containers my mother bought for the house and I'd never once seen used. A double cabinet was stuffed with files of yellowing papers, and a drawer was filled with rusted nails, broken pliers, candle stubs, and blunt, dirty scissors. Underneath the kitchen sink, a place I'd almost overlooked, I found a bucket of foul-smelling garbage, a collection of cleaning products, and some rags. I caught sight of a brass handle tucked behind them that I would have left alone if it hadn't been so out of place. Reaching as far back into the cabinet as I could, I lifted out a heavy black briefcase. In the process, I hit my hand on the cabinet divider, knocked over a bottle of furniture oil, and broke the last of my glass bangles, all at the same time.

Kneeling on the floor, I clicked open the latches of the old briefcase that resembled one my father once had. A strange smell wafted up, an unpleasant mix of rotting cauliflower, damp leather, and new banknotes. It took me a moment to grasp the contents, neatly arranged like the banker's tray in a serious Monopoly game. Covering every inch of the faded paisley lining were bundled stacks of rupees arranged in orderly rows. I'd never seen that much money before, and all of it was in hundred-rupee bills. When Yunis walked into the kitchen, I was clasping neat, solid bundles in each hand with my arms outstretched like the arms of the vegetable wallah's weighing scale. I dropped one handful on the floor, continuing to stare at the packet until Yunis retrieved it. He put it back in the briefcase, then gestured for me to replace the bundles I was still holding. I stood up to get out of the way so Yunis could return the briefcase to where I'd found it.

"Is it yours?" I asked him when he was finished.

"No," he replied.

"My grandfather's?"

"No."

He began scrubbing my breakfast dishes in the ancient kitchen sink that should never have been transplanted from Five Queen's Road.

"It's a lot of money," I said to his back.

Just then Sadiq swung open the kitchen door. He went to a counter littered with used and unused orange halves and began to squeeze juice by hand.

"No need for juice, thank you," I said, hoping to get Sadiq's attention. He continued to squeeze until most of the juice ran over the top of the plastic lemon juicer. Had Hanif liked oranges? Had Sadiq ever made juice for his son? "I would not like juice, please," I said as formally as I could.

"Khatam." Yunis walked over to Sadiq and removed the oranges from the counter. The way he said *finish* made me aware that he wanted Sadiq not only to finish what he was doing, but also to leave the room.

"Sadiq?" I began gently as Yunis led Sadiq to the back door. "Do you know about the briefcase of money underneath my grandfather's sink?"

Sadiq stopped in his tracks and replied, "Yes."

"The money is yours?"

"It's my brother's."

I was sure the bundles of hundred-rupee notes added up to at least 50,000. It had to be Sadiq's settlement money, and he'd given it to Yunis.

"Why? Is it Yunis's?" I demanded, but neither of them said another word.

A part of me wanted to pull the briefcase from the cabinet and give it to my grandfather for safekeeping. But if I did, questions about where the money came from would arise immediately, and I was afraid someone would discover my knowledge of the settlement and the money. My grandfather was a kind man, but he was also stern, as I'd seen in his dealings with my father. I couldn't risk lying to him. Moreover, I desperately didn't want Sadiq discovering I knew about Anne Simon and the settlement. The shame I felt at my betrayals, more than anything, kept the briefcase in the cabinet underneath the kitchen sink. I was good at keeping secrets.

The next morning, my last in Lahore, I didn't go into the kitchen but called out my breakfast order to Yunis from behind the kitchen door. After breakfast, my grandfather took me to the Old City to replace the glass bangles. On the way back, I suggested he keep his house locked during the day. He laughed off my suggestion, claiming there was nothing of value in the house, and as long as that was the case, thieves were welcome to help themselves.

"Then why did you have grills put in the windows?" I asked.

"Silly girl . . . to protect *us*. Not my *things*." When he saw my confusion, he offered a long whisper of consolation. "You understand that I lock the door at night when we are home, right?"

A few hours later, when the early night air was overpowered with the scent of jasmine, Yunis and Sadiq left for the bus station, where Sadiq would catch the express bus to Islamabad. And my grandfather and I left for the airport for my flight. No one locked the doors.

When I first returned to Islamabad, I worried that someone in Lahore would steal the money hidden underneath my grandfather's kitchen sink. If that were ever to happen, Sadiq would have lost both his son and his money, which amounted to everything he had. But when he appeared in our kitchen one morning with kohl lining his eyes, I realized I had more immediate cause for concern.

"Is that Jamila's kohl?"

"Don't you know that kohl wards off evil spirits?"

I looked at him, a grown man who'd painted his eyes and filled his head with superstition. Right then, it occurred to me that possibly, Sadiq had already lost everything.

SEVENTEEN

August 1979

W elcome home, Mama!" It was early in the morning and I stood
in the doorway, gathering my tangled hair into a knot away
from my face. I'd missed my mother and was excited to see her, but I
was also looking forward to the gifts she would bring.

The fact that my mother was different always struck me upon her
homecoming. Her accent was pronounced and nothing like my father's
or mine. "Lieverd!" she said, beaming, using a Dutch endearment for
me. "I missed you so much!" On the steps next to my father, my mother
was white. Her dark hair made her less white than Lizzy or Anne Simon,
but white nonetheless. She threw her arms around me in an embrace
distinct from the fierce bear hugs my father reserved for us. "Amir sent
you presents."

"Clove cigarettes? The ones you smell of?" I joked.

"Of course not," my mother said, briefly annoyed.

"You're not smoking those again, are you, Irene?" my father
demanded.

"Of course not."

"You know they aren't even cigarettes, right?" my father asked.

Most parents prayed for their children to stop smoking, but my mother encouraged my brother, as if the habit would prevent him from becoming a strict Muslim. The only time she smoked was when they were together, and she struggled with the slim clove cigarettes he provided, while he smoked Marlboros.

Mushtaq, the driver, carried her red hard-shell Samsonite suitcase and matching rectangular beauty case—old gifts from my father—up the stairs as Sadiq came to receive her. He touched his fingertips to his temple in greeting and broke into a wide grin. My mother smiled back just as enthusiastically, pleased to be home and surrounded with this much of her family.

In the evening, I conveyed the latest to my mother. Anne Simon had selected a name for her baby: Mikail. She reacted exactly the same way I had when Anne Simon told me. "You mean, Michael?" she asked.

"No. Mikail," I said, the second syllable rhyming with *sail*.

"A Pakistani name?" my mother said, very surprised. "Her child is her responsibility. Names and all, you see." I'd heard her say, "Her child is her responsibility," when we'd discussed Anne Simon's role in Hanif's death.

"Yes."

"What do you think of that?" my mother asked my father.

"Forget about it," my father said, greedily eating his dinner after having fasted all day during Ramadan. "Let them do what they want."

Sadiq came in to fill our water glasses. "Giving their son a Pakistani name is just strange," my mother added.

"Maybe they're trying to make amends," I suggested.

"They'll have to do better than that!" my mother said and caught herself.

All of a sudden I lost interest in the name choice. Plenty of foreigners were caught smuggling crates of antiques and suitcases full of ancient coins out of the country. Some even took their servants back with them, which put stealing a name into perspective.

Three mornings later, on the day before Eid, our household was fully absorbed in preparations for the celebration marking the end of Ramadan. It was the only time of the year that my mother opened our home to whoever visited, whether friends, relatives, or WAPDA staff. My mother had already made her special marmalade roulade, two loaves of Dutch ginger cake, dozens of chocolate hazelnut cookies, and a cream cheese coffee cake. She'd done all this despite the unbearable humidity the monsoons had left behind. Sadiq had polished the silver and laid out dessert plates and forks, along with the lace napkins my mother used on Eid. The trolley was set with teapots and matching milk pitchers and sugar bowls, ready for the guests the following day.

When I joined my mother in the kitchen, she'd finished preparing halva and seviyan and had only apple strudel left on her list. I picked out walnuts drenched in lemon and brown sugar from the filling and asked if I could ride my new bicycle to Lizzy's. My mother said she would drive me to Lizzy's house so she could drop off something for Anne Simon.

Once we arrived at Anne Simon's house, with my bicycle and a picnic basket in tow, she greeted us warmly.

"Come in! Come in!" Anne Simon's excitement made her look larger than ever.

"No, thank you, I know you must be busy," my mother said. "But tomorrow is Eid, our holiday, and I thought your family might enjoy a few of the delicacies we prepare specially for the occasion."

My mother placed the basket on the marble floor just inside the foyer and unwrapped a small bowl of seviyan and another of gajar ka halva from the cloth in which Sadiq had packed them. They were the only two Pakistani desserts my mother could stand. I'd never seen my grandfather do anything in the kitchen, but supposedly he'd taught her the recipes many years ago.

"I also brought you this." My mother handed Anne Simon a small box. Inside lay a silver rattle, an ornament from her favorite handicraft store in Covered Market.

"Oh, my!" Anne Simon cried. "Thank you! Wait till Jack sees this! Girls, look!"

"Honestly, it's not much. Just a small thing," my mother said, and I fidgeted with my earrings. It was unnerving to watch my school life and home life mingle.

"Don't be too late this evening, Aliya," my mother cautioned. My mother had been hesitant to let me have a bicycle, but so far I'd been good about staying off the streets after dark.

"Why doesn't she stay for dinner?" Anne Simon asked. "We'll put the bike in the car after we're finished and drive her home."

"Thank you," I said but immediately turned to my mother. "I'll call you when I'm ready." I'm sure she knew I didn't want the Simons' car coming to our house again, for fear of Sadiq seeing it.

"I wanted to ask you something," Anne Simon said, walking my mother to the door. "I'm looking for a maid to help with the baby. Perhaps you know of someone?"

"I can't think of anyone off the top of my head. But if I hear of someone, I'll let you know." My mother was friendly, but I knew it bothered her that foreigners seemed to expect her to keep rosters of potential servants to roll out at moments such as these.

"Maybe you could ask your servants," Anne Simon said.

"I will," my mother assured her, and I was positive she would not.

A few mornings later, without my father's knowledge, my mother violated the terms of Sadiq's house arrest and gave him permission to bicycle to the market to fetch garlic and onions. He was gone longer than an hour and, as a result, lunch was late. I had my suspicions about where he'd been but kept them to myself. After all, he had returned home without incident.

At the kitchen counter, where the steam from simmering lentils blended into the season's humidity, Sadiq peeled garlic cloves at a snail's pace. Once he started slicing the onions, he couldn't stop, and he minced them so finely they were an unusable soupy mess that upset my mother.

"Bohot cutting hai," my mother said in her English-Urdu pidgin.

"Pyaaz bahut bareek kata hai," Sadiq responded in Urdu as if he were correcting me.

"What?" my mother said.

"Don't worry about it. He's talking to me," I said, trying to cover for him.

My mother relieved Sadiq from the chore she hated and began to slice the last of the onions he'd brought home.

Sadiq washed his hands and dried them on the kitchen towel my mother reserved for drying dishes.

"Sadiq!" my mother cried.

"Maaf kijiye," Sadiq said.

He took the dirty kitchen towel to the laundry room, where he sorted our clothes, preparing for laundry day.

"Don't you have homework to do, young lady? Go and get your French book and let's work on verb conjugation. Vite, vite!"

I returned as my mother dropped sliced onions in the sizzling oil, the first step in caramelizing them. "Sadiq," my mother called, already thinking of the next task. "Kitna loads hamare paas hai?" She'd given up being embarrassed by her poor Urdu, as it was sufficient to know Sadiq understood what she meant.

He appeared in the doorway, holding his back as if it were in pain, and told her there were six loads of wash. His posture reflected what I knew was true: He was breaking under the weight of his burden.

"Mama, I'll help him."

"Sit down and open your book."

My French textbook fell open and I began work on the first assignment, composing a sentence that used two different tenses of *to be*. "This is how Sadiq's life is, but it is not how his life was meant to be," I wrote in French.

I didn't mind if my mother saw the sentence, but before I handed the assignment to my teacher, I changed Sadiq's name. School was school and home was home, even if it no longer felt that way.

EIGHTEEN

August 1979

I delayed visiting Lizzy for as long as I could after the baby was born. She called me the same day with the news that the baby was a boy, and I told her my mother didn't think it was a good idea for a newborn to have a lot of visitors, so I wouldn't visit immediately. She called the next day and invited me again, but I repeated the same thing. When she called three days later and said, "Leeeeeya! Come on! Are you scared of babies?" I told her that was not the case, but I was on my way to a doctor's appointment. The fourth time she called, my mother answered the telephone, and when Lizzy asked her how I was, my mother said, "What do you mean?" and put me on the telephone to explain myself. "I'm coming to see the baby today because I'm fine now," I whispered. That's how it happened that I finally went to visit Mikail, even though I didn't want to.

Before I left for Lizzy's house, and with the ease of someone who spent her days compiling lists of instructions for servants, I asked Sadiq to clean my closets and separate my winter clothes from my summer clothes. Winter was months away, but my motivation was to keep Sadiq occupied. I told him to retrieve all my wrinkled clothes and iron them. I thanked him, even though I was aware that unlike the English, the *thank-you* in Urdu was in the grammar, and it was awkward and redundant if repeated separately. My mother said *shukriya* over and over again, and it didn't matter how many times she was corrected. "It's important to thank people when they do things for you, and I don't care if it's already in the grammar of the sentence." Sadiq had taught me the most polite and formal tense for verbs, so I'd learned not to do it, except that morning, my separate *thank-you* was appropriate.

"Does Begum sahib know you are asking me to do all this?" he asked.

"Yes," I lied, but it was worth it to pretend my mother knew. I needed to be certain that when I saw Mikail for the first time, Sadiq would be far too busy to wonder where I was or to consider strolling to Embassy Road.

It took me eight minutes on my new red bicycle to complete the down-hill ride from Margalla Road to the corner of 87th Street. It happened to be during a scheduled load-shedding period, and the lack of electricity across the city rendered Islamabad virtually silent. But as soon as I turned into Lizzy's street, I was greeted with the drone of generators powering air conditioners in bathrooms and bedrooms in all the foreigners' houses.

I didn't see Mikail right away, but Lizzy immediately shared the details. As expected, the baby had been born in Polyclinic, the government-run hospital not too far from Lizzy's house. This had been the plan all along, but it was still surprising. Months earlier, when Lizzy had told me Anne Simon planned to have her baby in Pakistan and I'd shared this with my parents, my father had laughed. Americans never received medical care in Pakistan if they could help it. In emergencies, they were "medically evacuated" to Germany or other places, and in nonemergencies people made plans for treatment during home leaves or holidays abroad.

"Who chooses to have their babies in Pakistan if they don't have to?" he said.

"What do you mean?" my mother said. "There's nothing wrong with Polyclinic."

"All right, then," my father said. "I won't remind you about the time Aliya was admitted to Polyclinic for dehydration, and you swore you'd never go back."

"Oh, *that*," my mother said. "Having a baby is different!"

"Yes," my father said, still laughing. "A lot different than being in the hospital for dehydration, but in Polyclinic it can still kill you!"

"I hope you have some good PR people working for you," my mother said, "because you're one hell of a fan of your country."

Lizzy told me her mother's water had broken, just as we'd been taught in health class. Her father had called the new embassy nurse for help, but by the time the nurse arrived at the hospital, Mikail had already been born. Lizzy said her father was furious at the hospital because it didn't allow him to be in the room for the birth, and he'd had to wait to see the baby. Lizzy was permitted into the delivery room as soon as the baby was born. She told me that the conditions were gross, the room stank, there were five or six women lying in a row of beds in various stages of nakedness and labor, and their linens were soiled. Both her mother and the baby were fine, but Lizzy said Mr. Simon had been right to say she should have gone to the States to have the baby.

When I'd been to the hospital, I refused to go to the bathroom because the toilets were so filthy. "You have to bring your own sheets and food and buy syringes from the market to take with you to Polyclinic," I said, as if there was still time for my advice to be helpful.

"What kind of hospital is that?" Lizzy asked.

"Who does the baby look like?" I asked, changing the subject.

"Like me. Want to see?"

Mikail lay in a deep sleep while the twins ran around and Lizzy and I studied him. He was perfect except for the purple birthmark on his forehead.

"He does look like you," I said to make Lizzy happy, but the wrinkled baby did not look like anyone yet.

Anne Simon was wearing a long-sleeved shirt and what might have been a shalwar. She hugged me when I congratulated her and looked happier than I'd ever seen her.

"Let's hear you say Mikail," she said to me.

"Mikail."

"That's it! That sounds better than when we say his name," she said to Lizzy.

"I say his name right," Mr. Simon called from the other room.

"No one's going to call him that anyway," Lizzy said, ignoring her father. "They're just going to say Michael."

"Not in this family."

"Good luck with that," Lizzy said. My mother would have sent me to my room if I'd spoken to her like that.

"It's not hard," I told Lizzy, but I knew what she meant. It had been difficult to learn to say the *L* in Urdu just right. American *L*s were sloppy and loose, as if the speaker couldn't be bothered with the effort.

"It's a stupid name anyway," Lizzy said when we were in her room. "I mean, who's going to call him that when we get back to New York?"

She wasn't interested in an answer, so I asked another question. "Are you going back to New York when your dad's posting in Islamabad ends?" Generally, foreigners stayed in Pakistan two or three years before moving on to their next post. In the back of my mind, I'd been keeping track of Lizzy's stay in Pakistan and was sad to realize the Simons had already been in Islamabad for a year and a half.

"I guess," Lizzy said. "Will you come visit?"

"Why not?" I replied, happy to be invited.

When I got home, my mother was waiting at the front door.

"Did you give Sadiq all those things to do?" she asked me.

"Did he do them?"

"Aliya, he's not *your* servant. He only does what I ask him to. If you want him to do something for you, you go through me first. Understood?"

"Yeeees," I said, and my irritation crept into my voice.

"Looks like you've been living in Pakistan too long," my mother said, glaring at me.

I changed out of my sweaty clothes and went to find Sadiq. When I found him in the kitchen, he was standing over the ironing board and pouring vinegar into a juice glass. The smell made me nauseous.

"You aren't going to drink that, are you?" I asked, alarmed.

He looked up and said, "I'm cleaning the iron."

The iron plate was dotted with a paste of salt, but odd as that was, it didn't hold my attention. Sadiq had a bright red burn near his thumb.

"Did you show your burn to my mother?" I asked, and Sadiq ignored me.

"Did you do the chores I asked you to do?"

He took a step away from the ironing board and said, "How many months before winter arrives?" It took me a second to understand that he was drawing attention to the summer and winter clothes I'd mentioned in my instructions.

Just then, my mother entered the kitchen.

"Sadiq!" my mother cried. "What in God's name have you done to your hand?"

"Koi baat nahin," Sadiq mumbled.

I was surprised by my mother's anger. "It's your fault he burned himself," she said. "You had no reason to ask him to iron your clothes. Does he look like the dhobi?" she added, referring to the man who came to our house every Sunday and ironed our clothes on an ironing board set up for him in the servant quarters.

"I'm sorry," I said, including both my mother and Sadiq in a quick glance, and I really, truly was.

Just when I thought I couldn't bear one more day of the summer holidays, the beginning of the school year arrived and I started eighth grade. Our bus was unusually loud during the morning ride as friends were reunited and summer gossip was exchanged. Ten minutes from the school, as Lizzy was telling me about new students she'd already met at the embassy, and we were keeping an eye out for the first glimpse of the school compound, I thought the bus driver had taken a wrong turn. The previously unpaved stretch of road, which began at a cluster of mud huts and marked one boundary of the boys' spitting games, had been transformed into a modern two-lane artery. As we approached the school, the column of yellow school buses ahead shared the road with white minivans, black-and-yellow taxis, and a red city bus, which had never happened before. The new railway station was visible a few hundred feet from the nearest school gate.

"They weren't supposed to build the station so close to the school!" Lizzy complained.

"Why?" Everyone knew the answer, but I was curious to hear my best friend say it.

"Because of the kids' safety or something," Lizzy replied.

Our bus joined the others on the school grounds. One of the school's few chowkidars stood at attention with an empty rifle slung on his back, waving at the students; one or two waved back. I was always hesitant about being too friendly with the Pakistani staff for fear of drawing attention to the Pakistani part of me, but I hoped he would interpret my slight nod as a greeting, and he did.

As much as I had looked forward to school all summer, I'd conveniently forgotten the discomfort of the first day. As I stood in the aisle waiting to get off the bus, I steeled myself against the familiar discomfort of being half-and-half. I could see the railway station a few hundred yards ahead, and even though I wasn't American, the proximity of the railway station to my school *was* unsettling. I'd liked it better when the American School of Islamabad was located off a dirt road in the middle of nowhere, and it was easy to forget I was even partly Pakistani. I disagreed with my mother, who'd opposed the school's decision to extend the walls as a result of security concerns. I didn't mind the extra height that put more distance between me and the people roaming on the other side. Who knew if the scary man who'd accused me of being Amrikan was in the neighborhood?

Mr. Hill, the new principal, who'd been Mr. Simon's friend in Iran many years ago, made an announcement during school assembly that the chowkidars would keep the gates to the school closed during the day. As always, students were forbidden to leave the campus, and if they disobeyed, they would be suspended. My first impression of Mr. Hill, in addition to the fact that he was the tallest man I'd ever seen, was that he was what my mother would have called a "no-nonsense character," and he promised to be much stricter than previous principals. At the end of his first day, he was in the parking lot directing new students to their buses, encouraging others to do their homework, and warning one or two of the older ones that chewing tobacco on the buses would no longer be tolerated. I wondered how Mr. Hill might react if he learned of the spitting games. But it did not occur to me then, or ever, to be the one to inform him.

Within a few weeks, Mr. Hill had a problem on his hands. The science teacher was diagnosed with a serious case of hepatitis and was medically evacuated from Pakistan. It took the principal a few weeks, but he was able to convince Anne Simon to be a long-term substitute for the rest of the semester. I'd been at Lizzy's house for Mr. Hill's first call to Anne Simon, who had protested that she didn't have teaching qualifications, that she'd just had a baby and had given up her nursing job to spend more time with her children. But Mr. Hill didn't give up easily. He offered to rearrange the science schedule so she would be in school only part of the day, and he suggested she bring Mikail and his ayah, the nanny, to school with her. Lizzy didn't want her mother to accept the job, because she was a typical thirteen-year-old, and none of us wanted our mother sharing our school day. She sulked for the first day or two Anne Simon taught, but soon she was asking her mother if we could take Mikail from Parveen, the ayah, and hold him while we ate lunch.

I liked Anne Simon, and although she didn't teach any of my classes, her presence at the school was a comfort to me for a special reason. If Sadiq chose to violate house arrest and find his way to the corner of 87th Street again, he would not find Anne Simon at home. At least not on school days when she was forty-five minutes away, teaching Biology and Chemistry.

If only there was school on Fridays.

Sadiq could not have tried harder with his work. No one, not even my father, would have said otherwise. When we woke up in the morning, he was already in the house, at work with his dustcloth. He sorted laundry, vacuumed carpets, and did dishes without being asked. He even remembered to pick cilantro from the herbs growing in the servants' quarters and to squeeze juice from the tiny limes that grew on bushes along the driveway to freeze for later use. At some point, he went back to making me halva and pooris on Fridays. In fact, he was more occupied with household duties than he'd been in months. And while he didn't stop making mistakes the rest of us corrected, he tackled his chores with a new single-mindedness, as if he recognized that the sum of his chores was keeping him intact.

Even so, he strained with the effort of each task, whether climbing a ladder to clean a ceiling fan or bringing in laundry from the clothesline. It sometimes seemed as if the effort had him struggling against an invisible force that was as real as the water Lizzy and I struggled against when racewalking in the shallow end of the swimming pool. It made us want to help him, and soon, my mother and I had assumed much of what Sadiq had once routinely accomplished on his own. It was easy to forget what Sadiq had been like before Hanif died. I asked my mother whether she noticed that Sadiq seemed to be doing everything in slow motion, and she simply asked me to leave the fellow alone.

I couldn't know for sure, but my guess was that the arrival of Anne Simon's baby accounted for some of his behavior. When I finally asked my mother, "Do you think he knows Anne Simon had her baby?" she didn't even have to think before answering.

"Is anything a secret in Islamabad?"

I hated it when people answered my questions with questions of their own. Besides, her question was stupid because we all knew Islamabad was full of secrets.

Sadiq was a different person in the garden. We'd thought my father unwise to fire the mali and pass on his responsibilities to Sadiq, but it turned out he was right. Not only did the fresh air do Sadiq good, he happily assumed the responsibility. Pushing a lawn mower or wheelbarrow, or watering the rosebushes, he seemed free of the weight bearing down on him inside the house. One day he retrieved a variety of tools from the servants' quarters and dug up a front corner of the garden. By the time I came back from school, he'd already built a rock garden and created a small pond and was trying to convince my father to buy a water pump.

"For what?" my father asked suspiciously.

"A fountain."

"What do we need a fountain for?"

Sadiq thought for a moment. "For beauty?"

My father shook his head and went off to consult with my mother. "OK," he said when he returned. "I'll have an engineer from the office stop by tomorrow with a design that won't waste water or electricity."

"A WAPDA engineer is going to design the fountain?" Sadiq asked, amazed.

"I am the chairman of WAPDA, and I can't have people saying that my household wastes water and electricity. Therefore, yes, an engineer will come by tomorrow."

"Daddy, let him build it the way he wants," I interrupted. "It'll be fine."

My father's response was lightning quick. "The man can't even set a table correctly, and you want me to trust him with constructing a fountain?"

"Standing water breeds mosquitoes," I muttered under my breath, perfectly aware that this fact had nothing to do with the issue at hand.

Sadiq didn't understand much English, but my father hadn't said anything beyond Sadiq's comprehension, and I was embarrassed that he'd probably understood our exchange.

It took only a few days for the fountain to become operational. Sadiq's crude pond had been replaced with a kidney-shaped black plastic tub set deep in the ground. A small fountainhead sprayed a stream of water a few feet high. Lizzy would have loved it. The first time we stood in front of it together, Sadiq smiled proudly and claimed to be responsible for creating the Margalla Road Shalimar Gardens. He planned to lobby my father for a spotlight so we could see the fountain at night, but I told him not to get his hopes up.

For the rest of October, the days fell into a safe rhythm, and it was possible to believe that the worst was behind us. One afternoon, without consulting anyone, my father sent Mushtaq, the driver, to Rawalpindi on a special mission. My mother and I didn't think much of it until he returned with two plastic bags bulging with water and goldfish. Early that evening, Sadiq and I released the baby goldfish into our pond and, like magic, the swimming orange fish turned golden in my favorite light.

NINETEEN

Early to Mid-November 1979

I hadn't exactly followed in Sadiq's footsteps and given up the news, but really, what could be as important as the hanging of the prime minister? I spent my breakfasts ignoring the newscasts blaring from my father's black-and-silver Zenith radio in our kitchen, until one morning I heard a surprising combination of words, *American hostages*, surface through the hum. A second later, as if my visiting grandfather also heard the BBC newscaster's precise articulation of *Teheran*, he looked up from the hard-boiled egg on his fingertips and motioned for me to relay the headline. My parents joined us while he was attempting to read my lips for the second time: "American hostages have been taken in Teheran." My father fiddled with the dial and lost the radio announcer in his never-ending and fruitless search for a static-free bandwidth. My mother stood beside him for a moment contemplating the news before exclaiming, "Amazing!" Only Sadiq walked around the kitchen oblivious.

I didn't know much about Teheran, but I'd seen television images earlier that year of a tearful Shah fleeing a few days before the ayatollah's triumphant return. When I was small, Teheran was also the place airplanes refueled on trips from Vienna to Karachi. The proof was buried in a family album in a black-and-white photograph of us on the airport tarmac, impressive mountains looming in the background.

Sitting next to Lizzy on the bus that afternoon, listening to the urgent voices surrounding us, I tried not to appear too interested in the sixty-six hostages that had been taken at the American Embassy in Teheran. Talk alternated between the few students who'd lived in Iran and those who hadn't and involved a slew of English and Urdu profanities to describe the captors. *Fucking animals. Goddamn gandus. Behenn chuuts.*

Except for this, the ride was like any other, with the boys in the back turning to their games as soon as the bus rounded the first curve on the newly paved road. Suddenly, from the opposite direction, two buses and a truck rushed by in quick succession, very nearly grazing our bus.

"My dad says we need to be careful," Lizzy commented.

I agreed. The morning's newscast had warned Americans to use caution in their host countries.

We were interrupted by jeers from the back of the bus. One of the boys' spitballs had hit a man, and he'd fallen off his bicycle and collided with another cyclist. Our bus slowed down while the driver studied the rearview mirror and watched the two tangled men get to their feet. For a few minutes, an argument ensued about how many points the hit was worth until a new student, the son of the new American deputy chief of mission, shouted, "Shut the hell up!" and put a stop to the ruckus.

"Juveniles," Lizzy said, and I dared to nod in agreement.

After a minute, talk quickly returned to the hostages.

"Bomb the goddamn country," someone said.

"And their oil fields," someone else said.

"Fuck, yes!" two or three replied in chorus.

Lizzy whispered in my ear, "They're embarrassing." For the rest of the journey, she kept a watchful eye on her twin brothers a few seats in front of us and didn't say much besides reminding me that her father had lived in Teheran.

I imagined the embassy in Teheran as a duplicate of the Islamabad embassy, a red-brick building planted in a corner of the city, where a giant plain joined Margalla-like hills. By the time the bus ride ended, faraway Teheran and sleepy Islamabad sat side by side in my head, but the evening television footage immediately informed me I'd been wrong. The American Embassy in Teheran was nothing like Islamabad's; it was whitewashed buildings on a busy, tree-lined downtown street.

The next day, classes were interrupted for an emergency school assembly, an event that had only happened once, years earlier, when students had broken into the principal's office during the school day and issued a false alarm using the secret emergency radio connection between our school and the American Embassy. As a result, armed American marines had stormed the school, the students responsible for the false alarm were nearly expelled, and an assembly was called to explain everything to us. But no one could guess the reason for the assembly today. When the auditorium was filled and the students quieted down, Mr. Mancini, the assistant principal, read a prepared statement. At first I thought I'd misheard, but the audience rippled, and the music teacher sitting in the row behind me gasped. The principal of the school, Mr. Hill, a man who'd barely served out three months of his contract and was responsible for Anne Simon's job, was among the hostages in the American Embassy in Teheran. Almost as an aside, Mr. Mancini offered an explanation for Mr. Hill's presence in Teheran. He had taken one week of leave to retrieve some personal effects from his former school in Teheran, including a fountain pen that was a family heirloom. He'd also hoped to confirm that his former students' school records were properly moved from one building to another.

"Dad's going to be so worried for him," Lizzy said, but she was the one who sounded very worried.

"I bet they'll let the hostages go really soon, and Mr. Hill will be back in no time," I said.

"I don't know," Lizzy said doubtfully.

I was sad for Mr. Hill and for his wife and children, but all through the day my primary focus was on the fountain pen. What kind of a pen could it have been for Mr. Hill to board an airplane and fly to another country to retrieve it? And to do so while school was in session? The story sounded like a fairy tale to me, but it wouldn't have been so inconceivable if the pen had secret qualities, like something Maxwell Smart might have used in a *Get Smart* television episode. *That was it!* Mr. Hill was a spy, and the fountain pen was his Maxwell Smart or James Bond secret tool. Mr. Hill, the CIA spy, was my idea before I heard it implied by Uncle Imtiaz a few days later. He visited our home with a copy of *The Muslim* fresh off the presses underneath his arm and joked with me about Mr. Hill. "I'm sorry for the man," he said. "Must have been a very special fountain pen, eh? Irreplaceable! But between us, what kind of an undercover operation is he running at your school? Not to mention, what message is he sending to his students? Their leader jumps on an airplane to recover nothing more than a fountain pen?"

Mr. Hill hadn't made much of an impression on me either way. I'd seen him in friendly chats with students and playing basketball a few times with the older boys, but I couldn't recall exchanging a word with him or noticing much about him except for his height and the fact that he could dunk the basketball with one hand into the regulation-height basket. Had it not been for the hostage crisis, I would not have realized how clearly I remembered his face. Whenever I listened to news of the crisis, in my imagination, I saw sixty-odd Mr. Hills blindfolded and bound in different corners of a red-brick building, surrounded by an army of angry students.

A new sign appeared every day next to the principal's photo in his office window to let us know how many days he'd been held hostage. Our classroom display cases were filled with newspaper clippings about the hostage situation, but the teachers avoided speaking directly about Mr. Hill. Almost two weeks after the emergency assembly, around the time thirteen hostages were released—none of them Mr. Hill—the social studies teacher unrolled his world map and taped it to the blackboard. He traced the outline of Iran's borders with the rubber tip of his pointer. He located the tiny star that marked Teheran and enumerated the distance it lay from neighboring countries. "Twelve hundred miles from Pakistan," he said, and went on to inform the class that Pakistan shared a long border and the name of a province, Baluchistan, with Iran. He asked if the class knew how wide the Atlantic Ocean was, and when no one answered, he chastised the students, most of whom traveled the route at least once a year. He wrote the number with chalk on the blackboard, made a few silent calculations, and ran his pointer in a direct line from New York to Teheran to Islamabad. "Eight thousand miles," he said before dropping his pointer and dismissing the class early.

"No wonder the flight from here to my grandparents' takes so long!" Lizzy whispered.

Eight thousand miles didn't seem remarkable to me. The distance was shorter than the one my family's shipment had traveled from Vienna to Islamabad. Our container had traveled on a ship up and down the coasts of Africa because of a six-day war that closed the Suez Canal for years, including the summer our belongings were making their way to Pakistan. My father had us study the world atlas so we could see what twelve thousand miles looked like on a map. The number had seemed so huge it might as well have marked the distance between two planets. But in light of what my social studies teacher had said, twelve thousand miles had shrunk.

When I asked my father how long it took to fly from Teheran to Islamabad, he estimated it would be perhaps two or three hours, longer than the trip from Karachi to Islamabad.

"Don't worry about your principal," he added.

"Why not?"

"The Iranians won't dare harm United States citizens."

"Why not?"

"They're from the United States, after all," he said, exasperated with my questions.

"Did I tell you Mr. Simon was once posted in Teheran?" I asked. It occurred to me that if it weren't for the few years between then and now, Lizzy's father might have been a hostage that very minute. My father mumbled an unintelligible acknowledgment and returned to his newspaper.

Sadiq arrived to clear away the empty teacups, but before he could leave the room, the television captured our attention. In the midst of a sea of people, an American flag was doused with gasoline, lit from opposite ends, and curled in flames. Sadiq, clutching a copper tray heavy with dirty dishes, was hypnotized along with the rest of us. In the black-and-white television footage, a few of the sixty-six hostages walked with their captors into the crowd, hands tied behind their backs, their slow shuffles suggesting bound feet. Although they had no choice, it was shocking to see adults allowing themselves to be led, rocking slightly in their steps as if they were reassured by the presence of their captors at their sides. The blindfolds, rags really, covered most of their faces, and what was left for us to see—chins, beards, bald heads, and hair—was strangely separate, not parts of faces. One man, whom my mother declared had a dancer's posture, came to a stop, tilting his head toward his captor, straining to hear what was being said to him. He turned, as if he could see his captor, and replied. *Was the response in English? Farsi? Did Americans in Teheran speak Farsi?* The blindfolded man, the wide collar on his short-sleeved shirt open, spoke calmly and without hesitation, seemingly courteous, and I wondered if that's how a grown American man was taught to speak if he knew he might be killed.

In the financial report toward the end of the news, the newscaster announced that the Americans had stopped importing Iranian oil and had frozen billions of dollars of Iranian assets in American banks.

"You'd need a separate building to hold that much money. Or at least a whole lot of briefcases!" I was quickly hushed and left alone to contemplate how much Mr. Hill, my principal, was worth in terms of ransom money or, if he was killed, settlement money. How would such an amount be determined for each American hostage? *Were they all worth the same amount? Was the figure one million rupees? Two million rupees?* Then I realized the transaction would probably be made in dollars, and whatever the amount, it certainly would be more than the 50,000-rupee value ascribed to Hanif's life. The fact was that Americans were always and unquestionably worth more than Pakistanis or anyone else.

The news broadcast ended without a glimpse of Mr. Hill, and my father turned off the television. He joined me on the couch to gravely say, "I hope you haven't forgotten that you must stay away from the embassy."

"No, I haven't," I replied, annoyed at being reminded of a rule that I'd made for myself long ago.

"I wouldn't be surprised if your school changed bus routes and schedules now," he said.

"Why?"

"There's scarcely a more visible US symbol in the entire city of Islamabad than the buses with the name of your school boldly painted on them. And the daily bus routes and schedules are as predictable as my watch."

"What do you mean?"

"You get home every afternoon at 3:58. Did you know that?"

"How would you know? You're never even here!"

He sighed. "All I'm asking is for you to be a bit more cautious."

"Why? *Nothing* ever happens here."

My father gave me a skeptical look and said, "For the moment."

A few minutes later, I went to the kitchen to pour myself a glass of water. Sadiq was unloading dirty dishes from the heavy copper tray and shaking his head in silent disagreement with something to which we were not privy.

Finally my mother asked him what was wrong.

"Kuch nahin," he said gently. Nothing.

In a burst of unwarranted aggravation, my mother stomped her foot on the marble floor the way she sometimes did when frustration got the better of her.

"Then don't shake your . . ." my mother said, but stopped midsentence when she saw me by the refrigerator.

Sadiq looked up at her and waited in case she intended to complete her thought. When she didn't say anything more, he filled the sink with warm water and began washing teacups more slowly than seemed humanly possible.

TWENTY

Wednesday, 21 November 1979

The VOA newscast was somberly announcing the headlines, and I wondered aloud why we were listening to VOA instead of the usual BBC. The morning newspapers scattered on the table shared the same glaring headlines: The Grand Mosque in Mecca had been seized by gunmen, and President Jimmy Carter had ordered the USS *Kitty Hawk* to the Persian Gulf. There was no mention of Pakistan, which should have been a relief, but I sensed otherwise.

A minute later, as if I had asked, my mother explained, "*Kitty Hawk* is not a person. It's an American ship."

"With nuclear weapons," my father added.

"For war?" I asked.

"God forbid," my mother said, distracted by my grandfather as he slurped the last of the milky tea from his saucer.

Sadiq arrived looking more besieged than ever, all because of my grandfather. In the weeks since our servant had arrived, my grandfather had persisted in adding to his misery. Sadiq had a dustcloth and broom in hand and had already spent hours working.

"Did you hear the news?" my father asked Sadiq.

"God have mercy," he replied, shaking his head in slow motion, and everyone but me supposed he was talking about the gunmen in Mecca. Only I knew he'd given up the news.

Before the school bus came, my grandfather and parents disputed a VOA detail that blamed Iranians for the mosque's seizure. They said it wasn't reasonable to believe that fellow Muslims in Iran, even if they were Shia, would occupy the holiest mosque in the world. Although I was only thirteen and not entirely sure of the differences between Pakistani Sunnis and Iranian Shias, even I understood that the occupation of the mosque was sacrilegious.

It happened during science class.

My first clue should have been the school bell. The bell, which marked the end of one class and the beginning of a new one, rang during our science test and wouldn't stop. I'd never thought of the bell as particularly shrill or annoying, but it was both this afternoon. We all assumed it was broken, even when the new substitute teacher left the classroom to investigate. As soon as she did, we swapped test answers, and Lizzy, who was sitting next to me, gave me her iced animal crackers left over from lunch. She caught a simple math mistake in one of my calculations, and I pointed out an incorrect definition on her test. The morning had been long and slow in anticipation of the Thanksgiving holidays scheduled to start the following day. We'd already had one test, albeit in gym, where we were timed on our ability to hang from a bar with our chins well above it. I'd failed to reach the "presidential" standards for this exercise, whatever that meant, and it would be noted on my report card, as it was each semester.

My second clue should have been that when the teacher returned a few minutes later, she ignored the talking she'd expressly forbidden and instructed us to form a line by the door. Delighted that our test had been interrupted, we caused the ruckus we reserved for substitute teachers. Suddenly, one of the students declared he heard shouting. The teacher confirmed that an emergency was under way and scolded the student for being slow to get in line. The questions came from every direction.

"What do you mean by emergency?"

"What's wrong?"

"Where?"

The teacher screamed to be heard. She explained that a small crowd of angry locals had gathered outside the school gates, and as a safety precaution, our assistant principal, Mr. Mancini, had ordered all students to assemble in the auditorium. When two boys shoved each other, the teacher ignored them, along with the tests left on our desks. Another student joked that we were all about to become hostages, which made the teacher lose her temper and order him to shut his mouth. As a rule, teachers never spoke like that, so her remark immediately silenced us all.

I was reminded of the false emergency alert a few years before. From inside a classroom in the elementary school quad, I'd watched the marines and Pakistani police form a circle around the buildings. I hadn't been afraid at all. The marines and their precise maneuvers seemed more silly than anything else, and the Pakistani policeman running behind them, shouting, "Sir, sir!" was even sillier. I was younger then and didn't believe in the possibility of a real school emergency. Besides, the marines were only at the school for a few minutes before the principal informed their commander that their efforts were being wasted on a false alarm.

This time was different. More than a few minutes had already passed, the school bell had become a never-ending alarm, and our substitute teacher was fretting. I expected the incident to be a hoax, just a more serious one that would get students expelled, and when our class was assembled in the quad, I told Lizzy as much.

The final clue was the parking lot. Two or three young Pakistani men jumped over the newly extended wall, where they joined a handful of others on the school grounds. They were shouting, but in the confusion of the moment, their words were lost on me. A few teachers, including Mr. Duval and the Pakistani field hockey coach, had formed a line of defense. Some chowkidars stood by, uncomfortably holding their guns, afraid or reluctant to put them to use. Some of the older students, along with the captains of the football and soccer teams, conferred near their lockers. One had a baseball bat in his hand, and another nervously bounced one of the school's premium basketballs. Baseball bats and field hockey sticks were being distributed to the older boys. I was terrified.

Amir once told me that during his senior year, the school roof had been patrolled by teachers trying to catch students smoking. Shah, the prime minister's son, was caught like this, although the school didn't suspend him as they did all the other culprits. I'd never heard of teacher roof patrols since. I glanced up, but as far as I could see, the roofs were empty except for green air-conditioning units and, presumably, painted American flags. We'd all heard rumors that when the school was first built, flags were painted on the roofs as a precaution so that if the Indian air force ever attacked Pakistan, the pilots would see the American flags and spare the school. I didn't believe the story, but it was lodged deep enough in my consciousness to make me look to the sky, as if help, not necessarily from the Indians but from *someone*, was meant to drop from above.

Lizzy dug her fingernails into my arm. I hadn't fooled her; she knew that whatever was under way wasn't a hoax or a mini-royit, and she, too, was terrified. Fear worked like that. Once it got hold of one person, it spread to everyone else.

"What's happening?" she asked, as if Pakistan was my country and, therefore, I would know.

I couldn't think of an answer. Instead, I pretended to know more than she did and said, "The police will be here in a minute."

"Oh my God! Where are the twins?" Lizzy asked, further alarmed. "I've got to call Mom!" Anne Simon was not in school that afternoon.

I knew she had left for the embassy with Mikail for a doctor's appointment because we hadn't been able to play with him during lunch.

"It's going to be fine," I insisted.

We waited in line while the classes ahead of us filed into the auditorium building. Although the parking lot was no longer in view, I counted the number of strangers I'd seen there from the image in my memory. Counting in Urdu required a lot of concentration and helped me not panic. I'd reached trais, twenty-three, before someone cupped my head with a large hand. I jumped and turned around, and as I did, stumbled into the girls ahead of me. When I regained my balance and looked up, I was staring at an old man wearing a crumpled shalwar kameez and swinging a car jack at his side. He looked like a madman. And he was my grandfather.

"Dada Abba!" I cried.

He kissed my forehead as he did every morning, and I didn't wipe away the moisture his kiss left behind.

"What's wrong? Is Daddy OK?" I was consumed by fright and had barely managed to form the questions.

The presence of my grandfather on the premises escalated the emergency beyond my imagination. Had my father died? My mother? Had Lehla been killed in a car crash, or had Amir been murdered? What could possibly be so wrong that he'd come here?

"Problems. Embassy burning. Cannot ride bus," he whispered in Urdu in what was staccato, even for him.

It took me a moment to absorb his words. "Is Daddy fine? Mama? Amir? Lehla?"

"Yes," he said and repeated himself. "Problems. Embassy burning. Cannot ride bus."

"What embassy?"

"American," he said.

"Fire?" I asked.

191

"Attacked." He hadn't said much, but I got the basic idea. It wasn't much of a leap to recognize that his information also explained the emergency at my school, the *American* School of Islamabad.

I suddenly remembered Lizzy standing next to me. "Remember my grandfather? We're going to get a ride home with him." My grandfather hadn't said anything about taking Lizzy home, but I wasn't going to leave her behind. I didn't give her a chance to respond, just grabbed her hand and began walking.

Our substitute teacher approached and asked me where I thought I was going. Pointing to my grandfather—who, I had to admit, looked slightly deranged in his rumpled shalwar kameez, car jack in hand—the teacher said, "Who is he? He isn't even supposed to be here." I felt sorry for her, a new substitute, starting on a day like today, but her disdain toward my grandfather offended me. Rather than worry about him, shouldn't she have been more concerned about the growing crowd of troublemakers in the parking lot?

We were interrupted with a sudden crash and, subsequently, what could only be described as a roll of crashes. Some students were slamming the lids of industrial-size tin garbage cans into the pavement, and the noise momentarily drowned out the emergency bell and, by then, the chanting men. Did the boys really think their noise would return everything to normal? It helped to be deaf sometimes. My grandfather continued to pull me with him, I held onto Lizzy, and the three of us, virtually holding hands, left the vicinity of the auditorium.

The teacher didn't give up. She ran after us, angrily demanding, "Where are you going?"

"Home," I answered.

"You," the teacher said, pointing to Lizzy, "cannot go with them."

"Why?" I asked.

"All Americans must stay right here."

Lizzy looked around nervously, weighing the teacher's words. Her clear blue eyes shifted from the chowkidars to the strangers, the boys and their trash-can lids, and finally me and my grandfather. She tugged on her ponytail, this late in the day uncharacteristically high on her head.

"Says who?" Lizzy said forcefully, narrowing her eyes, and I was proud of her.

The teacher backed up a few steps. "If you leave, you'll be in serious trouble," she threatened Lizzy.

"No, she won't!" I replied.

We hurried away, but then Lizzy stopped and shouted, "My brothers!" She ran in the direction of the kindergarten classroom, my grandfather and I following close behind. The sign outside the principal's office had been changed that morning to reflect eighteen days of captivity. We found Lizzy's brothers almost immediately in a group of sobbing children who were covering their ears and shuffling toward the auditorium.

While Lizzy informed their teacher that she was taking them home with me, I had a few words with my grandfather. I pulled his face right next to mine and spoke in Urdu so only he would understand me.

"How do you know about the embassy?"

"Saw smoke. Confirmed by BBC."

"Why was the embassy attacked?"

"Americans involved in Grand Mosque siege," he answered, and I didn't understand what he meant.

"What? Will they burn the school, too?"

My grandfather's *No* wasn't convincing, and without being asked, he reached to pick up one of the scared twins. Lizzy crouched down so that her other brother could climb on her piggyback-style, and the five of us hurried to the parking lot.

"You drove here?" I asked, shocked at the sight of my parents' old Toyota Corolla. "Where's Mushtaq?"

"Office," he said, and I knew my grandfather had taken the car without my mother's permission, for she never allowed him to drive in Islamabad.

We arrived at the car in time to see some young men wielding sticks and throwing rocks at the school-bus windows. Mr. Duval was clutching a field hockey stick, looking like he was getting ready to take a swing. The Pakistani staff, who sorted the school's mail, made tea, cleaned bathrooms, and trimmed the lawn, were confronting the growing crowd, angrily shaking their fingers at the unruly men.

More cars had arrived in the parking lot, all of them local with black license plates, and drivers and fathers emerged from them. Had Americans asked their Pakistani friends or neighbors to pick up their children? Or were there more Pakistanis than I'd thought at the school, and these were their parents? A man who'd already packed his wagon with several young children and was leaving, waved at my grandfather as if they knew each other. At the gate, the man opened his car door and shouted at the mob in Urdu, "The police are going to beat the shit out of you!"

A rock struck his rear windshield, and as he drove away, I was able to decipher the men's chant: "Amrika Murdabad." Death to America. The chant was both absurd and chilling. It was hardly possible to kill a country, but being bold enough to demand this was horrifying. I wondered if the scary man from my bus stop was among the crowd.

Lizzy and I sat in the backseat of my mother's car, each of us with an unhappy twin on her lap. Again and again, my grandfather turned the ignition without any luck. Our yellow school buses were parked in a row on the opposite end of the parking lot, as they always were during the day. A few hundred feet away, two school employees appeared to be feverishly working on a few of the school's white minivans. When one employee stepped away from a van, I saw he was holding a yellow CD64 license plate. Our engine finally caught, and the car sputtered to life at the same time I recognized the men were trying to conceal the fact that the vehicles were American.

"What are they doing?" Lizzy asked, pointing to the Pakistanis wielding rocks and sticks.

"Scaring us," I answered, my heart pounding.

When we'd safely exited the school gates, I thought it only fair to share the news of the burning embassy with Lizzy.

"Oh my God!" she exclaimed. Biting her lip, she held back tears as she reminded me that her mother had planned to spend the afternoon at the embassy so Mikail could get his shots.

"It's probably just a burst gas main," I said, fabricating an absurd possibility.

"What happened at the embassy?" Lizzy asked, but she wasn't talking to me. She had turned to the only adult in the car, my deaf grandfather. When he didn't respond, she stopped looking as if she was going to cry and announced there was no reason to burn the embassy. Therefore, I had to be wrong; the embassy couldn't be under attack.

"Right, boys?" she addressed her twin brothers.

Our car was among several in a caravan on Peshawar Road retreating from the school, and I was thankful that the cars ahead dictated my grandfather's unnaturally slow speed. The twins kept themselves busy playing a game of I Spy that Lizzy and I also joined.

Half an hour later, when we neared Embassy Road, I gave my grandfather Lizzy's address, 87th Street.

I said it twice, each time bending over the front seat so he could see me, and apologized to Lizzy. "He's deaf," I said earnestly, but we unexpectedly dissolved into a fit of giggles.

"Does he have a hearing aid?" Lizzy finally asked.

I nodded, withholding the fact that my grandfather had not one hearing aid, but a cabinet full of them, all in Lahore. "He refuses to use it," I whispered.

My grandfather drove right by 87th Street.

"That's my street!" Lizzy cried out.

My grandfather indicated for me to come closer and whispered in Urdu, "Where are her parents?"

"At the embassy," I told him, my answer dictating a course of action he didn't need to explain.

"My grandfather doesn't think it's safe for you to go home if your parents aren't there. You come to my house instead, OK?"

"OK," Lizzy said wearily while the twins protested.

We were still tumbling out of the car when my mother opened the front door and raised her voice before she saw how many of us there were.

"You could have been . . ." she said, then changed her mind. "Thank goodness you're all safe." She hugged each of us, including Lizzy's twin brothers.

We sat in the kitchen while my mother made us hot chocolate by boiling the local vacuum-packed milk with her special Dutch cocoa and several spoons of sugar.

"I don't think they'll drink that milk," I whispered.

"Don't worry. You'll see. They won't know the difference," my mother said under her breath. "Dutch cocoa is the best in the world."

"They only drink commissary milk!" I insisted.

My grandfather reappeared a short time later with pastries from United Bakery. He placed the box of sweet rolls, almond cake, and chocolate squares on the table.

"You took the car again?" my mother asked in a tone that indicated how displeased she'd been the first time. My grandfather swung open the kitchen door and left.

Lizzy sat at the kitchen table with her brothers. My mother put a mug of hot chocolate in front of each of us and added floating ice cubes to the twins' mugs so they wouldn't burn themselves.

"You boil your water, right?" Lizzy asked hesitantly, worried for her brothers. "Ice, too?"

"Of course," my mother said, surprised at the question because this wasn't Lizzy's first time as our guest. "It'll be fine, sweetheart," she said, putting her hand on Lizzy's. "Now let's phone your parents so they know where you are."

Lizzy tried calling home, but the servant said her parents were not there. Then she sat on the kitchen counter for fifteen minutes while her hot chocolate got cold, continuously dialing Mr. Simon's office telephone number without making a connection. The twins were happily eating the round almond cake, which my mother had sliced through its entire width as though it were a round loaf of banana bread. She'd cut the slices in half, shaken confectioners' sugar on them, and served them to the boys on small plates from a hand-painted tea set.

"More, please," the boys kept asking, until the cake was almost gone.

"I think the telephone is out of order," Lizzy finally said.

"That happens more than we'd like," my mother said, and her comment annoyed me. Did she have to say *we*? She was wrong to put all of us in the same category.

Lizzy tasted each of the pastry selections on her plate but didn't finish any.

"She's not much for sweets," I said to my mother.

"Never mind. Can I get you some fruit instead?" She put a basket of bananas and apples next to Lizzy, who selected a banana and ate the whole thing.

"Where is he?" I suddenly asked my mother. I'd just remembered Sadiq.

"Dada Abba?" she asked.

"No."

"Daddy?"

"No."

"Oooh," my mother said knowingly. "He went out and will be back later." We both looked at the clock, which indicated it was exactly four. I wondered how long Sadiq had been missing.

Lizzy moved one of her brothers' mugs away from the edge of the table and followed our exchange. "Whom are you talking about?" she asked.

"The servant," I quickly replied, without saying his name. Initially I was relieved Sadiq wasn't home. I was happy that my grandfather had helped Lizzy and her brothers leave school, and that they were all safe at my home, but their presence heightened my concern for Sadiq. It was a Wednesday, not even a Friday, yet Sadiq wasn't at home as he should have been.

Lizzy jumped when the phone rang. It was Mr. Simon. My mother answered and confirmed to Lizzy's father that his three children were with us. He'd heard from someone at the school that they had gone home with me. "Yes, they're all safe," she said, looking over at the children and giving them a smile. Handing the telephone to Lizzy, she explained that Mr. Simon was not at the embassy, but at their house.

"Are Mom and Mikail all right?" she asked him. The twins clamored to speak to their father, and when the conversations with his children were over, Mr. Simon requested my mother keep the children until he decided it was safe for them to be driven to his house.

Lizzy tried to be brave. "My mom and Mikail are at the embassy, but Dad says they are safe."

"Can we call her?" my mother inquired.

Lizzy shook her head, her bangs falling into her eyes. "The phones aren't working there. Dad spoke to her on the radio from the house."

"You have a special radio at your house?" I asked.

"Dad uses it for work. The radio connects to certain places. To the school, too."

"Really?" I replied. I'd never seen a special radio or any radio, in fact, in their house, but I stopped short of asking where it was kept. That would not have been good manners or, for that matter, my business.

"The important thing is that your father has spoken to your mother, and she and Mikail are fine," my mother said.

"I want Mom," one twin wailed, before the other joined him.

My mother distracted the boys with the possibility of toys and led them on a search around the house.

As soon as they left, Lizzy cradled her face in her hands and wept.

"Please don't cry," I said, wrapping my arms around her, but she did anyway. I got her a box of tissues, the local kind that scratched your nose, but she didn't notice.

When my mother returned, the boys had two shoe boxes of Amir's old matchbox cars, and my mother was carrying my forgotten dollhouse that had been gathering dust in a storeroom for almost as long as we'd lived in Islamabad. We moved to the lounge, where the twins assumed that the slanted dollhouse roof was a perfect ramp, and the open-faced structure was really a parking garage. In a minute, careening matchbox cars skidded across the length of our cocktail table and crashed onto the marble floor.

Lizzy and I sat silently watching. "Please don't worry about your parents. I'm sure they'll be fine," I said.

"Why would anyone set fire to the embassy?"

"I don't know. Do you want to do homework?" I brought in our book bags and rummaged through mine for the English assignment we were meant to complete over the coming weekend. After we found our notebooks—Lizzy's American soft-covered, college-lined spiral one and my hardbacked, wide-lined local one—they just sat on our laps. Lizzy chewed her pencil, and I doodled on my cover.

I was embarrassed that my mother kept checking to see if anyone was hungry or cold or tired enough for a nap. She popped a batch of popcorn on the stove, an unusual occurrence in the house, and seemingly unconcerned about the potential mess, set a bowlful on the floor next to the boys. I was sure that the strong taste of Nurpur butter (the foreign Lurpak had been out of stock in the stores for weeks) would dissuade them from having any, but they seemed not to notice, happily helping themselves from the bowl. Every so often, Lizzy called her father for news about her mother and brother, but there was never anything new.

Finally, around six in the evening, my father walked into the lounge as if he were expected, clapping his hands with delight and acting surprised at the company. He picked up some matchbox cars that the twins had long since discarded, pretended to rev their motors, and sent them rushing to the twins, who were sitting side by side, irritable and unhappy, finally exhausted by the events and their parents' absence. He sat down on the sofa next to Lizzy and put an arm around her. "Please don't worry. Your mother will call any moment."

"That's what my dad says," Lizzy replied. Her eyes were red with strain and brimming with tears.

"You'll see. Your mother and brother will be fine," he said confidently. "Lucky for all of you, there's no school tomorrow!"

A short while later, I looked up at the window to discover Sadiq in the strange light of the back garden. He was engaged in his regular evening chore, making a round of the house to confirm each window was securely fastened for the night. As much as I was relieved at his return, I was immediately concerned about keeping Sadiq and Lizzy apart. Before he could reach the lounge window, my grandfather appeared beside him. He pointed at Sadiq's clothes and began steering him toward the servants' quarters, which Sadiq resisted. I left the room, telling Lizzy I'd be right back. I opened a back door and stepped into a haze of smoke that had carried all the way from the embassy and, possibly by then, the school on to Margalla Road.

"I'll check the rest of the windows," I said to Sadiq in Urdu. When Sadiq did not move, I said, "See?" and walked briskly to the lounge windows, doing what Sadiq had done every night for years, confirming that the windows were indeed closed and locked. I waved at Lizzy and the twins inside, and mouthed, "I'll be right back." Up close, I saw that Sadiq was not himself, if he had been himself at all since Hanif's death. His clothes were soiled and torn on his chest, his hands were dirty, and he smelled of smoke. "Please go with Dada Abba," I pleaded, hardly able to contain my alarm. I didn't want Sadiq in the house and, more than that, didn't want Lizzy and her brothers to notice him standing outside.

When I was back in the lounge, Lizzy asked, "Who was that?"

"Sadiq." Caught off guard, I'd said his name. "The servant. You remember him, right?"

"Oh, yeah."

"He was just doing something for my grandfather."

The two nighttime chowkidars, beginning their rounds, crossed paths outside, and before Lizzy could ask me why we had two chowkidars, my mother called for her. "It's your parents!"

Lizzy grabbed the telephone. "Mom? Dad?"

I left the room with my parents. "What really happened at the embassy?" I asked my father.

"The embassy burned," he replied, giving me information I already had.

"Is her mother OK?"

"Yes. And so is the baby. Thank God," my father said, but his brow was wrinkled, and he didn't look reassured.

"What happened?" I asked.

"Later," he replied, keeping an eye on the kitchen door, where Lizzy was still speaking to her parents.

My mother told the twins their parents were on the telephone. One of them was almost caught in the swinging door as they pranced out of the lounge. They gripped the receiver with two pairs of hands, their identical heads pressed against the single earpiece.

Finally, my father spoke to Lizzy's father again, in the formal manner he adopted for strangers. "Certainly, certainly, we'll bring the children home. We'll depart momentarily."

My mother bundled the twins into the backseat, berating my father for the thousandth time for never having had seat belts installed.

"See you tomorrow for Thanksgiving, right?" I said. Lizzy smiled weakly, and my hope sounded silly even to my ears.

"I should be driving," my mother lamented. "I'm a much better driver than he is, and wouldn't it be awful if something happened along the way?" My father reversed the car, and my grandfather rested his hands on her shoulders in case she ran after him. "And you! You could have been killed! You took the car to the school when I told you I would drive."

"They'll be fine," my grandfather whispered, ignoring her complaints.

"Fine, fine, fine, fine, fine, fine!" I suddenly exploded. "That's all anyone says around here. And it's not true. *Nothing* is fine. Why aren't you saying what happened?"

My grandfather bent down to my ear, until his breath was a loud rush in it. "As I said, the American Embassy was burned to the ground. Now there's nothing left of it."

"How do you know there's nothing left?"

"Your father said so."

"Who did it?" I asked.

"Terrible," my mother interrupted. "Buildings burning, people attacking. What for?"

"Who did it?"

"Thank God you're safe," my mother said and attempted an embrace.

"Why doesn't anyone ever answer questions around here?!" I shouted, pushing her away and running to my bedroom.

I slammed my door and threw myself facedown on the bed. My shin hit the wooden bed frame, and I cried out in pain. I wanted nothing more than for the terrible day to end. Burying my face in my pillow and closing my eyes in a losing battle to hold back tears, I remembered Sadiq, his clothes, his smell, and his reluctance to follow my grandfather. My dread was so overwhelming, it rang in my ears. A wave of nausea followed, and running to the bathroom, I had a single thought.

Where, oh where, had Sadiq been?

TWENTY-ONE

Thursday, 22 November 1979

When I awoke the next morning to my heart pounding as furiously as if I'd been running a race, I hoped I'd dreamed the events of the previous day. I immediately sought out the morning newspapers in the kitchen. I had skimmed through most of them before my parents joined me, and I was surprised to learn that American centers and consulates in cities like Lahore, Karachi, and Peshawar had also been attacked, although not nearly as badly. But unless I'd missed something, none of the newspapers offered a solid reason for why the general had not sent help to the burning embassy. Staring at me from the front pages of the newspapers was a photograph of the general on a bicycle with the cumbersome caption "General Zia-ul-Haq inaugurates a campaign to conserve gasoline and sets off on a 'Meet the People' tour on a bicycle to set an example for the people." Rather than worrying about rescuing people from the burning embassy, the general was on his bicycle conducting civic lessons?

The day's headlines included "President's Deep Concern over Mecca Incident," "Zia Urges People to Become True Muslims," and the obvious, "US Embassy Set on Fire in Islamabad." For the most part, reports suggested that the attack was a response to Iranian rumors that the CIA had seized the Grand Mosque in Mecca. False rumors of American involvement had spread through the country during sermons following afternoon prayers at mosques. How odd that an event in a different country thousands of miles away would rally people in Pakistan! Could Pakistanis have been so offended by the possibility of Americans dishonoring the holiest mosque in the world that they attacked American symbols in Pakistan? Who had orchestrated all the attacks? One article suggested that the Soviets had rented the blue university buses and paid students to seize the embassy.

Beginning with Uncle Imtiaz's visit later in the day and continuing into the months and years ahead, I heard all possible explanations. The general had not been informed of the attacks. He did not want responsibility for a rioting crowd's reaction to an army presence. He simply was at a loss for what to do. A common hypothesis was that by not getting involved, the general was teaching the Americans that, good and mighty friends though they were, they could not control everything that happened in Pakistan.

When my father appeared, he turned on the radio and took his seat at the head of the table, among an excess of table settings. His mood was subdued and he did not reach for the newspapers. He sat with his chin resting on a steeple of intertwined fingers, so deep in thought, I was startled when he finally spoke.

"Yesterday's news is dreadful. The US Embassy was burned to the ground. Apparently, nothing is left of it. Some people died . . ."

"Who?" I interrupted.

"We don't know yet. The police are going through the area now."

"Why?"

"You mean, why are they going through it now?" my father asked.

"No. Why did it happen?"

"Who knows?" he said. He focused on the radio, as if the answer might be at the top of the news hour that was just beginning.

The annoyingly formal BBC newscaster stated that Ayatollah Khomeini's government strongly denied American claims that Iranians were involved in the Grand Mosque siege in Mecca. Unsubstantiated Pakistani rumors blamed Americans for the mosque's siege and had led to countrywide attacks on American establishments. In the next minute, the perfectly enunciating voice recapped the attack on Islamabad's American Embassy, describing Americans escaping the hostile crowd by locking themselves in a vault on the top floor of the main building. Two Americans and four Pakistanis were dead. The newscaster continued, "Students at the American School were attacked," and mentioned the torching of the school auditorium and an unruly crowd ransacking classrooms and breaking windows with the school's cricket bats. Our school did not have a single cricket bat, and while I'd left early on, I couldn't help wondering if the attack on the school had been as serious as the newscaster detailed. The next sentence gave me pause. It made reference to the "evacuation of dependents and nonessential US personnel," and I worried what that might mean for Lizzy and her family. Not to mention, in case Mr. Simon really was a spy, would he be classified as essential or nonessential personnel?

Backtracking to an early detail in the newscast, I asked my father, "What kind of vault holds one hundred and thirty-seven people?" The only vault with which I was familiar was a bank vault lined with safety deposit boxes.

"Sorry?"

"The newscaster said the Americans fled to a vault."

"Perhaps it's a large room where they keep confidential papers, special equipment, or . . ."

"With enough space to hold one hundred and thirty-seven people?" I asked doubtfully.

My father cleared his throat and changed the subject. "Things will be different once US citizens leave the country . . ."

"Why are they leaving?"

"Standard diplomatic procedure, I think. When there's serious trouble in a country, diplomatic personnel, especially dependents, leave for a while until things calm down."

"Why will things be different once the Americans leave Pakistan?"

"For one thing, there are so many of them," my father said.

"Will all of them leave?" I asked.

"Most, I imagine. Your friend Lizzy and her family, too. I don't know if her father is considered essential to the staff. In any event, your school will certainly be closed for a while," my father said.

"You're up early," my mother said, joining us. She rearranged the place settings, folded the newspapers I'd read, and placed them next to my father. "No school today, remember?"

"I know."

"We'll have to determine what to do with you when the school closes," my father said.

"How long will it be closed?"

"I doubt anyone knows," he replied. Under any other circumstances I would have been thrilled with the news.

"How many gundas were at the school?" my mother interrupted. *Gundas* was my mother's favorite Urdu word to describe troublemakers. "I knew that extending the school wall was a complete waste of money."

Sadiq entered the kitchen through the back door, and when he noticed us, brought his fingers to his temple in greeting but kept his eyes lowered. Unable to look at us, he appeared guilty of something and that fed my suspicions about where he'd been the previous day. Where else could he have been except at the American Embassy? Why had he been there and what had he done?

"And how are you today?" my father asked Sadiq in an attempt to break the uncomfortable pause.

Sadiq flipped up his palms to the ceiling, suggesting the answer could be anything.

Just then, my grandfather walked in. "Tea," he ordered, not addressing anyone in particular.

"Yes," my mother said, getting up.

My grandfather caught her wrist. "He'll do it," he said, and she sat back down.

"But he never makes it hot enough for you!" she complained.

"Give him a chance," he responded, as if none of us, at any time, had ever thought of giving him a chance.

I did my best to avoid Sadiq for the rest of the morning. When he brought the vacuum cleaner to my room and moved the furniture off the carpets, I took the book I was pretending to read and left. Sadiq stank of singed hair and smoky wet clothes. It seemed at first that I was the only one who had noticed, but by eleven o'clock, I discovered my grandfather was also aware. Shortly after the shops opened, he presented Sadiq with a gray shalwar kameez and a piece of fabric meant to replace the one he used to wrap his head. Sadiq accepted the gift, but when he returned to serve lunch, he hadn't changed his clothes.

"Please tell him to shower and change," my mother appealed to my father, who'd taken the day off.

When he did, he also suggested Sadiq accompany him and my grandfather to prayers.

"Why? It's not Friday," Sadiq said, staring down at the sink, where pots were submerged and his hands and forearms were hidden beneath a mountain of soapsuds. Sweat stained his armpits and bled into the back of his kurta.

When the men left for the mosque, Sadiq complained to my mother of a terrible pain in his head. I translated the word *throbbing* for her.

"Where did you learn that word?" my mother asked.

"You really didn't know what dharakta meant?" I said, throwing back a question in reply.

My mother would not touch Sadiq's forehead to see if he had a fever, so she asked him to do it himself. "Is it hot?" she inquired.

Sadiq shrugged as if to say *I don't know.*

She gave him aspirin and waited until he'd swallowed the chalky tablets before leaving him to the dishes. Fifteen minutes later, I was in my bedroom when she slipped on the wet floor, slid feet first across the marble, and crashed into the table. Sadiq had abandoned the kitchen, leaving the faucet running and causing dishwater and soapsuds to flood the floor. We spent the rest of the afternoon on our knees using towels to direct the flood out of the back door, and by the time we were done, my mother's shins were purple from the fall.

I'd been invited to Thanksgiving at Lizzy's home, and the apple pie that my mother had baked for the occasion was sitting on the kitchen counter, cradled in red cellophane bought especially from London Book Co. But I was certain there would be no Thanksgiving dinner. Believing the news about the imminent American evacuation, I was sad I might not see Lizzy again. Over the years, I'd said good-bye to many friends, knowing I'd never see them again, but I'd always been able to prepare for their departures. In fact, I made it a point early in a friendship to inquire how long a new friend expected to be in Pakistan. Some parents were on three-year tours, others only on two, and once in a while, their contracts were extended. I knew Mr. Simon had only a year left in Pakistan, and I'd already begun hoping his stay would be extended. Instead, Lizzy would be leaving on hardly a moment's notice.

All day I thought about calling her but didn't. I couldn't have said precisely when it had happened, but the previous day had changed me. Before, I was half-and-half, but now I was suddenly Pakistani. It was confusing, because in light of Pakistanis burning the embassy and terrorizing schoolchildren, I felt shame. I did not feel the triumph of being claimed by a category or of belonging, despite the fact that I'd longed my whole life for exactly that. It was perverse and unexpected to feel claimed by my country at such a time. And I couldn't call Lizzy.

I couldn't speak to her or anyone else in her family because I was afraid they would hear the difference in my voice.

Late at night, when all the lights in the house were off except mine, I heard a car pull up at our gate followed by light footsteps on the driveway. Had I not already been awake, I wouldn't have heard the muffled knock. When the visitor knocked again, I got out of bed and hurried to the door, wondering whom the chowkidars would admit at this time without seeking permission from my father.

Lizzy was out of breath, as if she'd run from her house to mine, rather than having been transported by her driver in the white Buick. She seemed to be carrying her quilt, wrapped in ribbons like a gift. We tiptoed into the living room and, afraid of waking my parents, I did not turn on the lights. The room was cast in a dull yellow sheen from the lit gas lamps outside the house that were my father's newfound solution to intermittent power outages. Lizzy said she could only spare a minute, and we didn't sit down.

"We're leaving in a few hours."

"I heard on the radio."

"I wanted to say good-bye."

Lizzy handed me the quilt.

"You don't have to give me this," I said, trying to return it to Lizzy. "Your mom made it for you."

"I want you to have it," Lizzy replied.

In a flash, I ran to my room and came back with a supply of neverworn glass bangles my grandfather had brought me from Lahore. "Take these with you."

Neither of us said anything. The Buick's engine was still running and I wondered whether her parents knew where she'd gone.

"I'm sorry I didn't call before. It was just . . ."

"Mom was in the vault during the fire. Mikail was with Parveen in someone's apartment when the fire started, and when the alarms went off, Mom wasn't allowed to go back and get him," she said hurriedly. "She's fine, like everyone else. Except the marine who died and another American."

"And the Pakistanis." The BBC newscaster was right. There had been a vault, and Anne Simon had been in it.

I reached for Lizzy's hand and held it until our hold grew damp. Lizzy said she had to leave, and we hugged each other more tightly than ever before. Near the front door, which I'd forgotten to close, I said, "Write to me."

When Lizzy was at the bottom of the stairs with her back to me, I felt the distance surge like an ocean of waves between us. Lizzy was only a few feet away, but she might as well have been standing in a snowdrift on her grandparents' land in central New York. It astonished me how completely the distance, deep and full, had moved in between us. And partly because of this, I called Lizzy's name, throwing it out into the open as if it was bait. She stopped to look at me, and then I almost said it. Not because I was vengeful, but because I believed it would bind us together, forever. *Your mother killed our servant's son.*

But when Lizzy turned to look, I swallowed the words that would have kept the ocean from washing her away.

"I'm sorry," I said instead.

"For what? You didn't do anything!" Lizzy smiled and waved.

She disappeared down the driveway into the night, her shawl sweeping the asphalt behind her. The chowkidars stood at the gate watching us, taking a risk that my father wasn't using his lightbulb device just then to check on them.

TWENTY-TWO

Very Early in the Morning, Friday, 23 November 1979

At two o'clock in the morning, the crescent moon hung in the sky like an ornament. Islamabad was quiet, asleep in a way Lahore never was. But on this night, smog finally lent it the veneer of a true Pakistani city. From the back, Sadiq's new kurta hung like a tent, and the pleats of his shalwar swung back and forth at odd angles as he hurried. His polished winter sandals clicked furiously against the pavement, and he reached 87th Street in record time. He collapsed under the first tree, sending a slight breeze into the scorched air.

Cars without license plates rounded the street corner too quickly and came to a halt near the same house. Nervous Americans spilled from the cars to count their children and baggage. 87th Street had been transformed into a makeshift bus station. Car doors slammed, young children sprinted between vehicles, suitcases were dragged across the pavement, and worried parents repeating *Shush! Shush!* compounded the noise. The line of idling blue buses resembled those of the American School, save the color and missing identification.

After the frenzy, in which everyone who was expected seemed to have finally arrived, the street fell into a relative and momentary calm. Drivers chatted quietly, and chowkidars resumed their night beats. Suddenly, and seemingly out of nowhere, a woman appeared on the scene. At first, her shapeless silhouette hid who she was, but as she walked toward the working streetlamp, the baby against her chest became visible. In close proximity to the single police officer at the scene, she switched the baby to her opposite shoulder. The streetlight illuminated her high cheekbones, extraordinary eyes, and platinum hair, and instantly confirmed that the woman was Anne Simon.

I watched from a hiding place a short distance away. My bicycle and I were safely concealed by a cluster of bushes straining with the weight of flowers. Sadiq had his back to me and his hands dangled at his sides. Anne Simon was twenty or thirty steps from Sadiq on the same sidewalk, her face clearly visible.

As tired as I'd been earlier, as much as I'd wanted to escape into sleep after Lizzy had left my house, the sounds of Sadiq in his bathroom had awakened me. By the time his soft footsteps were moving up the driveway, the gate carefully opening and closing, I'd put on a shalwar kameez and grabbed a chaddar to throw around my shoulders. I hid behind my new bicycle in the carport until the chowkidars were patrolling the opposite side of the house, then I left the driveway. One quick look in each direction was all it took to find Sadiq, and I followed him from enough of a distance so he wouldn't notice me. Because it was obvious he was going to 87th Street, it was easy to trail him in the darkness.

I considered intercepting Sadiq many times. I knew he'd had something to do with the attack on the American Embassy. He'd disappeared from the house while making lunch and not returned until after the drama at the embassy ended. He and his clothes stank, he couldn't look us in the eye, and he hadn't accounted for his absence. My father was so certain Sadiq had been at the burning embassy, he hadn't even insisted on an explanation. I'd heard him late at night arguing with my mother.

"What good would it do to ask him? He should be fired!" My mother, the most forthright of us all, didn't ask Sadiq either. None of us mentioned it, but we were all caught in the same predicament, lured by the false hope that truth could be kept from being true as long as it wasn't spoken aloud. What would happen if Sadiq told us what he'd done and we were forced to admit we had an arsonist or, God forbid, a murderer, on our hands? Regardless of what he'd done, I needed Sadiq to remain the person I'd always known, doing what was expected of him, like making my tea, washing my clothes, teaching me Urdu, and being my friend. Yet the closer we drew to 87th Street, the more violent the possibilities I imagined became. Sadiq would break into Anne Simon's house. He would kidnap Mikail. He would hurt Lizzy or Anne Simon. He was carrying a knife. Or a gun. Then Anne Simon's street was upon us, and I disappeared into blooming bushes.

Lizzy had told me that her street would be the meeting point for an American evacuation, so I wasn't surprised to see it filled with school friends, teachers, and parents. As worried as I was by whatever Sadiq might have been planning, I was also thrilled to be a spy and a witness to the evacuation, knowing that Americans did not flee countries every day. But when I saw Anne Simon, I knew that the right thing to do, the only way to put a stop to whatever calamity was about to befall us, was to jump from my hiding place and create a disturbance. Instead, I disappointed myself. I didn't have the courage to reveal my presence, and worse, I was embarrassed, even in a moment such as this, to be seen in a shalwar kameez by an American who might recognize me.

Initially, Anne Simon, who was still some yards away on the same sidewalk as Sadiq, did not take notice of him. She appeared to consider which direction she might stroll next, before her gaze finally settled on him. As if he'd been waiting all along for this moment from where he sat on the ground, Sadiq pulled something from his pocket and began waving it at her as he rose, a broken twig and a crushed leaf falling from the seat of his crumpled kurta. Anne Simon moved toward him, hesitating only when the chowkidars outside the safe house, puffing on K2 cigarettes and cradling their rifles, cautioned her in broken English not to stray too far. With Mikail fast asleep against her chest, she walked briskly toward Sadiq, and in a matter of moments stood within his reach.

If Sadiq was surprised, nothing in his body language conveyed it. His back was toward me, so I could not see his face, but he stood tall, leaning slightly into Anne Simon, as if he were about to take her into confidence. Sadiq cleared his throat, a nervous habit that signaled he was about to speak. It didn't make any difference to me that Anne Simon would not understand his Urdu; the very idea that he would address her was alarming. I dared not breathe as I waited in cold dread for his words. The chowkidars had gone back to smoking cigarettes, playfully kicking a small rock between them, and the sound of stone scraping asphalt was unbearable. With Sadiq's back still turned, I noticed a small movement of his arm, as if he were offering Anne Simon whatever he was holding. But the strain of trying to hear them speak suddenly blocked out every other sound and muddled my senses, leaving me unsure of what I was witnessing.

"Excuse me?" Anne Simon said.

Sadiq had spoken, even if his turned back made what he'd said inaudible to me. And while Anne Simon could not have understood him, she gauged it important enough to respond.

The bottom of Sadiq's kurta remained crumpled, as it had been when he'd risen from under the jacaranda tree. He pulled back his shoulders and made himself as tall as he could.

"Pardon me?" Anne Simon cocked her head as if the movement might magically translate his Urdu.

While the two still faced each other, Sadiq reached across, his left hand reaching for her left side, his body turning slightly and providing me with a momentary view. Sadiq touched the fold of Mikail's baby blanket hanging below Anne Simon's elbow. His gesture wasn't threatening; if the two of them had known each other, it could even have been construed as kind, but because they didn't know each other, his bold gesture was confusing. Inexplicably, Sadiq's hand moved upward and grazed Mikail's face, and when it lingered, Anne Simon gasped and pulled away. She took a single decisive step backward, but a far smaller one than I would have expected. Mikail whimpered and she patted the baby without looking down or taking another step.

A moment later, Sadiq again thrust something in front of Anne Simon, and as he did so, it fell from his hand. The baby's blanket caught it; Anne Simon jiggled Mikail, and the piece of paper seesawed to the ground. The streetlamp cast light on it, and I watched Anne Simon's face register what she saw. One by one, her features were affected as if a mask were taking shape—her forehead, ears, nose, mouth, chin, each sculpted anew.

Sadiq's back was toward me again, and his fists were clenched. Anne Simon brought Mikail to her shoulder and rubbed tiny circles on his back. She peered intently at Sadiq, but it was impossible to know what she was thinking.

The scratch in Sadiq's throat made me think he was about to speak again. Instead, the sound that escaped his lips transformed into a sob. It seemed to catch him by surprise, and he spun away from Anne Simon and into full view. My reflex was to try and escape, but I had nowhere to go, and my back hit the iron fence hard behind me, bruising me in a crisscross pattern that would last for days.

The disturbance caused the chowkidars to shout and run toward Anne Simon. In what amounted to a lightning flash of activity, she bent to the ground without breaking her hold on Mikail, picked up whatever Sadiq had dropped, and slipped it into his kurta pocket without touching him.

I was certain she whispered something, but between the chowkidars' ruckus and the sudden commotion, I could not make sense of what she said.

Sadiq reached for her, but she was already gone.

My bicycle clattered to the sidewalk as I ran across the street. I was too slow for the chowkidars, who were already standing next to him and gripping him by his elbows when I reached him.

"What are you doing?" I demanded of the chowkidars in perfectly accented Urdu.

It occurred to me that no Pakistani would have missed the fact that I looked like a foreigner, despite my shalwar kameez. Still, had I not been short of breath, out alone in the middle of the night with my chaddar dragging on the ground, they might not have paid me much attention.

"What are *you* doing?" they asked me.

"I'm with him," I replied, as if stating the obvious.

Suddenly we were interrupted by the deep and authoritative voice of an American marine in front of the safe house, asking Anne Simon if she was all right, then Mr. Simon, who was swiftly on the scene, shouting at her, "What are you doing?" It was ironic that the same question was being thrown around at everyone without any answers. I quickly turned away, praying I wouldn't be recognized. The chowkidars had released Sadiq, but they continued to hover near him with their hands on their rifles.

"He's not well," I told them.

"Then he shouldn't be out on the streets," they replied, adding sternly, "And neither should you. How old are you? Where are your parents?"

I touched the hem of the kurta my grandfather had bought Sadiq the day before. It was already worn and stained, but I was thankful it didn't smell of smoke. I couldn't bear to imagine that the chowkidars would suspect Sadiq of being involved in the embassy fire.

"Where do you live?" the chowkidar asked, and I pointed in the direction of my fallen bicycle, hoping to suggest I'd come from around the corner.

When I looked in the direction of the safe house, I saw men loading suitcases and trunks through emergency doors onto the buses. Children I rode to school with every day, boys and girls whose voices were familiar but whose names I suddenly couldn't remember, began boarding. Sadiq remained perfectly still next to me as I got my first good look at the vehicles. Although the arched roofs of the vehicles signified they were American, they had been painted the blue of Islamabad's university buses. The familiar lemon-yellow of my school bus with the school name printed on the side had vanished. Then it dawned on me. The buses had been painted blue in order to pass as local buses and conceal the American departure. I marveled at the foresight and wondered who was responsible for the brilliant idea.

I tore my gaze from the flurry of activity to focus on Sadiq, who was standing next to me, motionless as a tree.

"Come," I urged him, desperate to leave before I was recognized by Lizzy, Anne Simon, Mr. Simon, or anyone else.

The drivers put the buses in gear and released the brakes.

"Let's go," I pleaded with Sadiq. "We have to hurry!" I cried.

But he refused to move.

I had difficulty catching my breath and broke out in a cold sweat just as my ears began to buzz and further panic set in. I didn't know what role Sadiq had played in the embassy events, but I feared that he'd be found any second and arrested for conspiring to kill Americans. Since Sadiq wouldn't obey me, it was useless to issue commands. The bus engines revved, and I was running out of time. In a moment, they would drive right past us. What else could I say that would persuade him to leave 87th Street with me? A few lines of a Tot Batot poem I'd once heard Sadiq recite flitted through my mind, but in the end, with a bus starting to roll toward the intersection, I pinned all my hope on the truth.

"That was Anne Simon," I said, and I hadn't yet finished speaking her name, when my words had the desired effect. Sadiq moved.

Emboldened, I continued, "That was Anne Simon, who is the mother of my best friend, *Leezy*." He pivoted to face the Margalla Hills, all but buried by night. "That was Anne Simon, who is the mother of my best friend, Leezy, and one November night last year she drove the white Buick." Together, we took small steps to my fallen bicycle, and in the eternity it took to get there, the blue buses lined up at the intersection, ready for the journey to the airport. I picked up my bicycle. After a slight hesitation in which I considered that it was inappropriate for me to touch him in such a familiar way, I took Sadiq's good hand and wrapped it around a handlebar. A few steps later, as I was preparing to add to my sentence, Sadiq interrupted my thoughts.

He spoke, "That was Anne Simon, who is the mother of my best friend, Leezy, and one November night last year she drove her white Buick into Hanif and killed him."

In my surprise, I let go of the bicycle, but Sadiq already had a solid grip on it, and it did not crash to the ground. His sentence was as long and complicated as some of those in our Urdu lessons, but it was not profound, and it did not say anything either of us didn't already know. In fact, his added clause was the one I'd been about to utter. Yet, buried in what could have been an Urdu lesson was more truth than we'd ever had the courage to reveal to each other, and I didn't want it to end.

I clutched the handlebar again, and with the bicycle lodged like a child between us, we started home. Soon, I took a chance. I slowly repeated his sentence but concluded with an additional clause, "That was Anne Simon, who is the mother of my best friend, Leezy, and one November night last year she drove her white Buick into Hanif and killed him, and as a result you received 50,000 rupees from Anne Simon in a legal settlement, which you hid in a briefcase in my grand-father's house." There. I'd laid bare an unspoken secret between us, and as unsurprising as it was, at least it had been spoken.

I heard a shout coming from the last bus leaving the intersection. I imagined a reckless boy perched on luggage at the back of the bus, his head hanging from the window. I pictured Lizzy and her family in the front squeezed together on seats that had always been ours.

When the spitball hit my hair, I prayed Sadiq had been spared. I pictured the boys arguing, *Two! One! Two! One! Two!* in a vigorous point dispute no one attempted to halt. Then the pale blue buses disappeared, and we walked home through the night, the spitball dribbling ever so slowly down my long and tangled hair.

Our house glowed like a movie set. In what must have been a frantic search for us, every light was switched on. A neighbor's chowkidar shouted for my father as soon as he recognized us, and my parents ran a block in their robes and slippers to meet us. My mother was much faster than my father and reached me first. She'd lost her composure and her cheeks were shiny with tears; it was such an unnatural sight that for a moment she didn't look real.

"Where have you been?" she screamed. Her four words contained more anger and relief in one sentence than I'd thought possible.

My father, close at her heels, tried not to shout, but his voice cracked. "Thank God you're all right."

Without much of a pause, he focused on Sadiq and bellowed so loudly that all the neighborhood chowkidars came running to witness the scene. My mother locked arms with me just as my father began his rampage. "How dare you take my daughter anywhere? Where the hell did you go? What were you thinking? Come with me, you goddamned idiot! Move!" When it became clear that Sadiq would not take a single step, my father resorted to the stupidest curse of all, ulloo ka patha! It meant little compared to all my father had already said, but it was said with the most venom, and it offended me the most. My mother and I had almost arrived at the top of our driveway, but I slipped out of her grip and bolted back to Sadiq's side.

Once again out of breath, but pretending a steadiness and calm, I addressed Sadiq. "That was Anne Simon . . ."

"What the hell are you saying?" my father said, angrily cutting me off, but Sadiq took a step.

"That was Anne Simon, she is the mother of my best friend, Leezy . . ."

"What?"

". . . and one November night she drove the white Buick," I continued, and Sadiq took another step.

"Enough!" my father commanded, raising his hand.

The three of us were crowded on the sidewalk while a host of neighborhood nighttime chowkidars watched our every move. It wasn't the way I'd wanted my father to discover my proficiency in Urdu, if he'd noticed at all. My mother stood forlornly in the distance until my grandfather magically appeared. The man was deaf and unable to speak above a hoarse whisper, yet he assumed command. As if he'd been with me on the corner of 87th Street, he wrapped his long arm around Sadiq and whispered, "That was Anne Simon . . ." Within minutes, he'd maneuvered Sadiq to the house.

After my father recovered, he directed his attention to me. "You were on Mrs. Simon's street? With Sadiq! Have you gone mad?"

I couldn't think of anything to say, which gave us time to consider each other.

My father's expression softened. "We were worried to death. My darling, never, never do that to us again!"

I wanted to collapse. "I'm so sorry," I said, burying my face in my father's chest. When he caressed my head, I swatted at his hand. "No!" I said, afraid he would touch the spit.

An hour or two later, I lay on my parents' bed, consumed by an exhaustion more exacting than any I'd experienced. The pounding in my head mimicked revving bus engines, and I couldn't imagine ever taking another step with my aching feet. My mother sat next to me and tried to coax me to eat a pastry generously sprinkled with powdered sugar. My father's fingers got caught in hair tangles as he ran his fingers through my washed hair and encouraged me to divulge the details of when Sadiq and I had gone missing. Neither of them had any success. The last thing I remembered was my mother suggesting I call Lehla, but when I heard her name I couldn't picture my sister's face.

I felt like Sadiq. I didn't want to move, much less speak, and before I knew it, I'd sunk into a deep sleep that would carry me into the afternoon.

TWENTY-THREE

Afternoon, Friday, 23 November 1979

My sleep was shattered by a crash. Strangely, the noise even had a smell, wet like sharp iron, and a color, the dull gray of hurtling boulders. It spun my room at a dizzying speed that refused to slow, even as I hugged my knees to my chest.

I used the furniture to help me steady myself, navigating from my bed to the door with the help of my night table, desk, and bookshelves. I pulled a sweatshirt over my head and opened my door just as the racket began all over again. From the corner of my eye, I saw a heavy silver object rip through my parents' bedroom window screen, slam into the marble floor, and break apart. The lid of my mother's pressure cooker hit the wall and the tiny weight knob bounced off the dresser and flew toward me. I stepped out of the way and cried, "Mama!"

"I'm here," my mother replied from beyond the empty window frame and in the driveway. "Stay where you are!" she commanded.

I could not see glasses crashing against the walls in the servants' quarters or pots and pans flying in every direction or a patio chair being thrown against the wall. But at least I knew where the tremendous noise was coming from, and I wasn't dizzy anymore.

Eventually the racket was replaced by a heated argument in Punjabi. Because I'd never heard him yell, it was not immediately clear that one of the voices was Sadiq's. At least two other men were involved, and I assumed they were our nighttime chowkidars until I glanced at my parents' alarm clock and realized it was far too late in the day for them to still be at our house.

There was a swell in the shouting, and I became petrified by my inability to identify the voices. I could imagine only one explanation for what had happened: the police had finally arrived at our house to arrest Sadiq for the crime he'd committed at the American Embassy. Someone kicked the aluminum garbage bin, and the crash hurt my ears.

I saw Mushtaq, my father's driver, sprint toward the servants' quarters with a cricket bat in hand.

"Allah, Allah!" someone shouted.

Suddenly the habit of invoking God at every opportunity struck me as ridiculous. God had nothing to do with what was happening in my house at that very moment. Truth be told, Islamabad hadn't been on His radar for days.

I inched toward the broken window screen, frozen in a wave against the wall. As I peered out from behind my parents' freshly laundered curtains, the familiar smell of detergent nauseated me. Both my parents were beyond the end of the driveway and in the servants' quarters, standing at a slight remove from the men. My mother's posture, ever straight, was alarmingly perfect in the face of such disarray. Three men surrounded Sadiq. One was Mushtaq with a cricket bat still in hand, and I recognized the two men with rifles slung across their backs as our nighttime guards, even though they were not in uniform. Given the unfolding scene, the absence of policemen failed to provide me with much relief.

In the next moment, my father's panicked voice rose above everyone else's. He flailed his hands, lucky to miss my mother, and ordered the men to restrain Sadiq. Anger shrank his lips, drawing them away from his teeth and transforming him into a man I didn't know.

For the first time in my life, I doubted my father's omnipotence.

Mushtaq dropped the cricket bat, stepped behind Sadiq, and locked him in a hold in which his arms were useless at his sides. I half expected Sadiq to be lifted off the ground and hurled over the nearest wall. As if seeking permission for such a maneuver, Mushtaq looked over at my father, who punched the air in the direction of Sadiq's room. It was obvious Mushtaq didn't require any help, but the chowkidars joined in, and the threesome escorted Sadiq to his room.

I hopped through the broken window screen and onto the driveway.

Whatever was left of the servants' finely crafted chair was lying in pieces on the patio, along with dented cooking pots, a kettle missing its lid, and a carpet of broken glass. Every item in Sadiq's miniature kitchen appeared to have been smashed to the ground. My father's hands were back in his pockets, and my mother was shaking her head.

"Sadiq!" I shouted, hurrying toward him.

"Bibi?" he answered calmly, as if he'd been interrupted in the middle of a boring household task.

"Stay away from him!" my mother erupted.

"Obey your mother," Sadiq agreed, continuing to be led to his room.

"Shut up!" My father barked his reprimand at him.

"You did all this?" I asked Sadiq, who couldn't see me nudge one of my mother's old cooking pots with my bare foot. I took a step toward him, and my father sprang to life, yanking me back and hurting my arm.

"Don't you dare!" he exploded.

"Ow!" I cried.

"Leave her alone!" My mother ran to my defense.

"Didn't your mother tell you to stay in the house?" he demanded.

I screamed like everyone else. "He has a lot to be angry about, you know!"

Before stomping back to the house, I sneaked one last look at Sadiq, just as he was pushed into his room.

My grandfather had been sitting in the kitchen for the duration. When my mother began to tell him what had happened, he nodded his head impatiently and whispered, "Yes, yes, I heard."

"But you're deaf!" I said.

"Aliya!" My mother was upset, but so was I, and it helped to focus on the inconsistency in my grandfather's hearing rather than the ache in my stomach. Besides, either my grandfather was deaf or he wasn't.

My grandfather replied, "Being deaf doesn't mean not knowing what's going on."

It would have been easy to miss his soft whisper, but I didn't, and in return, I offered a weak smile. My grandfather always knew what was going on because he was the smartest adult around.

A little while later, we were all still in the kitchen when my father strode back into the house, pretended we weren't there, and lifted the telephone receiver. None of us dared ask whom he was calling. In a moment, the slow clicking of the rotary face dial coming back to rest, *one-two-three-four* and *one*, made it obvious he was dialing 41, Lahore's city code. On the other end of the telephone line, Yunis answered the call. My father's instructions were concise: Yunis was to come to Islamabad immediately so that he could accompany Sadiq back to Lahore.

"You are firing him," my mother said at the end of the short telephone conversation.

"I should have done it long ago," my father complained and described what the nighttime chowkidars told him had happened.

The motorcycle intelligence officer had paid a visit the previous night and asked to speak to Sadiq. When the chowkidar told him that Sadiq had gone missing, the spy asked a barrage of questions, among them an accounting of Sadiq's comings and goings. The chowkidar could not say where Sadiq had gone, but to appease the spy, he gave him a log in which records such as those were kept. The spy also wanted the list of foreign-license-plated vehicles that visited our house, as per WAPDA regulations, and the chowkidar gave him that too. When Sadiq discovered the chowkidars kept a log of his movements, he slapped one of them and cursed the other. In response, they called him a stinking village idiot and various other names my father said he wouldn't translate for us. Like an animal gone wild, Sadiq lost his temper and threw everything within his reach at them, including the special servant's chair. Regardless of what the chowkidars had done to provoke Sadiq, my parents could no longer ignore the sobering reality that there was an unstable man living on their premises.

"Oh no, Javid!" my mother said, but I knew she didn't disagree with my father's decision. Like me, she'd wished for things to turn out differently.

Her words had the unexpected effect of igniting my father in a way nothing else had. *"Oh no, Javid,"* he mocked my mother. "Yasmin, look what listening to you has gotten me into! My daughter kidnapped in the middle of the night, and the US Embassy burned to the ground. We'll be lucky if General Zia himself doesn't arrive at our gate and arrest us all!" My father addressing my mother as Yasmin made it clear that he was furious.

"I *wasn't* kidnapped!" I interjected.

"You . . ." my father started, and my grandfather slammed his fist onto the table and sent teacups ricocheting across the surface. The distraction lasted long enough for everyone to take a breath.

"It's not like you to get carried away, Javid. The general didn't give a damn yesterday when the embassy was burning, and I doubt he has changed his mind today," my mother said.

My grandfather accused my father of being a negligent employer and blamed him for enabling Sadiq. My grandfather had been retired from the courts for years, but he made his case with the learned deliberation of an experienced lawyer. He said that the servant ought to have been sent away at the first sign of instability. My father's failure to do that had put me at risk. "Case closed," he said, and my father was momentarily speechless.

"It will all be all right," my mother said, struggling to come to my father's assistance, despite his harshness.

But her comment enraged him further. "Don't patronize me! Don't minimize what's happened! You scoundrels want me to lose my job." I'd never heard my father call my mother or grandfather names, particularly not the one he typically resorted to out of frustration when referring to his lazy office employees. My father had once again transformed into a man without lips and, unaware of what he was about to do, I thought he'd never looked scarier. Then he lunged at my mother and pushed her shoulder so hard, if she hadn't had excellent reflexes she would have been knocked from the chair to the floor.

"Javi, Javi . . ." my mother cried, now using her affectionate nickname for him.

"Don't *Javi, Javi* me!" my father bellowed, and my deaf grandfather covered his ears.

My mother was undeterred. She rose from her seat to wrap her arms around his neck. She sank against him, as if her sheer weight stood a chance at calming him. "You're right to send him back to Lahore before it's too late," she whispered.

"Daddy?" I said, tears streaming down my face.

"Will you please be quiet, please?!" he shouted, but his arms were around my mother, and he held onto her as if he were holding onto life itself.

I'd never seen my father in such a state—like everything else in my life, he was crumbling into pieces before my very eyes.

The next day, my mother and I stood in the carport while Yunis and Sadiq settled into my father's office car. My grandfather kissed me goodbye, leaving me with the usual spot of moisture on my forehead that I dared not wipe away.

"I'm coming back to the village soon," he said.

"You do know this is the capital, right?" I teased.

"No!" he joked.

He embraced my mother and while he held her in his arms, he apologized for taking the car to my school.

"I was wrong," he said unconvincingly, winking at me as he spoke. "I shouldn't have taken the car without your permission."

"I was worried about you. You're not the best driver, you know, and Peshawar Road is terribly dangerous . . ." my mother began and went on as she sometimes did.

My grandfather smiled widely during her monologue, his top lip stuck above his denture. He wasn't even looking at my mother, who was still partially in his embrace, and he paid no attention to what she was saying.

"Are you trying to say thank you?" my grandfather finally said.

My mother broke out in laughter. "Thank you for bringing my daughter home," she said graciously, clearly intent on putting the worry of the last few days behind her.

Mushtaq had just closed Sadiq's car door and had gone to the front of the car to listen to my father's directions. I knocked on Sadiq's window and waved my good-bye.

My father finished instructing Mushtaq, who finally joined the others in the car.

"Allah janta hai," my father said as the car rolled out of the gate, and then added, "God knows what has happened," as if my mother or I might have use for the English translation.

My parents hadn't spoken to each other since the previous day, so I was surprised when she acknowledged him. "God knows your country has gone to pieces," my mother said.

"You think?" It was my father's standard response to her frequent generalizations, but with their horrible fight fresh in his mind, he appeared to consider her complaint more seriously.

"I do," she said and hurried away. She swung open the front door of the house with unexpected determination and was the first to reenter.

For one fleeting moment, I was tricked into believing that everything could be set right. It couldn't, of course, but it didn't stop me from wishing that absolutely everything had been otherwise.

TWENTY-FOUR

Saturday, 22 December, through Wednesday, 26 December 1979

My father, like my grandfather, was a Lahori in the truest sense of the word. Not only did we grow up with his insistence that the city was superior to any other city in the world, he was convinced that Lahore's magic could cure any crisis. He sent my brother, Amir, to Lahore when he declared his intention to study Islam in Cairo. He sent Lehla there when she was caught breaking curfew with her boyfriend in a Karachi nightclub during a school trip. He sent all three of us there for part of our first summer in Islamabad when my mother set up the house. Whenever he joined us, he'd say, "Lahore is your history," and drag us on the same sightseeing tour. Lawrence Gardens, the Badshahi Mosque, the Red Fort, the Old City, Government College, Lahore Museum, all were places that had to be visited; as if without such a pilgrimage, our family would fall apart.

So it happened that my mother, my father, and I had just arrived at Lahore's airport and were in the car on the way to Shadman. My parents informed me that Sadiq was living in my grandfather's house because Sadiq's wife, Jamila, continued to hold him responsible for Hanif's death and would not allow him to return home. We all agreed that Jamila was being unfair, but I was afraid of seeing Sadiq, not only because of what had transpired in our home the night before he left, but also because of my recurring nightmare.

In my dreams, Sadiq sat on a pirhi, a few inches from the floor, in a corner of my grandfather's kitchen so that Yunis could spoon-feed him unidentifiable orange mush. He sat collapsed over his knees, without a pagri, and was as white as it was possible for a brown man the color of my father to be. I tried to entice him to speak. "Aap ki pagri kidhar hai?" I asked. After waiting to be corrected, I changed my grammar and said, "Tumhari pagri kidhar hai?" In frustration, I finally asked in English, "Have you lost your turban?" Then I begged Yunis to tell me if Sadiq would ever speak again. His hopeful response, "Insha'Allah," only made me despair. The night before we left for Lahore, my nightmare extended into a sequence of scenes in which Yunis took to the task of caring for his brother with the same precision he fried our eggs, poured tea, or swept the driveway. He cared for Sadiq as if he were a child again, leading him to the toilet and washing his bottom before pulling the flush. Yunis combed and cut hair that had grown long and white on Sadiq's head. He dressed him in starched kurtas many sizes too big and held a cloudy plastic glass to his parched lips. After the day's long shadows became night, Yunis prepared Sadiq for bed. He drew back the bedcovers on a charpai pushed flush against his own and gently laid him down. Right before I awoke, he turned Sadiq's face in the direction of the Ka'aba so that God and His mercy might easily find it in death.

We were approaching my grandfather's neighborhood when I asked my parents how Sadiq was doing.

"Hard to know," my father replied.

"The man needs help," my mother said.

"With Hanif's death and all, you mean, right?" I asked her.

"That, and . . . listen, darling, we don't know what happened the day of the embassy fire . . ."

"We still don't know who did it?" I interrupted my mother.

"We know that there were a lot of angry and organized university students involved," my father said.

"Maybe other gundas, as well," my mother said but didn't explain who they might have been.

"I don't understand why they did it," I said.

"Supposedly, they believed that the US had seized the Grand Mosque in Mecca," my father said and shrugged his shoulders.

"I don't believe any of it. I don't believe anything anyone says about anything that's going on anywhere around here anymore."

That said, I took a deep breath and tried to focus because I needed my father's help. "Americans didn't seize the mosque, right?" Two weeks after the mosque had been seized, the affair had ended, and neither Iranians nor Americans had been involved, but Saudis themselves.

My father nodded his confirmation.

"But then *why* did they do it?"

"You see," my father said calmly, "what the students—or whoever—did was not right. This is not the way to behave. But what happened is a cause for concern, because it shows how angry people are."

My father went on, getting angrier himself as he was reminded of the hanging of the prime minister, a wretched general, and various other things. I tuned out and drew my own conclusions. Very simply, the world was a small place and what happened in one place affected the other. I was suddenly reminded of Klackers, the game of two balls suspended on a string. When one ball hit the other, the *click-clack* sent it careening. Countries were connected to each other the same way, which made our world a very scary place.

Finally, my mother interrupted him and steered the conversation back to where it had started.

"What we were trying to say, my darling, is that we don't know what happened the day of the embassy fire. Remember when Sadiq came home, he smelled of smoke? Not to mention that awful scene in the servants' quarters?" She inhaled deeply and said, "Your father and I think he may have been at the American Embassy the day . . ."

"So what?" I interrupted.

"Well, we think he might have been involved somehow."

"That's ridiculous. He didn't hurt anyone. I was there when he talked to Anne Simon. He didn't hurt her or her stupid baby and he could have!"

My mother wasn't dissuaded. "Sometimes, under certain circumstances, people are capable of things we can't imagine," she suggested.

"You really think Sadiq was in the crowd that set fire to the American Embassy?" I pretended outrage, even though I harbored the same suspicion.

"I don't think he set fire to the United States Embassy," my father said calmly.

"I *know* he didn't," I said.

"You can't know that, though, can you?" my father said dejectedly.

"He told me."

"He told you what?" my mother was quick to ask.

I was saved by my grandfather's truncated driveway and our sudden stop. "Never mind," I said.

"Aliya!"

My mother had an uncanny ability to detect her children's lies, and this was no exception. Sadiq, of course, hadn't told me anything.

Standing in my grandfather's kitchen, Sadiq had shed his pagri, exactly as he had in my dreams. I pretended to ignore my parents' warning to be careful around him, but I was aware that they were in the next room.

"Welcome," he said, putting down the silverware he was drying. He flung the dishtowel over his shoulder and stretched out his arms in an expansive gesture equal to his welcome, as if my grandfather's home was his.

"Hello."

"Welcome to Lahore!" he repeated, his enthusiasm a match for any television commercial.

"Thanks." Sadiq looked at me expectantly with a broad smile. I had difficulty reconciling the person in front of me with the one I had last seen in Islamabad. "But I didn't want to come to Lahore."

"Why?"

"I didn't feel like a vacation."

"Me neither," he said.

"You're already on vacation. Isn't Lahore a vacation for you?"

Sadiq waved away my question. "Thank God you were fine," he announced, after a moment.

"Why wouldn't I have been?" I had no idea what he meant.

"The school," Sadiq said matter-of-factly, referring to the day when something had actually happened in Islamabad.

"You weren't there. How do you know what happened?" I was suspicious.

"I wasn't *there*," he said. "But *you* were, though, and I'm glad you are fine."

"You live with my grandfather now?" I asked, changing the subject.

"With Yunis," Sadiq replied, as if there was a difference.

"Is your wife all right? Your children?" I asked carefully.

"Everyone is fine."

"You won't be coming back to Islamabad?"

"No."

"Well, we don't really need a servant anymore. I'm the only one home, and in a few years I'll go off to college, too," I said, doing a poor job of disguising my disappointment.

"You'll visit your grandfather, like always," Sadiq said, not taking offense.

"Maybe," I said. "And you? Are you all right now?"

"I'm fine." He answered as if I had no cause for worry at all.

"You know, breaking your things, the chair . . ." I didn't finish my sentence about his unraveling.

"Nothing wrong with getting good and mad once in a while," he said.

"Mad? You were a tornado." Not knowing the Urdu equivalent for *tornado*, I used the English word.

Sadiq was puzzled but didn't ask for a translation.

"By the way," he said, presenting me with at least a week's stack of newspapers from the kitchen counter. "Have you been practicing?"

"Have you?"

"I saved these for you," he said, ignoring my question.

"You're following the general again?" I asked, as if the country's leader was our common acquaintance.

"No, but *you* should. It's good for your Urdu."

"I'm sick of the news," I said honestly.

"Go select a story, then come back and read it to me," he said sternly.

I was back a few minutes later with a three-column selection that could have been written by Uncle Imtiaz. At first, I made mistakes to see if he would catch me, until he finally quipped I ought to stop insulting our intelligence. Then I gave the story my full attention, and although the news was as uninspiring as ever, and the general was issuing whatever directives struck his fancy, I was happier than I'd been in a while.

I had promised myself I wouldn't look in the cabinet. I made myself write the promise on a piece of paper and put it in my suitcase, hoping a written reminder would help me keep my word. In the end, my good intentions didn't stand a chance. One afternoon while my father was in a meeting, and my grandfather was rifling through papers in his room, I declined my mother's invitation to accompany her shopping. I wandered into the kitchen and stood in front of the cabinet below the kitchen sink, where a damp rag wove through the nickel cabinet pulls to keep it from opening. I unwound the rag and the doors fell open. The half-full garbage pail didn't smell nearly as much as it had in the summer. I reached for the shiny brass handle behind it, pulled out the briefcase and set it upright on the counter. I righted it so that the front faced me, took a sharp breath, and snapped open the buckles.

"What's that?" my grandfather whispered near my ear. Startled with fright, I jumped and banged my knee hard against the cabinet. The briefcase fell open, exposing carefully packed bundles of money.

"Pardon?" I asked. We stared at each other until my grandfather leaned down to match my height and took my face in his hands. I was so close to him, I could hear the click of his dentures when he began to speak.

"What's that?"

"I don't know," I said. We both turned to the overstuffed briefcase. Since the last time I'd seen it, some of the money had grown a film of mold.

My grandfather let go of my face and picked up a packet. "Money?" His single word conveyed alarm. "Whose money?!" and his whisper may as well have been a shout.

"I don't know," I lied.

I tried to close the briefcase, but my grandfather's hands were much larger than mine, and he gathered them inside his own.

In the afternoon, when my parents returned, the briefcase was waiting on the dining room table. They drew chairs around the table and stared at the briefcase before my father broke the silence and asked me, "You want to tell me what this is?"

I shook my head.

My grandfather opened the briefcase without laying it flat, and several bundles of moldy money fell out.

"What's this?" my father said sternly.

"Yes. What is this?" my grandfather whispered.

"It's a briefcase of money. I found it last time I was here. It belongs to Yunis."

"Yunis?" my father said, and then he erupted in shouts. "Yunis! Yunis! Yunis!" and when he came running, my father demanded, "Is this yours?"

"No," Yunis said.

"No?"

"No."

"Do you know whose it is?"

"Yes," Yunis replied.

He looked at the ceiling, the walls, the single window, his feet, anywhere but my father, while he uneasily related the story. He recalled how Sadiq had brought the settlement money from Islamabad to Lahore on the train and deposited it with Yunis, and the two had decided that the money would be safer from prospective thieves inside my grandfather's house than in the adjacent servants' quarters. The briefcase had sat untouched beneath the kitchen sink since then. Yunis glanced at me and must have immediately regretted it.

"You knew?" my father said to me.

"By accident. I found it when I was visiting in the summer."

"And you didn't tell us?"

"What was wrong with the briefcase being there?"

"The money was supposed to be in the bank!" my mother exclaimed. "With Sadiq. Not here in Lahore!"

Yunis went to fetch Sadiq.

Several minutes later, both men appeared. They stood next to my grandfather for a minute or two without anyone speaking. "What's this money doing here?" my grandfather demanded.

"Growing moldy," Sadiq replied, and I smiled.

"What about your daughters?" my father said. "They could use it for school and . . ."

"Fees, medical treatment, hospital bills, unforeseeable emergencies, surprises that make up life . . ." Sadiq sounded like he was repeating something my father had told him, or else he'd once given a lot of thought to what the money might have bought.

"Does your wife know?" my grandfather asked.

"She never knew about the settlement money."

"You never told her the Americans gave you money after they killed your son?"

How could Sadiq not tell his wife about the settlement? Didn't it belong to her as well? Evidently my mother agreed with me, because she told Sadiq as much while my father patiently translated for her.

"We'll clean off the money and you can take it to the bank," Sadiq was told.

"No," Sadiq replied.

The back and forth went on for a long time, but no one was able to change Sadiq's mind, and in the end, even my mother had difficulty remaining angry with him. She finally just shook her head until Sadiq admitted he was sorry to have upset her. I don't know if anyone else felt the way I did, but I was proud of Sadiq. His resolve confirmed the obvious: A little boy's life couldn't be bartered for money.

"After letting your riches rot, don't think you're getting a raise from me," my grandfather whispered, a halfhearted attempt at continued irritation.

"No, sir."

Later, my grandfather asked me privately, "Why didn't you tell me when you found it last summer?"

"I don't remember," I said.

"Is that the truth?"

"The money just seemed like a raaz is all," I clarified, using the Urdu word that had become my word for all the deceit surrounding Hanif's death: Anne Simon's identity as the driver, the 50,000-rupee settlement, the briefcase in my grandfather's kitchen cabinet, and on and on.

"How much of a raaz is it?" my grandfather gently prodded.

"I didn't count it. But if Sadiq didn't spend any of it, it's fifty thousand," I replied. "Not a very high price for a dead son, don't you agree?"

My grandfather moved his head in a gesture that was both a nod and a shake. Almost immediately, I realized my mistake, but my grandfather did not question my knowledge of the amount, and I was grateful that he did not make me confess I'd snooped in my mother's desk and read the settlement papers.

The next day was Christmas, my mother's holiday. Although she'd converted to Islam before marrying my father, her Christmas baking was legendary in our family and also in Yunis's, because over the years she'd made a habit of preparing extra cookies for his children. Since Muhammad Ali Jinnah, the founder of Pakistan, shared his birthday with Jesus Christ, Christmas was a holiday in Pakistan. As a rule, we celebrated a day late on Boxing Day, a British holiday, so my mother could spend the day working without being bothered by servants. She'd brought some ingredients with her, like her homemade vanilla essence, and my grandfather had scoured Lahore's bazaars to find others, like colored sprinkles and hazelnuts. On principle, my grandfather had little appetite for celebrations or the British, but he said that it was a good thing the British had the sense to set aside an entire day to celebrate my mother's baking.

For the holiday meal, my mother prepared Wiener schnitzel, a dish she'd adopted in Vienna as the hallmark of her festive day. Yunis made vegetable pulao with cinnamon sticks that unwound into flat bark; toasted cumin seeds; fat green peas I helped shell; sweet, shiny carrots my mother had grated; whole almonds; and perfectly caramelized onions. We ate dinner early, and everybody but my mother slathered chutney on the breaded veal cutlets.

"It's very good like this," my father said, passing her Yunis's renowned peach chutney.

"No, thank you," my mother said, a predictable response. "It's perfect the way it is."

Because I didn't want to hurt her feelings, I served myself mashed potatoes and shook pepper and salt all over the yellow mass.

"You're ruining it! You won't be able to taste the butter," my mother exclaimed.

"I taste the butter. I really do."

Dessert was the highlight, as it always was on holidays. My mother served Salzburger Nockerl, a delicious soufflé of eggs, butter, and sugar, of which there were never enough servings to please us all. At the same time she served us, she set aside helpings for Yunis and Sadiq.

Eventually, we retreated to the living room to sit in front of the black-and-white television for Khabarnama, the nightly newscast. I nibbled on Lehla and Amir's favorite cookies, and the announcer, with a dupatta covering her head, began the newscast with the religious preamble the general had made mandatory.

There was only one item of interest in the newscast besides the number of days, fifty-two, that the Iranians had held the American hostages. The newscaster announced that the Soviets were sending troops into Afghanistan. Estimates suggested that tens of thousands of soldiers had already been airlifted into the country, and fuzzy black-and-white footage showed convoys miles long crossing the border.

Watching the television news with us, Yunis turned to Sadiq and said, "The Soviets are godless, aren't they?"

"So is the general," my grandfather said and made my mother laugh.

"But he's a lucky man," my father added, waving at the television. "If the Russians stay, Pakistan will have lots of friends."

Either Sadiq or Yunis made the standard joke about General Zia's direct telephone line to God. There was mention of a new directive the general had issued, and it prompted my grandfather to whisper a more recent joke: The general telephones God with the latest update, and in response God pleads, "For God's sake, you're busier than I am. Don't you ever take a break?!" It was my favorite general joke, but at that moment it failed to amuse my mother, who chided my grandfather for trivializing war with humor.

After a while, I gave up trying to understand the fuss about the Soviets entering Afghanistan. As the television droned on with official Soviet statements that they were the guests of Afghanistan's government, I sank deeper into the sofa and craved Lizzy's chocolate chip cookies. I recalled my farewell with Lizzy as if it were a movie, slowing it down frame by frame, making it last, keeping Lizzy in our Margalla home. I imagined my friend tucked between flowing hills and crystal-clear lakes in New York, as far away from Lahore as possible, and wondered if I would ever hear from her again.

Then, at prayer time, the azaan rattled the windowpanes, my deaf grandfather cursed, my mother slapped her knee in frustration, and my father, unperturbed by the commotion, remained as focused on the television as ever.

EPILOGUE

My rule as a journalist these days is simple: I don't tell Pakistan's stories. Now, more than ever, they make people throw their arms up in despair. To this day, the same unsatisfactory explanations for who attacked the US Embassy and why are bandied about, and the only truth agreed upon is that anything can happen in Pakistan. In reality, today's War on Terror means that the country has much more immediate worries, including whether it survives tomorrow. A newspaper account comes and goes, but when it interrupts your life, it keeps you in its grip. This story of Islamabad, those thirty months during the Cold War that changed my world, made me who I am. Rules aside, I wrote what I remembered and found the other truth.

I first imagined telling this story when I was visiting New York, toward the end of 1989. Ten years had transpired; I was in my twenties and living in Islamabad, having cobbled together a number of part-time journalism jobs. However, every year I set aside four weeks of vacation time to alternate between visiting my sister, Lehla, in Syracuse and my brother, Amir, in Cairo. Lehla was a perpetual student at Syracuse University, where I, too, had studied, accumulating advanced university degrees the way some people accumulate cars. Amir was in Cairo, where he'd originally gone to study before settling there to make documentary films when he fell in love with his wife and the city, which my father says is Amir's second wife.

I had been in Syracuse only hours before I remembered its proximity to Cazenovia and fantasized about traveling the twenty miles to visit Lizzy's grandparents' home on the lake and finding Lizzy there, but our paths never crossed again. As it always did, travel sharpened polarities, and I was struck virtually mute by the different worlds in which my sister and I lived: I, back in Islamabad, trying to make a life writing about Afghan refugees, and Lehla, trying to teach her students where to find Pakistan on a globe. Every time I visited, I was amazed by the fact that it was almost impossible to conceive of a more disparate reality from Islamabad than Syracuse. In those days, Islamabad was still a relatively new, carefully planned city, where the green of the Margalla Hills and the blue of the crystal-clear sky looked like freshly painted scenery, and the scent of raat ki rani flowers on certain winter evenings was strong enough to pretend someone had just sprayed the streets with perfume. In contrast, Syracuse was a city rusting from the inside out, adjacent to a poisoned lake, and home to a merciless winter that seemed to last most of the year.

It was a few days before Thanksgiving. Whenever I happened to be in the United States during that time of year, my memory went into overdrive, bits and pieces of it shooting into awareness like determined swimmers coming up for air. Timing was everything: It was the day before another anniversary of the 1979 attack on the US Embassy in Islamabad, when it was burned, as it is commonly said, to the ground.

On this particular night, I found myself in a solitary cubicle in the basement of the Syracuse library, where I often spent the evenings when Lehla was in class. The place was badly lit, and the frigid winter wind might as well have been blowing drifts of snow on my already numb feet. The library was thousands of miles away from London Book Co., the English bookstore in Islamabad, where Lehla and I once spent our summer afternoons sitting on rickety shelves, poring over Archie comic books and driving the bookstore owner mad. But memory is slippery and plays tricks with us, and in a corner of the building thick with the smell of damp steel and must, I was suddenly transported to that dusty bookshop in Kohsar Market. I could smell the lingering cardamom and cinnamon of the owner's Kashmiri tea, mixed with the unmistakable scent of yet-to-be-opened glossy magazines. Suddenly, at *that* moment, the contrast between these worlds transformed into a specific and concrete urge. I had an essential and immediate need to read about what I had lived through in those thirty fateful months in Pakistan. I didn't need any confirmation; instead, it was critical to make my memories real, to see them before my eyes as I sat in a freezing, disintegrating city that rarely saw sunshine.

In the university's microfilm station buried in a corner of the library, turning a miniature wheel with a cool handle, I searched for an account of the day the US Embassy in Islamabad was attacked. The pages of the *New York Times*, reduced to a two-inch-wide strip of film, became a fast-forward blur of time on display: There were articles on General Zia's coup d'état, Ayatollah Khomeini and the Iranian revolution, Prime Minister Bhutto's hanging, the Iranian hostage crisis, the siege of Mecca, and Russians occupying Afghanistan. I scrolled backward and, to my surprise, the film stopped on an old photograph of a teenager hugging his mother upon landing in Washington, D.C. The lanky teenager was a schoolmate of mine who rode my yellow school bus in Islamabad. The photograph was juxtaposed with an article about the body of the marine killed in the embassy attack being received by his grieving mother. Scrolling 444 days into the documentation of the US hostages' captivity in Teheran, I found a photograph of the day they were released. It took me a moment to make sense of the grainy image, but buried in it was my former principal, Mr. Hill, his broad shoulders towering above everyone else's.

I stayed in the library deep into the night. On a long table, under a fluorescent light that turned the dark library windows into mirrors, I leafed through a heavy periodical index for 1979 that contained unbelievably detailed lists of bold and italicized subjects under the heading of "Pakistan." I found a listing for what could prove to be a useful piece in a magazine and retrieved the requisite leather-bound volume from the stacks.

The essay was actually a letter of sorts, cleverly titled "Missive from Islamabad." I didn't notice the byline at first, but as I began to read, an unexpectedly familiar voice and cadence, soft and loud at the same time, reverberated in my head. *By Anne Simon.* My breath quickened as I stared at the name. Could it be? Was the author the Anne Simon I knew? Indeed, the contributors' notes confirmed she was: "Anne Simon spent a year and a half in Islamabad, Pakistan, and now lives in Cazenovia, New York, with her thirteen-year-old daughter, a set of five-year-old twins, and a baby boy, while her husband, Jack Simon, is a public health officer in a hardship post in West Africa."

It took me a few minutes to recover from the byline. Wasn't Anne Simon a nurse? When had she become a writer? Since when did my best friend's mother use British words like *missive*? How long after the evacuation had she written the piece? Had Lizzy read it? I shook my head to clear my racing thoughts, ran my trembling hand over the page, and read it again.

I laid down the volume on the solid oak table at which I sat and contended with memories I'd let slip—a long white Buick, the corner of 87th Street. The synchronicity of my memories with the details revealed in the essay was dizzying. This is what Anne Simon had written in her detailed account of the day the US Embassy in Islamabad was attacked:

As she was finishing lunch with her friend in the dining room of the embassy, a security alarm sounded, and she was forbidden to return to her friend's apartment, where her maid was watching her baby. She was herded into the vault with everyone else, and over the next few hours, tiles cracked and carpets smoldered from the heat of the fire. She held wet paper towels to her mouth to protect herself from the smoke, and her husband's voice finally trickled in over a radio, promising that her three children, but not her baby, were safe with her daughter's Pakistani school friend. As the 137 people stood shoulder to shoulder in the vault, the Pakistani staff prepared to prostrate themselves at prayer time. Someone muttered curses at the muffled Allahu Akbars with which prayers began. She did her best to save a dying marine, but blood pumped out of him faster than she could stem it. Crowds chanted outside, and no one came to help. It was almost dark when they climbed out of the rooftop hatch of the vault and descended the tilted bicycle racks laid out like ladders to the ground. Her baby was found in the arms of the wondrous maid, who had saved him in a bathtub of water during the siege.

It was a strange place, this city she'd lived in, hemmed in by mountains on one side and the long expanse of plateau on others. And in her whole life, she'd never felt more out of place, despite the kind chowkidars who greeted her with salutes on her daily walks. On the morning the Americans left aboard a yellow school bus that had been quickly painted the pale blue of the morning sky, with her children and husband at her side, she felt her family had never been more complete. She stared from the bus window, contemplating a small part of her that was disappointed to be getting out and saddened that the rushed circumstances couldn't help but leave some business undone. She caught the back view of a young girl, vaguely familiar in a simple chaddar (the cloth made them all look alike), helping a man cross the street. After the two people put a bicycle between them, she assumed they were going home. Smoke was still rising from one corner of Islamabad as the airplane climbed into the sky, and the one thing the nurse-cum-writer was absolutely certain of was that she would never, ever, be back.

That was *her* story, plain and simple.

And, as you now know, it made me want to write *mine*.

~

Because my story and the story of my country are woven into one, I must tell you about Pakistan's intervening years.

It took eleven long years for General Zia's rule to finally come to an end with an unexplained airplane crash that claimed the lives of all passengers, including the US ambassador to Pakistan, who was a surprise guest on the flight. I will always remember waking up in New York at the same time as General Zia was falling from the sky in Bahawalpur, his face pressed to the cabin window of an airplane rising and dipping like the tail end of God's yo-yo. Within weeks, the elections that had been scheduled and rescheduled for eleven years were set for the last time, and Prime Minister Bhutto's daughter, Benazir, returned home to waiting crowds of hundreds of thousands of people before becoming Madam Prime Minister. She would be deposed not once, but twice in the years to come; three times, if her very last ascension is counted. She hadn't quite been reelected when she was killed some years ago, three days after Christmas, and her husband, Asif Ali Zardari, became president. In the back and forth and back and forth that counts for Pakistani politics, I am reminded of the metered nonsense of a Tot Batot poem I once knew. The list of generals, prime ministers, and presidents we have seen is a jumbled refrain, and the world of Pakistan molds itself to its pitch.

I traveled to Islamabad in 2008, the year after Benazir's death. In a reality no one could have foretold, billboards with year-old election posters still loomed over the roads near the airport: Gigantic images of the murdered Madam Prime Minister Bhutto sat side by side with those of her father, who'd been hanged twenty-nine years before. It was the first time since I was a child that his likeness, immense the way it had once been in my mind, had appeared on billboards in the country.

Prime Minister Bhutto, his two sons (including Shah), and his daughter Madam Prime Minister Benazir Bhutto are all dead and buried in the same remote parcel of Garhi Khuda Bakhsh. Their mausoleum climbs in impressive domes and arches above their graves, recently threatened by floodwaters. Some years ago, they were joined by Begum Bhutto, the prime minister's once-beautiful wife, whose mind was broken by Alzheimer's and impossible to reach. Her plight might have been the only sane response to the madness that has ravaged her family and our land. The prime minister's sole surviving child, a graduate of the American School of Islamabad, had her grief captured on camera at her sister's funeral, and her face, strewn across newspapers all over the world, has been made unrecognizable by so much loss.

The world surprised us, even as the Bhuttos, one after the other, predictably met their deaths. The Soviet Union retreated from Afghanistan before my first international journalism assignment. Not long afterward, the Berlin Wall came down and eventually marked the end of the Cold War. Since then, a parade of presidents and wars has come and gone the world over. But thirteen years ago, under a brilliant blue September sky, airplanes flew into buildings, and the world spiraled into a War on Terror that will never end. The United States arrived in Afghanistan and then Iraq . . . and stayed. Today, its drones travel the skies of Pakistan, some of the unmanned aircraft piloted from a control center at Hancock airport in Syracuse, New York, the small airport with which I was once intimately familiar. On the ground, Pakistan's cities are bursting with spies, but today they carry guns and do not drive cars with identifying license plates.

As for all of us, we're much older, and our lives have unfolded in unsurprising ways.

My father says that while his Zenith radio brought news into our home as we were growing up, it also made a home for the news in each of his three children: I write the news, Lehla teaches it, and Amir films it. My mother lives the news as the dramas of the world unfold in the kitchen on BBC newscasts, holding her breath at nightly war bulletins, bemoaning the state of the country, continuing to hold my father forever responsible in her accusation, *Your country.* But my father has taken to laughing and replying, "It's *your* country! Do the math! Count the years you've lived here!" Time and again she proves him right, whether she's visiting Amir in Egypt, Lehla in New York, or me, wherever I am. When she tells us, "Back home, brown sugar is brown *and* sugar!" or "Back home, vinegar does wonders for cleaning windows," and when she prefaces her sentences with *Back home*, she is referring to Pakistan rather than Holland.

My father lost his WAPDA job before General Zia lost his life, and because there was never any question of his leaving his country, he made a new job for himself in Lahore by founding a security business, capitalizing on a service whose need multiplies in the city by the day. Retired for several years, he now has lots of time on his hands to think about his country and where it landed all of us. He claims the WAPDA job was always thankless, and he pities the people in charge today who are blamed for Lahore's paltry electricity supply, a round-the-clock schedule of one hour of electricity followed by one hour without it.

Four years ago, the country's elections saw Madam Prime Minister's husband, along with Pakistan's famous cricketer, lose, and a different familiar name once again assume the post of prime minister. My father applauds the country's first peaceful democratic transition of government, but his lament is real.

"The odds are against the country," he says, while continuing to hope. "One day, there won't be war: Iraq, Afghanistan, Pakistan, Syria, anywhere. One day, there will be no refugees. One day, we'll stop fighting each other. One day, we'll eliminate corruption. One day, we won't be someone else's lackeys." Once in a while, I hear him using the catchphrase *If only*. "If only we weren't ruled by such idiots." This morning at a breakfast of halva and pooris that my mother prepared for us at my new home in London, he said, "If only we weren't killing ourselves."

My mother has no patience whatsoever for this. "Stop it, Javi. Saying 'If only this, if only that' is useless. God is not a general, and he doesn't orchestrate from above. We must help ourselves."

"See how you just said *we?*" he said, and we all laughed.

My grandfather is impossibly old and, finally, truly deaf. For years, he wrote his grandchildren, especially me, blue aerograms about the long-ago days when people fought the British, and the world, as far as he was concerned, was still being made. Now that my parents live with my grandfather in Lahore, they convey our news to him, regardless of whether he hears any of it. He is the only man older than one hundred years in the neighborhood. He has given up whispering and wearing dentures, but he reads every book my father brings him. He seldom leaves his room but attends Eid prayers every year at the mosque across the street, not because he has forgiven the amplifiers, but because at his age, so close to death, this is one of the few things God requires of us.

Sadiq is the only one of us who never returned to Islamabad. Shortly after the briefcase of rotting money was discovered, he stood on a street corner in Lahore's Old City and gave it all away. It took Sadiq and Jamila a few more years to make peace with each other, but now he lives with her, his children (two daughters and two more sons), several grandchildren, and one great-grandchild. He enlisted the help of my father in starting a taxi service with a single car, my grandfather's battered Toyota Corolla. The service grew into a business that today monopolizes the route from Lahore Airport to Shadman District. Now, when we visit, he ferries my children, my husband, and me to all the sites I'd been required to visit as a child. Once in a while on these drives, he tries to convince me to learn Punjabi, Lahore's true language. I have told him that my debt to him is too large to allow him to teach me another language, and that he ought to consider allowing me to teach him English. But we both know he has no need of it, and besides, I'm rarely home.

～

All the while, Sadiq never spoke of the day the embassy burned, those many hours when he was missing from the Margalla house—uncut chicken on the counter, onions and garlic sautéing in a pan, cinnamon sticks and cloves roasting in the oven. And none of us ever asked him, not the day it happened, and not once in the many years that have passed since then. We didn't ask because we couldn't bear to know what he had done, yet this didn't prevent me from assuming the worst. When I was still a teenager, I lay awake at night in my grandfather's house, imagining police kicking in the door, guns and batons flying from room to room as they came to take Sadiq away. My worst fear was that Sadiq was responsible for the deaths of two Americans and four Pakistanis. Regardless of his particular crime, I was certain that some Pakistani authority, whether policemen, soldiers, or intelligence officers, eventually would track him down.

It was the one missing piece of the story necessary to put the events of those thirty months behind me, once and for all. Whenever Sadiq ferried me around Lahore, I considered broaching the topic. I thought of asking in the presence of my children, as if they would make Sadiq's answer easier to bear. Once when we were alone, I brought up the topic of Sadiq's role with my mother.

"Don't you wonder?" I asked.

"I do not," she said too emphatically, and I left it there.

Then, after years of silence, and without any prompting, it happened.

On my last visit to Lahore a few months ago, I walked out of my grandfather's front door with an empty basket dangling from one hand and my crying nephew clinging to the other. My sister, who was also visiting, had left her youngest child with my parents for the day so that she and her husband could bury themselves in archives for their latest research paper. I hoped to entertain my nephew by taking him to the bazaar to buy made-to-order naans from the best naan wallah in the city. I called for Sadiq without realizing he was already near the car. He was deep in conversation with a woman who I assumed was his wife, although I hadn't seen her in years.

"Jamila! How nice to see you. How are you?"

The woman blushed, touched her forehead with contrition, and said, "I'm not Jamila."

"Who are you then?" I asked and had a fleeting thought that Sadiq was having an affair with this unfamiliar woman in my grandfather's carport.

Sadiq cleared his throat a few times, the nervous habit he'd never overcome.

"She's a friend," he said reluctantly.

I contemplated this information for a moment before brusquely inquiring, "Friend or *friend*?" the difference between the categories obvious to us all.

"No, no," he stammered. "Friend."

"I'm the ayah," the woman said.

"You work for him?" I asked, perfectly aware that he had no need for one, because his children had long since become parents themselves.

"No. I work in the area," she said, stumbling over her words, her eyes shifting here and there, and generally making a spectacle of herself.

After an uncomfortable pause in which the three of us eyed one another with suspicion, Sadiq finally said, "Let me explain." His tone was fully resigned, a signpost for the explanation that was about to come.

Late that winter afternoon, thirty-some years after the embassy burned to the ground, the final piece of the story found me. While Sadiq and the ayah spoke, the milkman next door tipped the tin canister hanging from his bicycle handlebars and measured out the neighbor's buffalo-milk order. Across the street, boys whose voices were at the cusp of breaking memorized a verse from the Holy Quran, even as a giggling band of children darted after cricket balls onto the mosque's lawn. In the shade of my grandfather's carport, while my nephew fell asleep on my lap and my grandfather's window grills cast longer and longer shadows on the house, the two friends told their story.

They had known each other since the day of the embassy attack. They used identical words to describe the place each had in the other's life. They were like brother and sister. The ayah was in the room when Jamila's youngest sons were born. No, she was not a midwife. She was family. When the house next to theirs became vacant, Sadiq and Jamila arranged for the ayah and her family to occupy it, because this is the sort of thing you do for family.

They first met one November in Islamabad. The ayah couldn't remember the year, but she recalled with certainty that she was eighteen. She'd been living in Islamabad for six months by then, having been sent to live with an aunt while her parents and brothers sorted out a family dispute in Lahore. The ayah's sister worked for an American family in Lahore, and that was how she found work in an American home in Islamabad. The baby she cared for was born in August to a family that had five-year-old twin boys and a thirteen-year-old girl. A few days after the ayah started her job, her employer, Mrs. Simon, began working at the American School. The ayah and Mikail accompanied her, spending most of their time in the teachers' lounge until she'd finished teaching and they all returned home. One day, Mrs. Simon, Mikail, and the ayah left early to go to the embassy, where Mikail was scheduled to receive his immunizations. After the doctor's appointment, the ayah took Mikail to Mrs. Simon's friend's apartment, also on the embassy compound, so that Mrs. Simon could enjoy lunch with friends in the dining club.

Mikail, generally an even-tempered baby, had only just stopped crying when the commotion started. It began innocuously and in the distance, with several busloads of people arriving at the compound for meetings at the same time. She'd peered from the window when the noise grew but couldn't determine its source. All at once, the origin was beside the point because she could make out the chants, "Amrika Murdabad," and she understood the baby was in danger. The gunshots unnerved her. They *were* gunshots because, like anyone who'd grown up in a certain section of Lahore, she was familiar with the sound. She smelled the fire before she saw it. Even inside the apartment, the stink of burning tires was suffocating, but she stayed frozen in front of the window until the mob made its way toward the apartment blocks. She did the only thing she could: She took a sobbing Mikail to the bathroom, opened the bath faucet, and sat in a slowly filling bathtub with the howling baby in her arms. Too late, she noticed the open window near the ceiling, but she didn't dare to get up and close it for fear the action might draw attention. Submerged in rising lukewarm water, her wet shalwar and kurta ballooning around them, she put her lips against the baby's ear and sang every children's song and lullaby she had ever known in an improvised medley that lasted hours. Not for one second did she stop praying to Jesus Christ, her Lord and Savior, that He would spare them.

Sadiq, on the other hand, did not have an explanation for how he arrived at the embassy. He just did.

He'd gone for a walk to the American woman's house, where, of course, he'd been forbidden to go. But grief had stripped him of sanity, and he went anyway. Instead of returning home, he walked and walked, catching snippets of sermons from mosques he passed. Along the way, an inordinate number of red city buses and blue university buses rushed toward the diplomatic enclave and made him want to see what the fuss was about. The passengers shouted "Amrika Murdabad!" and without question, he assumed the chants were connected to the morning's news that Iranians had occupied the Grand Mosque in Mecca and the revised news he'd just heard emanating from the mosques that the Americans had done so. Why, yes! He had *indeed* given up newscasts of all types, but when news of this nature broke, it reached absolutely everyone, without regard for level of interest.

Sadiq didn't remember being in a hurry. When he arrived at the American Embassy, he leaned against the boundary wall for some time before hoisting himself up and draping himself over the edge for a view. The scene startled him. Fire raged in uniform bands of orange and yellow in every corner of the sprawling complex. As if he were only now noticing them, plumes of black smoke appeared suspended in the air. The Margalla Hills were not visible, and this fact, rather than the rioting mob, made him understand the embassy had been under siege for hours. Suddenly a bus arrived and stopped behind him, although it was nowhere near an entrance to the compound. The unloading passengers promptly scrambled over the wall and pulled him with them. He landed on his belly with all the air knocked out of him. Nonetheless, he got up quickly to avoid the stampede and was immediately impelled by the mass of elbows and shoulders surrounding him.

He was absorbed by the horde of people moving toward the low buildings ahead. The carport was ablaze; automobiles and minivans were consumed by fire. A car burst into flame when the fuel tank ignited, but the tremendous roar of the fire drowned the accompanying noise. Buckets of fuel were transported from the gas pump to the buildings. The mob—of which he was now a part—arrived at the embassy apartments. Plants and chairs were set out neatly on patios, with tricycles, balls, and metal toy trucks nearby. As if the crowd that had carried him had had a singular plan all along, it exploded into action. Stones were hurtled through windows, water heaters were torn from the nooks beside kitchen steps, and patio umbrellas were overturned. As a result of the activity, he was momentarily released from the mob's pressure. He wove his way between the enraged rioters and escaped to the farthest block of apartments on the edge of the compound.

Although the structure stood only a few hundred yards from the others, it appeared untouched by the hazy blanket of smoke. He was alone on the patio, and despite the deafening roar of the nearing fire, he detected the most unexpected sound.

The ayah caught Sadiq's gaze and held it for more than a moment before he continued.

Sadiq listened for the sound again and had it not been immediately familiar, having spent many a night listening to Hanif cry as a baby, he would have doubted himself. But what he heard was a whimpering infant behind an open window. He pushed a chair beneath the window and peered inside. A baby and someone he assumed was an ayah were immersed in a bathtub of water, fully clothed. The ayah lifted the baby from the water to give it a moment's relief. How many babies have purple birthmarks high on their foreheads? It was Leezy's baby brother. The ayah jumped at the sight of Sadiq's face in the window, and the infant wailed. "Allah rehem kare," the ayah cried.

The mob was getting closer. Sadiq hopped away from the window and reached for the object nearest him, a propane grill. In a fit of mock rage, he threw it into the living room window, then picked up a child's bicycle and did the same with it. That way, he explained, he fit into the crowd and didn't have to worry about drawing suspicion to himself. The men were almost upon him when he joined the chants, "Jeevay Pakistan" or some such thing. The raging men and roaring fire drowned the voices of the baby and the ayah, who had joined in the wailing by then. A can of lighter fluid was lit on the patio, but the flame leaped up at a few men, causing others to come to their rescue and leaving Sadiq to his own devices.

Sadiq made his decision. He slipped inside the narrow opening between the detached water heater and wall, folded himself until he was completely hidden, and stayed there, waiting for the best time to rescue the ayah and her baby. As the hours passed, he expected the block of apartments to be engulfed by flames. At some point, for a brief moment, a low-flying helicopter interrupted the throbbing sounds of the pulsing crowd and raging fire, but it came and went without making any difference to the mob, which had moved to yet another set of apartments. Hours later and for no discernible reason, the crowd dispersed.

Sadiq was shocked at how easily the mob dissolved into people who became themselves again, sauntering away from the grounds with the same ease as if they were leaving a fair.

Sadiq stepped out from behind the water heater. He'd thought through his plan and wasted no time implementing it. He covered his mouth with his kurta and entered the apartment through the broken living room window. He found the bathroom door, and a quick kick to the door broke the chain lock. The bathtub was empty. The ayah stood in a corner with the baby wrapped in a shower curtain. She recoiled when she saw him, but when he beckoned her to follow, she obeyed. He helped her climb on the sofa and maneuver through the empty window frame. As soon as her feet touched the patio, the ayah ran as fast as she could for the farthest clump of bushes before she collapsed. Sadiq followed her, but a uniformed American caught sight of him, so he fled from the compound.

The American was dressed for war, the ayah remembered. He wore camouflage clothes and had a belt of ammunition strapped to his chest. He tried to take Mikail from her, and when she would not let go of the baby, he half dragged, half carried her away to a makeshift post. She waited with the soldier, more terrified than ever, and did not let go of the baby until Mrs. Simon arrived and lifted the dehydrated baby from her trembling arms. The others wanted to take her somewhere and interrogate her, but Mr. Simon demanded that the ayah be allowed to accompany them home. A short while after they returned to 87th Street, the other children arrived.

The ayah smiled. She pulled out a silver chain and a small lapis lazuli pendant from inside her kurta. Mrs. Simon had given it to her the next morning, despite the ayah's protestations that the baby was not alive because of her, but because of someone else.

"You speak English?" I asked. The suggestion that the ayah and the Simons had shared substantive conversations was too much for me.

"Please? Thank you? Like that?" The ayah laughed. "No English. I would never have lasted in that household if Mrs. Simon's husband hadn't spoken Urdu."

"What?" I asked.

She was puzzled. "You didn't know Mr. Simon spoke Urdu?"

The ayah's revelation stunned me. Speechless, I looked on while Sadiq and the ayah, unperturbed by the detail, launched into a separate Punjabi conversation. Left alone, I recalled details, the significance of which I'd once missed. Mr. Simon had always exhibited surprising facility with Lehla's name. He'd been the only one in his family to pronounce Mikail's name correctly, at least in my presence. I wasn't certain, but the longer I thought about it, the more convinced I was that he'd been equally adept with Pakistan and Afghanistan, and possibly also Khyber Pass, on that long-ago day he'd sat on the sofa with Lizzy and me and shared photographs of a recent trip.

I finally spoke, but stumbled over words that weren't audible above the ayah and Sadiq's lively chatter. "He spoke . . . he spoke Urdu?"

I thought back to when I'd arrived at Syracuse University and had discovered that Pakistan and Urdu were not even in the vaguest recesses of anyone's mind. This many years later, I had yet to meet an American who spoke fluent Urdu. Mr. Simon's mastery long ago was an anomaly, and that made it all the more astounding that his family had kept it a secret from me. If I had ever had any doubts, I did not have them anymore. Mr. Simon, malaria expert and father of my best friend, had been a spy in a city of spies.

"What's your name?" I asked the ayah, interrupting them.

"Parveen," she said. "You don't remember?"

Suddenly the weight of my sleeping nephew overwhelmed me. The ayah's name *was* familiar. I recalled learning it a lifetime ago, when Lizzy and I were caught playing with Mikail instead of going to our next class. Her name, more than the specificity with which she remembered the ages of Anne Simon's children or her description of petrol bombs, confirmed the veracity of their story. I struggled to change my sleeping nephew's position on my lap, and when he wouldn't budge, Sadiq lifted him from my arms and took him to the house.

Parveen studied me. "Now you know why he's my brother," she said casually, as if I'd asked or we'd been friends for years.

The possibility that Sadiq could be a brother to anyone besides Yunis was difficult to absorb. Sadiq was a solitary man and, despite the large family that grew around him over the years, I could not see him otherwise. So I focused on what accounted for their bond. "You think he saved you?"

"I know he did."

I gazed at her, taking in her simple nose ring, the matching crow's-feet along her eyes, and the slack of silver chain settled in the dip near her breastbone. She'd only been five years older than me when she was employed as Mikail's ayah. "That's quite a story," I finally said.

"Ye afsanah nahin hai, ye hamari zindagi ki kahani hai." This is not a tale. This is the story of our lives, she said, a little surprised.

After Sadiq drove Parveen to her place of work, we went to the naan shop and I quizzed him at last.

"Why didn't you ever tell us what really happened?"

Sadiq responded with his own question: "Why didn't you ever ask?"

"I didn't want to pry."

He shook his head, and for a moment, I thought that might be his only response. "Forgive me, but that's not true," he finally said.

"Well, why do *you* think I never asked?"

"I have nothing but the highest regard for you and your family," Sadiq said. Then he hesitated. "But all of you—you, your parents, your grandfather—thought I'd done something terrible."

I didn't bother to contradict his assumption. "Then why didn't you correct us?"

Sadiq took his time, pausing between sentences. "I did something I shouldn't have done. I wasn't supposed to be on 87th Street. I shouldn't have gone to the embassy. But you were just a child, and even you thought I'd done something much worse!"

"I didn't think that," I lied, and he knew it. "You could have just told us the truth."

He didn't take my denial seriously, and his response was swift. "I did not tell your family what had happened because it would have been humiliating to defend myself."

"Humiliating?" I never liked the word. In Urdu, as in English, it had the strange effect of transferring its meaning onto me, and I felt slightly humiliated. But why was Sadiq suggesting that our need for an explanation was demeaning if such an explanation would have absolved him?

Sadiq was in no hurry to elucidate. I wondered if he thought it odd to have such a frank conversation with me, when he'd once been our servant, a fact I often overlooked. As I waited, a thought slowly began to take shape in my mind. In the context of our suspicions, and given the uneven and generally unspoken power relationship between us, compelling him to explain himself was uncomfortable, and indeed, possibly humiliating.

"If you'd just told us, it would have saved us so much trouble," I insisted.

Sadiq momentarily appeared not to understand. "What trouble? Your wondering all these years?" He stifled a chuckle. "That's hardly trouble, you have to agree."

"Anyway," I finally said, "you're wrong. My grandfather never thought you set fire to the embassy."

Awkwardness settled between us, but I was more uneasy than he was.

"Is that what you thought? I struck a match and *boom*, people were killed, and the embassy burned to the ground?"

"My grandfather never thought that."

"You're right. He never thought that. Otherwise he wouldn't have let me into his home." Sadiq was careful to draw a distinction between my grandfather and the rest of us.

"How did you come to see the ayah . . . ? I mean, Parveen, again?"

"She's from Lahore. The neighbor's chowkidar on Margalla Road was also from Lahore, and her aunt knew him. Parveen came to the Margalla house to thank me after I left, and he struck up a conversation with her. One thing led to another, and when she returned to Lahore, she called on me." Sadiq still seemed amused at the serendipity.

I mulled over some details of her experience the day the embassy burned. "She must have been terrified that day," I said.

"She's the bravest person I know, and an excellent role model for my daughters and granddaughters."

As if I were still a child, or his wife needed defending, I almost said, "Jamila is brave, too."

At the naan shop, Sadiq placed our order and returned to the car with a hot, steaming naan for me to snack on while we waited, a ritual from my childhood. He passed it to me through my car window, then leaned against the car as we watched a man slap rounds of bread dough into the outdoor tandoori oven. I let the naan grow cold in my hands without taking a bite.

"So what did you say to the American woman the night you went to 87th Street?" I couldn't have asked if we'd been facing each other. The question was only possible because I was still seated in the car and Sadiq was still outside, leaning against it, his back to me.

"Mrs. Simon?" It felt strange to hear Sadiq refer to Anne Simon by name. "I showed her a photograph of Hanif," he continued.

As if it were yesterday, I remembered the paper seesawing to the ground the night I'd spied on Sadiq and Anne Simon. It was a photograph. In all the time since then, I'd never considered such a possibility. Had Anne Simon seen Hanif's face after she'd run over him? Could she have recognized Hanif in the photograph?

262

"Did she know she was speaking to the father of the boy she'd run over?" I probed.

Sadiq deliberated over my question. "I think so. Who else would have been shoving a photograph of his child in her face that night?"

"*She* didn't speak Urdu, though, did she?"

Sadiq shook his head.

"Well, what did you say to her?" I was insistent.

Sadiq rubbed his cheek and crossed his arms while he pondered and did not take his eyes from the naan being prepared. "I don't know. Nothing that made sense."

"What did she say to you?"

"You know I don't speak English, right?" He laughed, and I waited. "She said she was sorry." He said *sorry* in English.

"For what?"

"Wasn't clear."

"For running over Hanif?"

"I showed her the photograph and it fell from my hands. She picked it up and bumped into me," he said and gently slapped his palm against the car door to demonstrate. "Most likely she was apologizing for that." He had turned to face me, and we studied each other through my open car window.

"Why did you go there that night?" I asked.

He turned more circumspect. "Maybe I hoped she would acknowledge what she'd done."

Sadiq's claim was suspicious. The prospect of a meaningful interaction between the two of them wasn't plausible in the absence of a common language. "You weren't planning on hurting her, were you?" I asked, somewhat indignantly.

"Is that why you followed me?"

"No," I lied.

"Your following me got me fired," he said.

"It did not. Your scene the next morning did."

"But you shouldn't have followed me."

I could conjure every detail of that night. The blooming bush of upside-down flowers, the angle of Sadiq's arm as he reached for Anne Simon, the tenor of the marine's voice. I remembered. "You tried to grab her."

His face hardened. "You think so little of me."

"Well, if I were you, I would have wanted to hurt her," I said quickly.

Sadiq took his time responding. "You see, I didn't want their settlement money. That night, I didn't want to hurt her. I think I was after something else."

"Did you get it?"

I watched Sadiq carefully consider my question, his brows knit together, his eyes unblinking with the effort of deep concentration. "I don't know," he finally replied.

The naan wallah brought us our dozen naans wrapped in a morning newspaper. I put the package beside me, and before Sadiq had reversed out of our parking spot and onto the road, the heat began bleeding the newspaper text and accompanying photographs into an indecipherable mess.

We drove through Lahore's busy traffic as the sun set and the smog turned the sky an orange we rarely saw in Islamabad. There was one question left to ask. Now I was free to inquire about the intimate detail that would put my childhood worry to rest. "Did Hanif die the moment he was struck?"

Sadiq took a sharp breath. "Yes, Alhamdulillah. My son did not suffer, and the last few moments of his life were happy."

I remembered the prime minister, and the images of his stinking death cell and rotting abscesses rose in my mind with the same clarity as they had when I was a child. "Not like the prime minister," I mumbled.

The car lurched forward, and I knew I had startled Sadiq with the memory of Hanif's curious connection to the prime minister. At the next stoplight, Sadiq took both his hands from the steering wheel and lifted his open palms to the sky in a resigned gesture that mimicked his thought. *This is life.*

As if he'd spoken, I added to it. "This is the life where nothing ever happened, until it did."

"Bilkul," Sadiq said. Absolutely.

My grandfather's old Toyota Corolla sputtered as Sadiq shifted the grinding gears and drove us home.

POSTSCRIPT

The American Embassy compound, long since rebuilt, is in the new Red Zone of Islamabad, which is host to the entire diplomatic enclave, the Presidency, foreign office, and rebuilt Marriott hotel. The Red Zone, the highest security cordon in the city, borders Margalla Road and Embassy Road, Lizzy's old neighborhood. The city is almost unrecognizable, with new avenues and districts running seemingly forever along the foothills and filling the once-empty land before Rawalpindi begins. Buildings previously tall and imposing, much like the three-story blocks of the Blue Area market, are dwarfed with dense construction. On my last visit to Islamabad, despite my parents' written instructions on how to navigate the new underpasses and overpasses, I quickly lost my way and couldn't locate the street where Anne Simon had struck Hanif.

Outside the fortified gates and walls of foreigners' homes, Pakistani guards armed with automatic rifles lie in wait behind sandbag bunkers. Concrete barricades zigzag across the streets of foreign residences, so cars and people must thread the narrow gaps, each as slowly as the other. On my last day in Islamabad, I sought out the Margalla Hills, the only familiar, unyielding edge of the city. I walked steep and winding trails into the beautiful hills, passing armed bodyguards and their foreign charges, anxious to complete the descent before dusk. Finally arriving at Viewpoint, where Sadiq told me he and Hanif had once shared a bottle of 7UP, I surveyed the sprawling city below—streets, avenues, and districts stitched together in a blinking mess of lights. After a while, I gave up trying to find our old house, the landscape of my long-ago time in Islamabad almost but not quite forgotten.

Sometimes, all it takes is the hint of a certain shade of purple, the echo of a note bending downward, a flicker of a yellow lightbulb, or the smudge of newsprint on my fingertips to make my father's rosebushes, the melody of the azaan, the rooms of my childhood, and the newspapers of my life come rushing back to me. Other times, I will it all back. I close my eyes in the middle of a hectic day and conjure the crevices of the hills, the clarity of the summer sky, the crescendo of singing parakeets, and the clank of our gate catching the stopper. The layers of memories are endless, spaces and times for the taking, if only I try hard enough.

My home is a barrage of headlines. You see, my country is at war. My cities are burning. My capital is a police checkpoint where journalists disappear. My sector borders the Red Zone. My road is a sandbag bunker. My hills, my beautiful Margalla Hills, are an airplane-crash site. My Kohsar Market is the site where the Punjab governor was gunned down. Later today, tomorrow, or not until next week (if we're lucky), the list of headlines will have grown.

The Islamabad of my childhood is so remote there was only one way to keep it alive.

I wrote my home.

See? I tell my children.

ACKNOWLEDGMENTS

I am grateful to many people without whom this novel would not be what it is. My agent, Bill Contardi, for his exceptional patience and resolve. Carmen Johnson, my editor, for her wisdom and tremendous enthusiasm. Simar Puneet, David Davidar, and Ravi Singh for the Aleph edition. Douglas Unger, Laura Rhoton McNeal, and Lisa Loomis for crucial encouragement. Sehba Sarwar, Waqas Khwaja, Christine Kosmicki, and Pat Dutt for being early and important readers. Joel Dinerstein for a small but critical edit. Duncan Murrell for a long-ago insight that kept me in the story. Saeed Qureshi, Mehreen Saeed, and other family who indulged my random questions. My siblings, Omar Khan and Ayesha Khan, who tirelessly supported me, and Kamini Ramani and Ahsan Jamil, who did the same. My parents, Thera Khan and Munir Ahmad Khan, whose belief in me was immense and whose absence is profound. My children, Kamal and Shahid, who never begrudged the city or the story that preceded them. Finally, my husband, Naeem Inayatullah, who makes everything possible and to whom everything is due.

ABOUT THE AUTHOR

Photo © 2016 Barbara Adams

Sorayya Khan is the author of two previous novels, *Noor* and *Five Queen's Road*. She is the recipient of a US Fulbright award, and *City of Spies* was the 2015 winner of the Best International Fiction Book at the Sharjah International Book Fair.